DATE DUE		

BLOOD SOLSTICE

James Howard Kunstler

BLOOD
SOLSTICE

DOUBLEDAY & COMPANY, INC.
GARDEN CITY, NEW YORK
1986

Library of Congress Cataloging-in-Publication Data
Kunstler, James Howard
    Blood solstice.
        I. Title
PS3561.U55B56   1986   813'.54   85-16043
ISBN: 0-385-19697-0

This book is for Tim Belknap, who knows . . .

"God save the Republic!"
—H. L. Mencken

BLOOD SOLSTICE

CHAPTER 1

It wasn't the kind of homicide they're used to seeing around here. After all, this is not California. Around here, usually, some poor slob finds his wife in the arms of another guy and tries to clobber both their heads with a claw hammer, and there you have it: a simple, ugly crime of passion. Half the time, the killer turns himself in.

In this case pieces of a carefully dismembered body began to turn up at landfills across Vermont. The first piece was a leg, uncovered by a bulldozer operator at the Rutland dump. A search of the site failed to turn up any more body parts and the police were baffled. Then a torso was found thirty miles away in Woodstock, and two days later another leg was seen sticking out of a plastic garbage bag at the Middlebury dump. By this time a statewide search was in full swing, and soon a couple of arms were found at Waitsfield and Stowe. Finally the head was discovered in the possession of a large, male black bear at the Craftsbury dump. According to one stupefied witness, the animal held it in its paws "like a sort of hairy basketball."

It took the Vermont authorities another week to get a "make" on the victim's dental work. The information came from across the state line. His name was James F. Hurlbett, twenty-eight, of Lake Placid, New York. Jamie Hurlbett was my best friend.

* * *

Was my best friend. A long time ago. I haven't had any other best friends for quite a while, unless you call Barbara Frye that, and at the time of Jamie's murder she wasn't speaking to me anymore, so the relationship—friend, best or otherwise, lover, whatever you want to call it—was already defunct.

Jamie Hurlbett was my best friend in college. Sometimes it seems like thirty years ago but it was only seven. We were put together as roommates in the dorms our freshman year, and hit it off, and became fairly tight right away, in the way that only roommates or brothers or soldiers can be. For some people college is really the last opportunity to get close with people in a certain way. And you don't have to be a psychiatrist to suggest that he was a replacement for my real brother, Philip, who was accidentally strafed by our own goddamn planes in Quang Tri Province, Vietnam, in 1972 when I was seventeen. Anyway, we were tight.

Our sophomore year Jamie and I escaped the dorm and rented a place off campus, a wonderful old run-down farmhouse in the hills five miles outside of town. It was ideal. You could forget about college and the rest of the world out there in the corn rows and the apple orchards, plus it was a great place to throw parties. We had some wild ones there. Then in the fall of our junior year his twin sister, Lisa, showed up and moved in—to their parents' great consternation, especially their father, the doctor, who was a very domineering, disapproving sort of guy.

They weren't identical twins, of course, or they would have been the same sex, obviously, but they looked very much alike. Both had the same dark brown hair that gets streaky with reddish-blond in the sun, the same deep-set squinty brown eyes, same long narrow nose—not long in the sense that it stuck out, but long between the eyes and mouth. They sometimes reminded me of wolves.

They were complete opposites in terms of personality. Jamie

was an art major, very disciplined and focused on what he was doing. Lisa was all over the place. She'd started college out in Oregon and transferred to the University of Colorado before she landed back East with us. Jamie hadn't talked about her that much, but I was certainly aware of her existence. It would be a while before I realized that he hadn't especially wanted me to meet her at all.

Then, once she was there, it seemed inevitable that Lisa and I would become involved, living together so casually in that old house out in the snowdrifts. In the beginning, at least, I was under the impression that Jamie approved. Sooner or later your sister ends up with somebody—right?—and it might as well be your best friend. Then, one blizzardy March night I came home unexpectedly early from a canceled senior seminar and saw her hurrying out of Jamie's room without any clothes on. The next day, without any warning, she left. I didn't ask Jamie what had been going on between them—it was all too embarrassing and weird—but he finally told me all about it. They had been having sex together since childhood, he said. I was more amazed than hurt.

Somehow, we managed to stay friends and remained out at the Farm, as we called it, until graduation two months later. Then we went out into the world: myself to work for a newspaper in Rockville, Maryland, and Jamie to be an artist up in the mountains. I never heard directly from Lisa again.

* * *

You had to admire Jamie's integrity. Over the years he did whatever was necessary to keep painting, refusing to compromise, working crummy jobs when he had to. You could probably count on one hand the number of canvases he sold in his whole life, and I own two of them. In some ways he made it extra hard for himself. For instance, he refused to deal with the New York art world. He hated city life. Just being in Manhattan for a day made him "crazy," he said. So the only gallery that ever hung his work was this dinky tourist trap in Manchester, Vermont, where he lived for a while around 1980. By then I had moved on to a job with the Boston *Phoenix*. Later, when I came to the Capital as a reporter for the *Times-Herald*, Jamie had all but retreated from civilization, to a cabin outside Lake Placid in the heart of the Adirondacks.

What he liked to paint was landscapes. He could draw the human figure as well as anyone, but after college, where he was required to paint from human models, people rarely appeared in his paintings. The few that did looked dazed and out of place, as if the earth wasn't their natural habitat. But Jamie himself wasn't a cold individual. I can understand why he appreciated natural things more—especially in our ridiculous culture.

On the other hand, I hope you don't think his paintings were sappy because they were landscapes. They had a lot of genuine feeling—maybe a lonely, gloomy sort of feeling, Like Edward Hopper, but not clichés, like the junk they sell at a shopping-mall "art sale." I'm not even sure Jamie cared if people wanted to buy them or not. I suppose he had very mixed feelings about it.

So, anyway, in this period after we graduated from college, I was bouncing around the Northeast from the Washington suburbs to Boston and finally to the Capital, moving along in my journalism career while Jamie hid out in the mountains. I still considered him my best friend, even though we hardly saw each other anymore. You might think that being a reporter would lead to a glamorous social life, but the newspaper racket isn't what it was cracked up to be in the old *Front Page*, "stop the presses!" mythology—as you'll see when I tell you about the clowns I worked with.

It was pretty hard to dislodge Jamie from wherever he was living, so I used to visit him. One of these visits included a winter camping trip I dreamed up, which turned into a minor disaster for me because I caught frostbite and had to have my right pinky toe amputated two weeks later. I'm not a cripple or anything. I can do all the things that any normal person can do. It just looks a little strange. I'll go to the beach where you can stick your foot in the sand, but I tend to avoid swimming pools, where people stare at it and then ask you what happened. I guess I'm just self-conscious about it. It's nothing really. You don't need it that much or miss it when it's gone.

The last time I was actually with Jamie was at that gallery show in Vermont. He was one of four artists being exhibited. It was a rather wan affair. Only about twenty-five people attended the opening reception, and I think more than half of them were tourists who wanted to get in on the free wine and cheese. Afterward we went to one of those wormy-wood-paneled steak pubs they have for the skiers, and Jamie apologized through the whole dinner for making me drive up from Boston. I tried to reassure him and cheer him up. Then he got depressed all over again when I insisted on picking up the tab, because I was at least earning a regular salary and he was practically broke. After that I don't think he even tried to exhibit his paintings anymore.

And then he became really distant. He was never much of a letter writer and it was rather an effort on my part to keep up a one-sided correspondence. He wouldn't have a phone in his cabin—or couldn't afford one—so I wasn't able to call him. A few times he called me from a bar in Lake Placid. I still felt closer to him than anybody else, but it was all just memories by then. Finally I came to the Capital to be an investigative reporter for the Kaiser Corporation, publisher of "America's Family Newspapers." Sometime in May, Jamie Hurlbett was killed and chopped into pieces. It wasn't until early June that they found out that the victim of the so-called Landfill Murder was him.

* * *

If I could figure out what a "family newspaper" is, I would die happy.

Does it mean that it's suitable for children? What newspaper isn't? I don't mean the *National Enquirer*, or *Screw*, or *Midnight*. I'm talking about your ordinary daily newspaper, whatever city you live in. This kind of thing drives me crazy.

About a half mile from the Heritage Hills apartment complex where I used to live (no hills and about twenty-three months' worth of heritage) there was a small shopping center with a supermarket and a drugstore and a Fotomat. At the bottom of the big illuminated sign out in the parking lot was a smaller sign that said "Family Center." I drove past that goddamn sign every day for over a year and racked my brains trying to figure out exactly what that was supposed to mean. One day when I happened to be in there picking up a few groceries I asked the manager:

"Uh, pardon me, where's the family center?"

"It's here."

"You mean right here in the pet-food section?"

"No, the whole store."

"I see. Can you explain what it means—a family center?"

He shifted his weight from one foot to the other.

"It's, like, where the family can come," he informed me.

"Frankly, sir, I don't think I've ever seen a complete family roving around these aisles."

"Maybe not," he agreed, "but they could if they wanted to."

Obviously he didn't have the faintest idea what a family center was either, but it didn't bother him the way it bothered me. After a while I developed a fantasy about it. I imagined long lines of overweight consumer families being lured through a secret door in the snack-food department into a gigantic underground room full of disco lights and carnival rides, like the place where Pinocchio grew donkey ears. Suddenly, out of the sprinkler system nozzles on the ceiling, comes a cloud of green poison gas. . . .

Not that I'm a Nazi or anything. Please don't get the wrong idea. We all have fantasies that would sound embarrassing to talk about. I'm not a standard-issue liberal, by any means, but I'm certainly no right-winger. I've met quite a few ultraconservatives as a reporter, and a great many of them seemed clinically insane to me. If I had to pick a label, I'd describe myself as an independent. Basically I believe in the American system. The price you have to pay for a system that promotes individual liberty is that a certain percentage of one's fellow citizens are free to be assholes and lunatics—Grover Graff, the great humanist philosopher, that's me!

So, the Capital *Times-Herald* is a "family newspaper." As you can see, it's hopeless to try to figure out what they mean by that. But they seem to have taken to heart the old proverb that says "No news is good news."

Every day, for instance, our paper would run a huge four-column photo on page one of something totally irrelevant to the headline news: a girl with a pony or a chimpanzee with a funny hat on. I'm not kidding. Sometimes they would shoot a picture of a guy standing in a pile of leaves over a caption that said, "Joe Blow of Woosterville sure has his hands full with this year's crop of colorful autumn leaves," which would be particularly pointless since the photo was in black and white. If the Capital was the only city to survive a nuclear holocaust, you could bet the next day's paper would have a photo of a little girl with a pony on the front page, and next to it would be a one-column headline saying, "World Destroyed."

*　*　*

Now at the time of the Landfill Murder—Jamie's murder, that is—I was beginning an investigation of an outfit that called themselves the Children of Abraham. No, it wasn't a Hebrew charity organization. It was a so-called cult. Investigating religious cults had become sort of a specialty of mine. The Jonestown Massacre happened the year I started out as a reporter. It really spurred my interest—the idea that almost 1,000 people would kill themselves out of blind obedience to one nut. I got my feet wet in the D.C. area covering several crooked small-time evangelists. Then, in Boston, I had a field day. They had every kind of whacko outfit known to man there, from the Moonies to the Scientologists to devil worshipers. The series I did for the *Phoenix* on the Prabdajhanpur Study Center—an extremely wealthy Krishna group that was buying up half of Cambridge—was nominated for a Pulitzer Prize. Ultimately it led to the job at the *Times-Herald,* though as soon as I arrived they started subtly agitating for me to do different things—which is typical of the Kaiser Korp.

"People are bored with religious nuts," my boss, Charlie Boland, would say, which was bullshit. What he really meant was that it was too hot a subject and that the Republican Kaiser

Korp brass wanted me to steer clear of their Moral Majority bedfellows. Frankly, I was the one who was getting a little bored with investigating cults, like I was trapped in some area of expertise that I never planned on making a whole career out of. But the more Charlie Boland tried to nudge me off the subject, the more tenaciously I hung on to it. Actually it was foolish of him to hire me in the first place if he didn't want me to do what I was good at.

It's not that I have a personal ax to grind. Spiritually I consider myself an agnostic. I was raised in a religion-free household. I don't have a grudge against God—like a lot of atheists do—but I do object to people who use God to enforce their will on others, whether it's the fundamentalists trying to banish evolution from the classroom, or some Satan worshiper fucking the mind of a teenager, or a two-bit evangelist bilking old ladies out of their savings accounts. I am their enemy. But it's nothing personal.

I'd seen members of the Children of Abraham hawking their "literature" out in the shopping malls, though I wasn't prompted to look into their affairs until a contact of mine in the attorney general's office turned me on to information that they were under investigation for charity fraud. That's how a lot of these outfits work: they register as "nonprofit" organizations and then rake in the boodle without feeling obliged to account for it.

I remember this one grifter down in Maryland, for example, who blew into town, rented a storefront, and opened an evangelical-style "church"—one of those Holy Roller deals that feature "speaking in tongues," and thrashing around on the floor, and the rest of the hyperthyroid numbers the Born Agains go for. Naturally, the guy was bilking his flock out of fabulous quantities of loot. Some of it was cash and the rest was in the form of negotiable goods. Old ladies signed over their stock portfolios and Cadillacs. Others brought him jewelry, old coins, family heirlooms, you name it. I discovered that he was reinvesting a lot of the dough in a chain of rattletrap nursing homes that stretched from Baltimore to Hagerstown —which was especially ironic because one of the main tenets of his doctrine was that the world was about to come to an end. He even had a date set for it: April 3, 1979.

Of course it didn't happen. But when the Big Event failed to come off, do you know what this asshole did? Set a new date the following year. What balls. And his followers accepted it without batting an eyelash. This really says a lot about what some people's threshold for absurdity is.

As things turned out, my series of newspaper articles made things a little too warm for this bird. He closed up shop and lit out for the territories under the cover of night. I'd tell you his name, but I doubt it would do you any good because he's probably changed it half a dozen times by now.

* * *

The Children of Abraham's headquarters was located in a town house made of Geneva sandstone in the old section of the Capital, a few blocks away from the governor's mansion. Much of the inner city is a scungy moonscape of burned-out ghetto, but Old Dutch Hill, as the neighborhood around the state offices is called, is like a little slice of Georgetown. The three- and four-story row houses date from the 1880s and they've installed gaslights on the sidewalks to give it a "period flavor"—as the *Times-Herald* often put it. There are several gourmet food boutiques in the neighborhood, should anyone need a quick fix of brie or squid salad, and there's a fern bar where all the state flaks hang out. Basically, the neighborhood is chi-chi, upstate style.

I got the group's address from my contact in the attorney general's office and decided to drop by in person rather than call and make an appointment for an interview—to reduce the chance of being brushed off. It was raining buckets that day. Two weeks earlier, around Memorial Day, it had literally *snowed*. For about an hour, big wet flakes the size of silver dollars came down. It didn't stick to the streets, but the trees, all full of bright new leaves, were coated with the stuff. It was beautiful, of course, but you really get sick of the shit living up here. By May, after six months of winter, its aesthetic value is about zero. Anyway, this day it was raining buckets out.

Above the doorbell was a little brass plaque the size of a business card that said *The Lyman Foundation*. It threw me for a moment, but I checked the house number against the one I'd written down and it was 214 Union Street, all right, so I pressed the button.

The guy who answered the door looked like he had athlete's foot of the face—some sort of scabrous, eczematous, wormy-looking disease, all red with these flaky peelings of skin coming off. I don't want to beat it into the ground, but believe me, this was one terrible-looking dude. I kept thinking, it had to be the right place, because only a group that wanted to ward off snoops like me would let somebody who looked like that answer the doorbell. I actually winced when I saw him.

I told him my name and the paper I was from. It's unethical not to—I don't care how sleazy your assignment is. Besides, they'd figure it out themselves as soon as you started asking questions. There's really no way around it. You can't pretend to be from the census bureau or the Gallup poll. And you can't pretend to be a cop because (a) it's against the law, with stiff penalties, and (b) they'd demand to see your badge unless they were complete knuckleheads.

But you'd be amazed how people react when you say you're a reporter. Most of the time they're terrifically flattered that a newspaper would pick them to write about. Suddenly they're important! Interesting! Celebrities! What they say and do *matters!* I've even seen hard-core criminals react this way, guys who you'd think would be naturally publicity-shy. You just say you're a reporter from the *Times-Herald* and their eyes light up. It's stardom!

I could tell that even this spooky motherfucker with the motheaten face was taking the bait. For a few moments he just stood there as though he wasn't sure what to do. I was getting drenched standing out in the rain and asked if he minded if I stepped inside the vestibule. "Okay," he said nervously. I knew that investigators from the A.G.'s office had already paid a call on the group, and I realized that they might want to use the press to defend themselves against allegations.

"Wait here," the guy said and disappeared inside. My sports

jacket was soaked. Finally he returned, acting much less nervous than he had at the door, and invited me into the house.

"Leave your rubbers in the hall," he said.

I had rubbers on. I realize they're not terribly suave, but I was wearing these rather expensive English shoes that cost over $100 a pair and I didn't want to ruin them. If you had your pinky toe amputated, you'd be choosy about your footwear too. On the other hand, I didn't even own a proper raincoat, and my herringbone jacket from J. Press was sopped, and it cost *twice* as much as the shoes.

Anyway, I followed scab-face into a sort of living room or front parlor. Seated at one end of a plush sofa was a brown-haired girl, possibly a minor, anywhere from sixteen to twenty years old, wearing a blue skirt and a plain sleeveless white cotton shirt. She didn't wear any makeup but had a strong-featured, rather handsome face—like the salt-of-the-earth working women you see depicted in those Depression-vintage murals they have at Rockefeller Center—and she also had a good tan. I nodded hello and she smiled.

There was a sterile feeling about the room, as though it had been cleaned a little too strenuously. The furniture was all dark, fine old cherry and mahogany, including a loudly ticking grandfather clock that showed the phases of the moon in a smiling round face. Heavy brocade drapes blocked out the sights and sounds of Union Street, which is a fairly sedate thoroughfare anyway. I didn't see any religious paraphernalia, no portraits of Jesus, or deities with elephant heads, or photos of their spiritual leader. Scab-face, who appeared to be in his early twenties, gestured to the sofa and I took a seat there while he repaired to a wing chair across from me. To my left was a fireplace, unlit, of course, because it was June.

"Can I offer you a cup of tea?" he asked.

"Why, thank you, that would be very nice," I said, though I tend to get a little paranoid when people offer me refreshments in a situation like that. A guy I know from the Boston *Globe*, Tom Bethke, was slipped a whopping dose of LSD while he was investigating a Satanist outfit called the Society of the Dark Star. They put it in a hamburger. He recovered from it all right, but the experience was none too pleasant. Eventually the motherfuckers got nailed for it. But I wanted to put these people at ease, and not appear nervous myself, so I said fine, I'd have some tea. Besides, at this point they didn't know what I was after so it didn't seem terribly risky. In an abrupt manner he called loudly into the next room:

"Hey, Shitfingers!"

I was somewhat startled by the language. I do swear now and then myself, you may have noticed, but I was surprised to hear him use profanity, partly because it seemed a crass form of address for a supposedly pious person to use, and partly because if anyone was a candidate for a disparaging name it was this poor fucker with the decrepitating face.

The person who responded to this call appeared as noiselessly as a cat. He was an eerie, angelic-looking young man in his early to mid-twenties, medium height but frail, with blond hair that was practically white. At first I wondered if he was an albino, but his eyebrows were darker than his hair so he couldn't have been. His costume—black jeans and black turtleneck shirt—tended to accentuate his paleness. He looked like a young Andy Warhol, but with more delicate features. I couldn't see his eyes because he was wearing sunglasses, wire rims with round lenses, like a blind man's. You sensed that he wasn't blind, though, from the way he held his head and took in the room.

"Bring us a pot of tea," Scab-face said.

The other one smiled back—like someone who would just as soon push you in front of a subway train—nodded his head, spun around on his heels, and marched back out of the room.

"Now, Mr. uh . . ."

"Graff," I reminded him.

"You said you were from the *Tribune?*"

"No, the *Times-Herald*. They're the evening paper. We're the morning one. It's all put out by the same company, in the same building, but we have separate staffs. By the way, do you mind if I take a few notes while we chat?"

"Not at all," he said, but you could see him bristle. Most people get a little uptight when a reporter takes out the tools of the trade. It's like when the dentist lays out all those pointy steel probes on his round worktable—you know you're in for the business. I took a steno pad and a Bic pen out of my briefcase.

"I don't believe I caught your names," I said to him and turned to the girl next to me. I noticed that she wasn't wearing a bra under her cotton shirt, and that she had very nice breasts. The way she had her arm resting along the top of the sofa, I could see right into the loose sleeve hole like the opening of a cave. One wide brown nipple was completely visible. For a second her eyes locked on to mine. I suspected she was aware of what I could see, but she didn't shift her position in the slightest.

"It's Rebecca," she said.

"What a pretty name." I wrote it down. "And yours?"

"Isaac."

"Last name?"

"Just Isaac."

"Like in the Bible?"

"Correct."

"In the Bible wasn't Rebecca Isaac's wife?"

The girl giggled.

"Are you two husband and wife?"

"We're united in spirit," Isaac said.

"I see," I said, making a note. The clock ticked hollowly. Isaac shifted around in his seat and picked a piece of dead skin off his lap where it had flaked off his face. "I understand the attorney general's office—"

"Those stories are a lie!" he jumped up and hollered. If he presented a startling and unappetizing figure when he was laid back, you should have seen him in the throes of a tantrum. Gobs of foamy spittle started forming at the corners of his mouth. I should have been prepared for something like this. When you're dealing with psychologically marginal people, anything's liable to happen. It was quite a tirade:

"These people have no right harassing us. It's against the Constitution! It's Godless and unconstitutional for them to devil us with their damned subpoenas! We have done nothing wrong! We don't steal money. Every cent that comes into the Holy Spirit Center we can account for. Our people come here because they love the Holy Spirit. Nobody forces them. They can come and go as they please. This whole thing . . ."

Just then another strange thing happened. The blond-haired guy, Shitfingers, appeared in the doorway with a tray full of tea things. He was behind Isaac's back, but I must have raised my eyebrows or looked up, or perhaps Rebecca flashed him a sign, because as soon as he entered the room, Isaac calmed right down. He just quit fulminating and foaming at the mouth and returned to his wing chair as though he were taking a seat on the Metro bus.

I hadn't made any attempt to calm him down myself, because I've been in the same situation many times before, and it invariably only makes them more hysterical. It's really harmless animal-threat display behavior, like a baboon stamping its feet and barking. Usually you just sit back and wait until they run out of gas. But this was a new wrinkle on the old routine. Shitfingers put the tray down on the Queen Anne coffee table, gave me a sort of glowerly looking-over, and departed.

"How did he happen to acquire that name?" I asked Isaac, who seemed to be in control of himself once more.

"He misbehaved."

"What did he do?"

"It's not important. Just an internal thing."

"What was his name before?"

Isaac hesitated. "Esau."

"Esau was Isaac's son in the Bible," I said.

"He's not my son," Isaac gravely stated the obvious—anyone could tell they were close to the same age. Rebecca giggled again. Isaac glared at her reproachfully and she stopped.

"Is that his punishment—to fetch and carry?"

"To serve. He serves."

"Do you give him his name back after a while?"

"Maybe."

"You don't know yet?"

"It hasn't been decided."

"I see."

Isaac leaned forward and grasped the silver teapot. He poured three cups. During this operation a flake of skin fell off his forehead into one of the cups. He didn't seem to notice. I made it a point to pick up one of the other cups. When Rebecca reached for hers I felt her breast brush against my arm. The tea was a very robust red and the spicy flavor was familiar, though I couldn't name it.

"What kind of tea is this?"

"Sassafras," he said. "We blend it ourselves."

"It's very good," I said and put down my cup. Believe it or not, just that morning they'd run a feature in our paper's Lifestyle section listing common health-food items that contained known carcinogens, and sassafras tea was one of them.

"So, how are you going to write this up?" Isaac asked me in a peremptory tone of voice.

"Write what up?"

"Your story."

"Well, we've barely even begun to chat," I pointed out.

"Come on. Don't you have a story already written in your mind?"

"No. If I had, what would be the point of my coming down here?"

"So you could say you did."

"Wait a minute. I'm here to gather information by asking a few questions, and you're free to answer them as you see fit, or not answer them—"

"Yeah, but you can twist what we say."

"Look, Isaac. I can't promise unconditionally that you'll approve of what I write. That's the chance you take when you talk to the press. But there are some ground rules for your protection. For one thing, you can ask me to leave anytime you like. I'll leave right now if you want."

I stood up and jammed my notebook back into my briefcase, not angrily, but just to call his bluff.

"Wait. Don't leave," he said rather urgently and stood up himself. I waited a few seconds, then chucked my briefcase back on the sofa and loosened my tie. Meanwhile, he bustled across the room to a bookcase beside the fireplace and brought back a book. "You spoke to those government men about us, didn't you?"

"I had a conversation with someone on the attorney general's staff," I told him.

"Then this is what you want to see." He handed over the book very solemnly, but with no further explanation. The binding was high-quality red and black calfskin. It was impressive in a hokey sort of way.

"Go ahead," he insisted. "Open it and have a look. It'll tell you what you want to know."

"What is this?"

"Read it. It'll answer your questions. Go ahead."

I could tell he was getting wound up again, so I opened the book. It was an account ledger, purporting to be a record of all the group's income and spending for the year to date. Only it was so neatly done, with all the entries in the same handwriting and black ink, that I was fairly certain it was a fake. There was another strange thing about it. Most examples of simple bookkeeping have two columns of figures: one for money coming in and one for money going out. This ledger had three categories: "income," "expenditures," and "forsake all." By far the largest sums fell under the "forsake all" category.

"What does this mean, 'forsake all'?" I inquired.

"Oh, well, I'm glad you asked me that question, Mr. Graff, because I think we have a real opportunity to clear the air here. You see when new members, 'initiates' we call them, join the Holy Spirit Center they are required to give up their personal possessions, to forsake all. We believe that personal possessions are an obstacle to being washed in the"—something got caught in his throat for a moment—"in the blood of the Holy Spirit. So we ask all our members to give them up. They do it completely of their own free will. No one forces them."

"Where does it go, all this forsaken stuff?"

"It goes to the organization."

"Do you have some sort of treasury?"

"We have bank accounts."

"In the group's name?"

"It's put into a foundation account."

"The Lyman Foundation?"

"That's right. You must have noticed the nameplate on the door."

"It's not on the door, actually," I corrected him. "It's above the bell."

"I guess it is." He smiled uncomfortably. "You reporters don't miss a thing."

"Sometimes it pays to notice little details. But getting back to the book here, there sure seems to be a lot of forsaken stuff. Look—here's $12,500, and another lump of $5,220, and another one for $9,275, and here's a whopper, $14,000. Is this all cash, or what?"

It was a mistake to invite him to look over my shoulder because a few flakes of his skin fell off on my sleeve.

"Yes," he began to explain. "These two were cash. They were the bank accounts of two initiates."

"They simply signed them over to you?"

"Not to me. To the organization," he said, bristling. "There's nothing illegal about it."

"How about the other figures?"

"I'm not sure just from looking at the numbers. Possibly proceeds from the sale of a car. I can look it up."

"Would you mind terribly?"

"Not at all," he said and started over to the bookcase. But he stopped halfway and snapped his fingers. "Oh, I forgot. We gave those records to the gentlemen from the government."

"I see."

"But it's all accounted for. I just don't understand what it is we've supposedly done wrong."

"Large sums of money tend to attract attention," I suggested.

"We've been blessed. What can I say? But so were those who came here in doubt and confusion. Before, they were snotty-nosed godless little brats. Now they've been washed in the blood of the Holy Spirit. It all balances out. And even if they seem like large sums of money, I think I ought to point out a few things to you. First of all, just because it's $12,000 instead of $1.98 doesn't make it illegal. You write *that* down because it's important. Go ahead, write it!"

I took out my steno pad and wrote it down. He seemed very pleased that I obeyed his command.

"Second of all," he continued, "this Holy Spirit organization comprises a family of over sixty individuals, all of which have to be fed and clothed and everything else that individuals require. So, if you add up those figures, it might *seem* like a giant sum of money, but that money is going to support a lot of little souls, and if you average it out, you'll see that it works out to less than $5,000 a year per head, which, you may realize, is way below the poverty line established by the U.S. Department of Health and Human Services. And that's what I mean when I talk about you people twisting the facts, because this money is chicken feed when you have to stretch it like we have to. And make sure you include *that* in your story!"

He was getting all wound up again, so I told him he was making a really good point and wrote it down in my steno pad. Rebecca leaned over to check what I was writing, and in doing so literally rested her breast in the crook of my elbow.

"May I ask what your annual salary is, Mr. Graff?"

"It's around $20,000."

"$20,000. *$20,000!*" he echoed me, nodding his head gravely, lips tight. "To some people that would seem like a large sum of money. Is the government deviling you?"

"I don't claim to be a nonprofit organization."

"You see"—he ignored my remark and went on in a world-weary tone of voice—"not all of our brothers and sisters come from prosperous circumstances. Myself, for example. I didn't have anything when I came to the Holy Spirit Center. 'Take me in!' I cried from the doorstep, and they did. 'Forsake all,' they said, and I did. I emptied my pockets and gave them $14, which was all the money I had to my name. And I was accepted. I was loved. They didn't discriminate against me because all I had in the world was $14 where somebody else had $1,400. We are all loved equally here, and all forsake what they can. And everybody gets taken care of equally."

"Except Shitfingers—"

"He has nothing to do with it! He did a bad thing and he is doing his penance. He is doing it willingly, and when he is finished he'll resume his regular activities. But he is still loved, even in his time of humility."

"Isaac, are you the leader of this organization?"

"Leader? We don't have any leaders. Everybody does what they can."

"Then you're not in charge here?"

"I do what I'm good at."

"What are you good at, exactly?"

"I make sure that certain things get done."

"But you don't call that being in charge?"

"No."

"What do you call it then?"

"I call it being a good organizer."

"I see."

"And sometimes it works out that the other brothers and sisters are good at doing tasks that I organize."

"Where are the others, by the way?"

"Most of them are not here right now."

"Where are they?"

"We have a farm out in the country where we grow a lot of our own vegetables and raise some livestock, and quite a few of the family are there now, where we need all the hands we can muster."

"Did you say where this farm was?"

"Out in the country."

"Where?"

"About an hour away."

"Which direction?"

"Follow the righteous path."

"You don't want to tell me."

"I don't want you distracting them. They've got enough work to do."

"Fair enough," I said with a shrug. "Can you tell me where the members who live here are?"

"Out spreading the word of the Holy Spirit."

"You mean selling pamphlets."

"It's a perfectly legal way to generate income," he said. "And an excellent way to spread our message. We're not ashamed of it. Would you like to take some literature with you?"

"Thank you, I would indeed."

"Wait here," he said, as if otherwise I might get up and poke around the place. He ducked out of the room for a minute, leaving me with Rebecca and the grandfather clock, whose loud ticks dominated the room like a watchful human presence.

"How come you're not up at Century Plaza?" I asked Rebecca, alluding to the huge shopping mall where I'd seen some of the troops doing their thing.

"Because I'm here," she said with a rather wan smile. She looked into my eyes as though she wanted to enter the inside of my brain and hide in there. A second later Isaac noisily returned with a handful of pamphlets which he more or less dumped in my lap.

Each one was a booklet running from six to eight pages, printed in offset from photographed typewriter pages rather than composed type—in other words, strictly an amateurish printing job. The cover of each booklet was jazzed up with an alarming cartoonlike illustration. This artwork was rather deftly drawn, but really crazy.

The first one was a cartoon of a naked young woman with her shoulders hunched in an attitude of shame, while various authority-type figures—a Catholic bishop in regalia, a firm-jawed politician, and a middle-aged schoolmarm—all pointed their fingers at her. It was titled *The Sex Hex*. Above the title was a little banner that said "Abe-gram No. 9." I gave the text a glance or two. It related how down through the ages people have been made to feel ashamed about sex by the church and state. It went on to sketch out a "perfect society" where "the pleasures of love" would be freely available to all. There were even a few idyllic drawings of nubile youngsters making out together, with the genitalia artfully concealed. I handed the pamphlet back to Isaac.

"What does this mean—'Abe-gram No. 9'?" I asked.

"It's the ninth of a series."

"Yes. But who writes them?"

"The Prophet Abraham."

"You mean the Prophet Abraham who is spoken of in the Bible?"

"No, the Prophet Abraham who is the founder of the Holy Spirit Center."

"I see. Then this group does have a leader."

"No, I told you, there are no leaders. We have a *founder.*"

"He's the founder, but not the leader?"

"That's right."

"I don't get it. Is he retired or something?"

"No."

"Is he here now, by any chance?"

"Oh no," Isaac said with a cackle, relishing some humorous tidbit that must have gone over my head completely.

"Where is he, then?"

"Uh, Switzerland," Isaac said, as though he'd just thought it up.

"Are you sure about that?"

"Yes."

"Why Switzerland?"

"Why not?" Isaac said, gaining in confidence and clearly enjoying himself.

"I see," I said and made a note. "So, he prepares these booklets over in Switzerland—"

"That's right."

"—and sends them over here to you guys."

"And elsewhere."

"Elsewhere?"

"We have a satellite community in California."

"Where?"

"The San Francisco area."

"Can you be more exact?"

He smiled again, meaning he had absolutely no intention of being more exact. I stopped and made a few more notes. This seemed to annoy him. You could tell because he shifted around in his seat while I wrote in my pad.

"Does he ever come to America, this Prophet Abraham?" I resumed, taking a slightly different approach.

"No," Isaac said.

"He just stays over in Switzerland?"

"That's right."

"Have you ever seen him yourself?"

Isaac began to reply, then hesitated. "No," he said.

"Are you a hundred percent sure he exists?"

"I believe he does."

"On what basis?"

"I have faith. Besides, we keep getting the Abe-grams every two weeks."

"I see," I said, making another note. "This 'Abe-gram No. 9' seems to promote free love. Am I perceiving this correctly?"

"You're surprised, aren't you?"

"A little. But maybe I shouldn't be. Historically, quite a few spiritual groups have been into it."

"Oh, yeah?" Isaac brightened. "Which ones?"

"The Oneida Community. Many of the offshoots of the Transcendentalist movement, like Brook Farm. The Mormons certainly got very sexually active in the last years of Joseph Smith. He seduced quite a few of his followers' wives and then he proclaimed himself spiritually wedded to them when their husbands found out. Pretty soon the other Mormon elders got into the act, and in a few years it was made an official part of the religion, as polygamy."

"No kidding?" Isaac said, apparently enchanted with the idea. I have to admit I enjoyed playing the pedagogue.

"It sounds like more fun for the men than the women," Rebecca remarked. She had a husky voice, like someone who had smoked Camel cigarettes for twenty years. You couldn't help wondering about her sexual role within the group.

"This was back in the nineteenth century," I assured her.

"The Bible says be fruitful and multiply," Isaac pointed out, resuming his normal, bumptious manner of speaking.

"This is more a matter of the juice, not the fruit, if you know what I mean," I attempted a wisecrack.

"I know what you mean"—he pretended to appreciate it—

"but that's just another example of how people twist and distort things. You assumed that we condemn sex. Well, we don't. We believe it is healthy and natural, no more and no less. But you put a label on us and expect us to live up to it. See what *I* mean?"

"That's a really good point, Isaac," I said and took a few more notes. In a way you felt sorry for him. With his skin condition it was hard to picture him getting in on much action around there, even if they had a perpetual orgy going on when busybodies like me and the attorney general's people weren't nosing around.

I glanced through the other booklets he had dropped in my lap. These were actually more flipped out than the one about free love. The first was titled *Into the Pit*. The cover illustration depicted an elevator full of businessman types and their secretaries wide-eyed with terror. The elevator was plummeting down the shaft of this cutaway skyscraper—you could tell it was going down because the artist had drawn these action lines above it, plus the characters' hats were flying upward. The elevator was labeled "Godless Society."

Another booklet was titled *The Tale of the Comet*. The cover had a sci-fi flavor. It depicted a comet with a bearded old man's face at the head of it, sort of a wrathful God face. The text was a prediction that the comet Moclu-Vistla was about to veer off course and smash into the earth, thus putting an end to "Godless Society."

For those of you who don't remember, the comet Moclu-Vistla was discovered by two Romanian astronomers and was supposed to make for a spectacular sight in the sky last summer—they never said it would crash into the earth or anything of the kind—but the whole affair turned out to be rather a dud because it was barely even visible to the naked eye at its closest point. I held up the booklet to show Isaac.

"I guess this one didn't pan out, huh?"

He shrugged his shoulders, well fortified against any shake-up in his cosmological view.

"The Holy Spirit just decided it wasn't time yet," he said and rose from his chair. "You must have enough information for your story now, Mr. Graff," he added. Apparently this was my cue to buzz off.

"It's been very enlightening," I said, rising off the sofa and stuffing all the Abe-grams in my briefcase along with my notepad. "May I call you here in case any additional questions crop up?"

"What questions?" he retorted, growing visibly annoyed again.

"I don't know. They haven't cropped up yet."

"Whatever. Sure," he said, to placate me. "You just write it all up accurately, like I told you, and don't twist what I said."

"Don't worry, I won't."

He began steering me out of the room. Rebecca remained on the sofa.

"Good luck," I said to her on my way out.

"You too," she replied, nodding her head in an enigmatic way, without a smile this time, and running long strands of brown hair through her fingers. It unnerved me.

Isaac shepherded me down the hall to the vestibule. I put on my rubbers. Just as he reached for the knob, the door flew open, and in bounded an attractive redheaded girl with the kind of awkward energy only teenagers have. She was carrying a shoulder bag full of Abe-grams. I wondered if she was a runaway, but didn't broach the subject, since it was liable to open up a whole can of worms, and I was as anxious to get out of there as Isaac was for me to leave.

"Hi, Esau," she said as she barged past us.

Isaac flinched. "Hey, Nancy!" he called after her. She stopped and turned. "It's Isaac, not Esau," he corrected her sternly.

"Oh, sure," she agreed, looking flustered, and continued into the depths of the house.

"An initiate," Isaac explained when she had gone. "She doesn't even have *her* Holy Spirit name yet. Must be confused."

"How long has she been here?"

"Two days."

"Well, that's understandable." I pretended to dismiss the matter. "Thanks for the tea, Isaac."

"You mind what you write, now."

"Oh, I will," I assured him.

The rain had stopped. A hazy sun was out and suffocating mist rose off the pavement. It felt sticky and uncomfortable, like someone had poured pancake syrup down your shirt. There was a pink parking ticket under the windshield wiper of my Datsun. The meter's little red violation flag was up. I stuck the parking ticket in my glove compartment along with fifty others just like it.

CHAPTER 2

It was after five and there was no reason to put in an appearance at the office, so I drove home to go for a motorcycle ride. The bike was one of several gifts I'd lavished on myself after taking the job with the *Times-Herald*—the others being a color TV and new speakers for my stereo. For someone so generally scornful of the consumeroid mentality, I sure managed to buy a lot of things that year.

The ironic part is that I am so neurotically terrified of high speeds that I'd never even put the bike in top gear. It was a Yamaha 750 Virago, a real monster, and I drove it like somebody's grandmother. Still, it was lovely swooping through the hills south of the city on it, especially in the evening at that time of year, when the corn is up and the cows are browsing in the pastures.

I stayed out as long as daylight lasted—till about 9:30—thinking about things like how I was going to handle the Children of Abraham story, and about getting a job on a better paper somewhere else, and finally went back to my apartment. The Heritage Hills complex was only a couple of years old, and pretty well maintained, but it really depressed the shit out of me to be there, especially after swerving around all that sweet farm country. Anyway, I was back, fixing a grilled cheese and tomato sandwich and getting ready to watch the last few innings of the Red Sox–Detroit game on the cable when the doorbell rang. It was disconcerting because practically no one besides the maintenance man ever came to my place—which tells you something about my social life in the Capital. So, imagine my surprise to answer it and find Rebecca out in the hall.

"Hi," she said, as though I should have been absolutely delighted to see her. She had a big floppy bag with her, sort of a shopping bag made of canvas, crammed with stuff.

"What can I do for you, Rebecca?" I asked politely, but with a deliberate lack of cordiality.

"May I come in?"

"How did you find out where I live?"

She shrugged. "I called your newspaper."

"I see," I said. That really pissed me off. A newspaper should *never* give out the address of a reporter—especially one like me, who has dealings with quite a large number of unbalanced individuals. It just goes to show you the kind of clucks I worked with that she was able to get it.

"Is something burning?" she asked.

"Oh shit . . ." I raced into the kitchen and flipped the scorched grilled cheese sandwich out of the frying pan onto the countertop. Meanwhile, I heard the door clunk shut. When I looked up Rebecca was standing in the living room.

"It's nice and cool in here," she said.

"Air-conditioning."

"It's luscious." She put down her bag.

I popped a beer and brought it and my sandwich over to the sofa. My strategy at this point was to simply find out what she wanted without being either cordial or nasty. I left the ball game on the tube and pretended to be giving it an equal amount of attention.

"What brings you here?" I asked again, not even looking at her.

"I have nowhere else to go," she said.

"I don't get it."

"I split from the Children."

I swallowed and finally looked up at her. "You left the group? Between this afternoon and now?"

"Uh-huh." She nodded, making a helpless face.

"How did you get all the way out here?" It was about five miles from downtown to my place.

"I hitched."

"There's nowhere else you can go?"

She shook her head.

"You don't have any other friends or relatives in the city?"

"I'm from this little town south of Buffalo."

"Well, how did you end up here in the Capital?"

"I went to St. Agnes for one semester," she said, referring to this dinky Catholic college in town, "but that was more than a year ago."

"I don't mean to be unfriendly, Rebecca, but why don't you take a bus home?"

She giggled ruefully.

"There's no buses to Buffalo until tomorrow. I already checked," she said.

"Oh . . . ?"

"And the bus station is full of creeps."

She was certainly right about that. The terminal was a combination rogues gallery—wino lounge—and Ripley's Believe It or Not Museum.

"Do you mind if I sit down?" she asked.

"All right," I said coolly, trying to figure out what the hell to do about her. I admit I felt some urges to act chivalrous, despite my better judgment. She took a seat in this ratty old blue velveteen chair of mine that I got at Goodwill Industries and hiked the hem of her ankle-length skirt over her knees.

"It sure was hot out there, lugging all this stuff around," she said. Her suntanned legs were apart and she was fanning them with an L. L. Bean catalog that had been on the coffee table.

"I thought the Children didn't allow any personal possessions," I said, looking back at the TV screen.

"Well, God, a person's got to have *some*. You can't share underwear."

"What suddenly inspired you to leave them?"

She sighed and puffed out her cheeks. "A lot of things."

"Such as?"

"I don't know. I guess I got bored with it."

"It sounds to me like they have a jolly good time together—gardening, free love."

"Some parts were better than others."

"Did they abuse you in any way?"

"Oh, no."

"So, you just got tired of it, huh?"

"I think there's got to be more to life. That sandwich looks *so* good."

"Excuse me. Are you hungry?"

She nodded.

"You can make one for yourself if you'd like," I told her.

"Gee, thanks," she said and headed right into the kitchen. It was probably at this point that I started rationalizing—telling myself it would only be cruel to kick her out, that I might learn a thing or two about the Children's workings if I let her stick around, and that she could sleep on the sofa or something. Or something.

To be perfectly honest about it, I'd been celibate for several months, since I broke up with Barbara Frye—who was the arts editor of the evening paper, the *Tribune*—or rather until I did something stupid and she dumped me.

In a little while Rebecca returned to the living room with her sandwich and a glass of cranberry juice. The game ended—I couldn't tell you who won—and an old movie came on, *It's a Wonderful Life,* with Jimmy Stewart and Donna Reed, which I'd seen at least half a million times.

"Do you mind if I sit on the sofa too?" Rebecca asked. "It's hard to see the screen from this angle."

"You can have the whole thing," I said, getting up. "I'll bring you a blanket and a pillow."

"Do you have a cat, by any chance?"

"Yes."

"I think it's meowing outside."

The air conditioner must have blotted out the sound. I went

over to the sliding glass door that led to my ridiculous little slab of so-called patio, which I never even used, and let in Babe, my gray tiger. We'd been together since Boston, where I found her scraggly and starving under my stoop on Newberry Street. The vet said she'd already been spayed. But she certainly wasn't doing very well out in the streets, so we figured she'd been abandoned or run away. She still had a roving spirit and would disappear for a couple of days at a time, but she always came back. Anyway, I let her in, gave her a can of her favorite food, Taste o' the Sea, and then went to the bathroom to take a leak. When I returned to the living room, carrying a blanket and a pillow, Rebecca had Babe up on the sofa. She was playing a game with her, sort of boxing with two fingers, cuffing her on the muzzle, while Babe held up one paw in defense. I could tell by the way her ears were folded back that Babe was getting pissed off.

"Don't you think you're playing a little rough?" I asked.

"Our cat at home loves this."

Suddenly Babe hissed at Rebecca and swatted her with her paw before bolting off the sofa.

"You bitch!" Rebecca cried and sucked on the back of her hand. "Look what she did to me."

Two red lines, like a section of railroad track, ran diagonally across her hand.

"I told you she didn't like it. Here." I dropped the bedding on the sofa. "Help yourself if you want anything more to eat. I'll give you a lift to the bus station in the morning. The bathroom is down the hall."

"Thanks," she said, licking cranberry juice from the corner of her mouth. "Are you going to bed now?"

"Yes."

"Well, I'll see you."

I turned down the volume on the TV but left it on in case she wanted to see the rest of the movie, then headed for the shower. Though I kept telling myself that nothing would be allowed to happen, I found myself going through a lot of the ablutions that I usually reserve until morning—like shaving and putting on underarm deodorant—so obviously in some dark corner of my brain I was hoping something would develop.

I stepped out of the steamy bathroom into the air-conditioning of the bedroom, slipped between the cool sheets naked, which is how I always sleep, and picked up the book I happened to be reading: *Ironweed* by William Kennedy, which I was really enjoying. I'm a fairly high-strung person. Sometimes I have sleeping problems and so I usually try to read myself to sleep. Ordinarily the conditions would have been perfect for helping me wind down, but I wasn't getting drowsy, and I could barely concentrate on the book. Finally, in exasperation, I switched off the lamp and rolled over on my stomach. Through the closed door I could dimly hear Jimmy Stewart as he ran down Main Street in a state of hysterics after learning the fate of his loved ones had he not been born. I worried a little about Babe, whose favorite spot to sack out was the blue velveteen chair. I didn't want Rebecca bothering her. Oddly enough, my own well-being hardly concerned me at all. Besides, I sleep with an aluminum baseball bat between the night table and my bed—an old habit from Boston, where my apartment was burgled twice.

Eventually the TV went off. I heard the toilet flush. I lay there in the dark with my eyes closed, wide awake, the blood pounding in my eardrums. At the very least I dreaded the prospect of dragging my ass into the office with no sleep. I'm a basket case without at least four hours' worth. Finally what I dreaded most might happen—and secretly hoped for, I must admit—did happen. I heard the metallic sound of the doorknob turning. My left hand stole across the sheets searching for the bat handle. The door creaked. I opened my eyes and propped myself up on one elbow. Rebecca stood in the doorway, the ambient light of the living room glowing behind her. She was naked from the waist up, but still wearing her long skirt. The canvas bag was in her hand.

"May I come in?"

"I don't know," I replied in a phlegmy voice.

She stood there for what seemed like minutes on end, but was probably a lot less. Then she padded over to the bed.

"May I sit down?"

I didn't even reply this time, knowing that my silence would answer the question without me having to feel responsible for it. She lowered herself to the edge of the mattress and sat down. The frame creaked. She smelled like perfume and seawater. Her nipples stood out against the light, as big as the first joint of my pinky. I could feel the heat off her body.

"What's in the bag?" I asked.

She leaned over and rooted around in it, then straightened back up holding different objects in each hand. In the meager light I could just barely make them out: the round, flat case for a diaphragm and a tube of spermicidal jelly.

"You certainly come prepared," I said.

She shrugged her shoulders, opened the case, took out the rubber diaphragm, squeezed spermicide around the rim, stood up, lifted her skirt and one leg, and inserted the device. Then she sat back down on the bed.

"You wanted me to watch that," I said.

She shrugged again and shook out her hair.

"Squeamish?" she asked.

"No. Is this why you came here?"

"No. I told you why."

"Somehow, I'm skeptical."

"I'm not used to going very long without it," she said. "It's not normal."

"You'd be surprised."

"I was already wet when I put . . . the thing . . . in. My lips were wet."

"Do you realize that this is unethical for me?"

"Once I came thirty-two times in one day. I counted."

She drew one knee up over my legs and hiked her skirt way up.

"The ethical question doesn't concern you, huh?" I said.

"I'm concerned with how you're going to fuck me," she said and lowered her face down to mine. Her breath was all perfume, warm lips wet, breasts dangling against my chest. "I want you up inside me."

We made love. Or, to be more accurate, we fucked. I was

trembling all over when we were done, it had been such a long time.

"Are you cold?"

"Yes," I lied.

"Here." She pulled up the blanket and tucked it around me. "Did you like me?"

"A little too much, I'm afraid."

"There's no such thing as too much. You'll see. In a little while I'll suck your cock and drive you crazy again. You'd like that, wouldn't you?"

I didn't say.

"Or you can fuck me up the ass if you want."

"You talk like a professional, Rebecca."

"A professional what?"

"At sex," I said, not wanting to use the word *whore*. But she seemed to grasp my meaning, and in the dim light she looked delighted by the idea.

"I'm good at sex, aren't I?"

"Aren't you going to miss all the . . . all the fooling around that they did?"

"No," she said and giggled. "I can find all the pleasure I want on my own. Look, I'm doing it."

She left a damp track of kisses down my chest and belly and took me in her mouth. I was astonished at how exciting she was, and appalled, too, which probably made it much more exciting.

"You taste sweet," she said when it was over. "Not like some men." She nuzzled under my left arm, a sleek leg thrown over mine and her damp mound rubbing gently against my knee. "I'm fucking your leg," she said. "Oooo, it feels so good. In heaven you're always coming. Forever. Don't move." There was something poignant about her profligacy. What might have seemed unattractive in a Labrador retriever was somehow touching in her. Maybe it would've been different if she wasn't such a pretty girl. Finally, with a gasp and a shudder, her hips stopped grinding and relaxed. "That was super," she whispered. "You're hard again!"

Believe me, I was even more amazed.

"Fuck me up the ass now."

"I don't think so, Rebecca."

She climbed off me and assumed a kneeling position at the foot of the bed with her behind raised toward me.

"Please," she said. "I want you."

"I'd rather not."

"Why?"

"I don't like the idea of it."

"The *idea?* Did you ever try it?"

"No."

"Then how can you be sure?"

"I just am."

"You're missing something."

"It's not my style."

"Come in here, then," she said, her fingers parting the genital lips, and I arched forward over her, her back damp and a breast heavy in my cupped hand underneath her. It was exhausting in that position, and I collapsed to her side when it was over, feeling as though my brains had been pulled out through my nose. Soon the air conditioner made me shiver and I crawled back under the covers. The clock said 3:20. Rebecca returned to the hollow between my chin and shoulder.

"We smell like sex," she said.

"We do indeed," I agreed. My hamstrings ached.

"Are you going to write your story tomorrow?"

"Probably start it, yes," I said.

"Did you uncover a lot of interesting facts about them?"

"Enough for my purposes."

"Like what, for instance? Come on, you can tell me."

"What do you care? You're leaving."

"Just curious," she said, tracing her finger up my jawline. "How come you haven't pumped me for information?"

"I'm trying to keep this incident separate from my professional life."

"This incident. You mean us fucking?"

"Yes. Us fucking."

"How high-minded. If I was in your shoes, I'd ask me some questions."

"I'm not in my shoes," I said.

"I'd take advantage of a situation like this." She ignored my stupid quip. "After all, tomorrow I'll be far away and nobody will ever know I was here. I'd ask about a few things."

"Okay. Who's Abraham?"

That seemed to catch her up short.

"Does he exist or not?" I pressed her.

"I really don't know," she said.

"You're a regular gold mine of information."

"Ask me about Isaac," she said.

"Okay. What happened to his face?"

"He fell into a poison ivy patch."

"Doing what?"

"Trying to fuck me."

"How come you didn't catch it?"

"Just lucky, I guess."

"Were you his girl?"

"He thought so."

"Is that why you're leaving?"

"Maybe. How come you picked the Children to write about?"

"Some contacts of mine put me onto them."

"Do you hate them?"

"I wouldn't put it that way."

"Put it how you'd put it."

"I think there's probably a case against them."

"For what?"

"Cooking their books."

"What's that?"

"Lying about the money they've got coming in and where it's coming from and what they're doing with it."

"You're wrong. They're the most honest, upright, open, nicest people I ever met."

"Then how come you're splitting?"

"Maybe I'll come back. Do you want to fuck me one more time? I'm still wet and tingly."

"Thank you, Rebecca, but I couldn't manage it if I tried."

"Was I good? Did you like fucking me?"

"Yes."

"A lot?"

"Yes."

"I'll be right here in the morning for you," she said. "I'll send you off to write your story with a big smile on your face."

"That would be nice," I mumbled and spun down a dark velvety tunnel to sleep.

* * *

The curtains shut out the daylight. I hadn't set the alarm and the clock's glowing blue digits said 9:45. Rebecca lay curled with her back to me, all musk and stillness, tangled strands of brown hair fanned over the pillow. I desired her again, and remembered what she said about sending me off to work with a smile on my face. But I had to take a leak first, so I tossed aside my half of the blanket and swung my legs onto the floor. In the process I knocked over her canvas bag. A heavy rectangular object about the size of a pocket dictionary tumbled onto the carpet and broke open. A tape cassette fell out.

I glanced back at her. She didn't stir. As quietly as possible I picked up the recorder and the tape and tiptoed into the bathroom, marveling at what a chump I had allowed myself to be. In there, I turned on the ventilator fan and the shower to create as much background noise as possible, dropped the cassette back in, rewound it part way, and pushed the "play" button.

"Did you like me?" her voice asked, echoey but quite intelligible.

"A little too much, I'm afraid," my voice said.

"There's no such thing as too much . . ."

I rewound it to the beginning. The tape started when she had entered the room. Everything, all the heavy breathing, all the talking dirty, the moaning and creaking bed springs, was on the tape. I sat on the toilet-seat lid for quite a while trying to figure out what to do. One option was to erase the tape, stick it back into her bag, and send her trundling back to the Children with her mission bungled.

There was also a good argument for me *not* erasing the tape, but rather keeping it intact in my possession, in case there was ever any question of what had happened at my apartment—of whether I'd raped her, for instance. The tape would show pretty conclusively that she had seduced me. Of course, as a reporter it was still inexcusable for me to have been suckered in, but legally, in terms of potential lawsuits, I might need some hard evidence to protect myself—that is if I went ahead with the story.

Then I realized that they had already partially succeeded in their attempt to intimidate me, simply by making me doubt whether or not to go ahead on the story, and that *really* pissed me off.

I snuck into the living room and found exactly what the situation called for in the cardboard box where I kept all my tape cassettes: a recording I'd made of a B'52s album that started out with the song "Devil in My Car." It was even on the same brand of Sony tape as her cassette. I fast-forwarded it to the end, thinking they'd rewind it to listen, and stuck it in the pocket of my flannel bathrobe. Meanwhile, Babe was rubbing against my leg wanting her breakfast. I broke open a can of Sea Nip Dinner, another favorite repast, fed her, and tiptoed back into the bedroom.

As soon as I entered, Rebecca rolled over and opened her eyes. I quickly sat down at the edge of the bed, trying to figure out how to slip the tape recorder back into her bag without her seeing it.

"Sleep well?" I asked.

"Uh-hmmm," she nodded drowsily and shook the hair out of her face. A hand came out from under the covers and began foraging inside my bathrobe.

"You're hard again," she said.

In spite of everything she was still capable of turning me on. It was awful but I couldn't help it. The human race is pathetic.

"It's from thinking about you," I told her.

"Really?" she said, delighted. "About fucking me?"

"You love that word, don't you?"

"I love what it stands for."

I pulled the blanket down slowly, revealing her naked body.

"Well, darling," I told her sweetly. "I'm going to fuck you good."

She licked her lips and lifted her knees. I lowered myself onto her and managed to slip the tape deck into the bag and stand the bag back up. I'd be lying if I said I had to pretend she was someone else, but when we were done I couldn't wait to wash her off of me.

A half hour later we were headed downtown on Washington Avenue to the bus terminal in my Datsun.

"What time does your bus leave?" I asked as we drove past her alma mater, St. Agnes, in a part of town known as "the Yards," where several slaughterhouses used to operate until just before World War II.

"You can just drop me off at the station," she said. "You don't have to wait, or anything. I'll be all right."

"No, I want to wait with you and put you on the bus personally."

It was fairly obvious that she didn't want to get on any bus, but would have much preferred to skip back to the town house on Union Street. I gave her a big gushy smile and she showed me a slightly less enthusiastic one in return. She hadn't showered before we left and she smelled like a goddamn monkey.

The terminal stood in the shadows of the expressway that cut off the city from the riverfront that it owed so much of its history to. The usual assortment of glowering bozos, drunks, displaced persons, bag people, and released mental patients were on hand in the main waiting room. One enraged traveler pounded on a coin-operated TV built into her chair when it shut off in the middle of a "Mork and Mindy" rerun.

"I'll get you a ticket," I told Rebecca.

She smiled back gamely.

There were two buses to Buffalo before noon. One was a local that stopped at every jerk-water along the way, and the other was an express that didn't stop anywhere except its final destination. The express cost me eight and a half bucks more, but it was worth it.

"If you just give me the ticket, I'll get on myself and you can go off to your job," she suggested.

"I refuse to leave you alone here in the company of all these shady characters," I told her nobly.

I guess she decided to play her stupid bluff right out to the end because she dutifully, if a little sullenly, got on board the bus as it was getting ready to depart.

"Feeling sad to go?" I asked as she mounted the first step.

"I guess," she replied gloomily. "Well, 'bye."

"Bye, darling," I said and watched her struggle down the aisle through the line of sooty windows. As the bus backed out I blew her a kiss, and when it was out of sight on the expressway ramp, I walked back to my car.

CHAPTER 3

My story came out five days later. Essentially all I could do was report that the state attorney general was about to seek indictments against the Children of Abraham for charity fraud and outline the group's denials of those allegations based on what Isaac had shown me and said.

I managed to scrounge up a little more information from my contact at the A.G.'s office concerning the "founder" of the group, the so-called Prophet Abraham. He was thought to be a former tent-show evangelist out of Texas named Lester Trent who had started an outfit called "Teens for Christ" in the sixties and got into some trouble involving his female followers ("teen angels," he called them) that caused him to flee the Houston area. He rematerialized briefly in the Capital with an investment scam that got him in more hot water, and finally he left the United States altogether, theoretically for Switzerland, where a lot of the Children of Abraham's money was thought to be funneled.

Unfortunately none of this information about Trent's whereabouts could be substantiated, so it was less than good journalism to use it, but it was also obvious that he'd never be in a position to complain about it, so I went with it for the laugh value. The hardest task was trying to explain the group's theology. Since I derived my understanding of it entirely from the Abe-grams, I just picked out some of the more ridiculous elements and set them forth for the reader in an unabashedly sarcastic manner. It was a major shortcoming in the story.

Frankly, by my own standards it was pretty lame stuff. The whole thing had left a bad taste in my mouth and I'd pretty much made up my mind to take a vacation from religious nuts for a while to concentrate on other things. I was annoyed with the story and pissed off at myself for doing such a half-assed job. Of course it was fine by Kaiser Korp standards, except that they practically have no standards.

* * *

The morning my story appeared was the same day that the Vermont State Police got a positive make on the victim of the Landfill Murder.

I was sitting at my desk in the newsroom after lunch reading the New York *Times*. I really didn't have anything to do because I was pretty much responsible for cooking up my own assignments and, to tell you the truth, I was just goofing off that afternoon. It was Friday and I was planning to leave work around two and drive down to my parents' beach house on Fire Island for the weekend. My "big story" for the week was done, so I was just killing an hour reading the only newspaper that tells you what's going on in the real world.

To say that the *Times-Herald* newsroom was an unstructured operation is putting it mildly. You could sit around there knitting a muffler, or calling all your friends around the country on the WATS line, or writing personal letters on Kaiser Korp stationery, or beating your meat all day long and nobody would bother you. One of a reporter's main tools for gathering information is the telephone, but at the *T-H* it was a joke because at any given moment three quarters of the people present were on the phone to their grandmother in Kalamazoo.

The only thing I really had to do that day before I took off was make out my weekly expense sheet. This was a tally of all the miles you supposedly drove in your car on company business, i.e., gathering news. They paid us eighteen cents a mile. The idea was to pad your expense sheet by including all sorts of trips that you never made. It was dishonest, but everybody did it. Some people liked to justify it as a "blow against the fascist corporate state" but between you and me it was just simple thievery. And I did it, too, so I guess I was a crook myself—not that I'm apologizing, really, because these days eighteen cents a mile doesn't cover the cost of operating a car. Maybe we should just drop the whole subject. I'm sorry I brought it up.

Anyway, it was close to two o'clock and I was making out my expense sheet when Merle Lyons barged into the newsroom. It was impossible for him to just quietly walk into a room and sit down at his desk like a normal person. He was like Orson Welles barging into the newspaper office in *Citizen Kane*.

In fact he was about the same size as Orson Welles was in his later years, except that Merle was my age. He was terrifically ambitious and was considered one of the shining stars of the staff, which tells you a lot about the clowns I worked with, because Merle was a mediocre reporter at best. Frankly, I don't think he would've made it at the night rewrite desk of a halfway decent paper, like the Boston *Globe*. I think he resented me because I was allowed to operate independently whereas he was still tied to the city desk, and because I refused to vocally admire him like everybody else did. But unless you were a clown, there wasn't much there to admire.

Wherever Merle was there was always a big commotion. Unfortunately his desk was right next to mine. The building was fairly new, and the architects had designed the newsroom with all the desks bolted down to the floor, in cozy little groups, so you couldn't just pick up your desk and move it out into the hall if someone was disturbing you. And even though everybody treated him like the star reporter, nobody really wanted to sit next to him because he was such a noisy bastard that you could hardly concentrate on what you were doing, even if you were just writing a letter to your Aunt Sally, let alone working on a news story. He had already been there a year when I was hired, and I didn't realize what I was getting into when I chose the vacant desk next to his. By the time I found out what an obnoxious motherfucker he was, it was too late, and nobody would switch with me.

The other thing about him that used to drive me crazy was the guy's eating habits. Instead of eating in the cafeteria like everybody else, he used to bring a tray down to the newsroom and eat at his desk. And he always got the most gloppy, disgusting thing on the menu. Spanish rice. A hot pork sandwich. Or this repulsive macaroni and hamburger dish that upstaters refer to as "goulash." He always got *two* desserts, like tapioca pudding and cherry pie, or cheesecake and ice cream. Sometimes, when he was on a "diet," he got two Jell-O's. To tell you the truth, I've never seen such a fucking pig in all my life. No wonder the guy weighed over two hundred and fifty pounds.

The reporter on the other side of my desk was another winner, but compared to Merle he was as smooth as Noel Coward, and nowhere near as noisy. His name was J. Roland Tuttle—or just plain "Rollie" around the office. Nobody knew what the "J." stood for, and Rollie wouldn't say. I used to try to trick him into revealing it by calling him Jasper or Julius or Jackson and see if he would turn around, but it never worked.

Unlike Merle, Rollie was blissfully devoid of ambition. He was pushing forty and for about ten straight years had covered various suburban beats for the *T-H,* which meant, mainly, that he sat through a lot of zoning board meetings. Once in a while the city desk might send him out to cover a two-alarm fire or a highway fatality if there was nobody else around. But what would have been a nice change of pace for someone else, or even a minor opportunity to shine for a kid starting out, was just a pain in the ass to him. He didn't like to have his routine interrupted. He enjoyed his zoning boards and his school budget disputes. He was a simple salary slave who was grateful for the job he had, and who got a Guild raise every eighteen months, and who had no desire to rock his little boat.

He was a little bit tubby, but nowhere near Merle's class, and not a slob either. In fact, he was quite a dapper fellow for an upstater who had probably never set foot in a decent men's clothing store. He always wore a three-piece suit, and even though he bought them at Monkey Wards, the colors were at least in good taste. And unlike a lot of our fellow staffers, he was acquainted with the art of dry cleaning. The finishing touch was his gold pocket watch, which he wore on an old-fashioned fob. It was a "sportsman's" model that you see in the outdoor catalogs, engraved with a tableau of ducks winging over the wetlands.

This watch was the key to his inner life, because secretly he considered himself J. Roland Tuttle, *sportsman*. He spent a huge percentage of his salary on expensive hunting and fishing gear, including a four-wheel-drive Ford Bronco with every luxury option you could imagine. On especially dull days at the office he would take me out to the parking lot to show me how to cast with a fly rod, which he kept at the ready in the back of his car at all times. He was constantly inviting me to come along with him on his weekend excursions. The one time I gave in and went it rained cats and dogs all day Saturday and I lay in a smelly two-man tent listening to him recapitulate every lunker he ever landed in a lifetime of angling. At least I didn't lose another toe.

He was married to a woman who looked like one of those dolls you win at the carnival for knocking over iron milk bottles, and the two of them lived in a bungalow in that depressing section of the capital that had been the suburbs in the 1930s but which had been absorbed into the city since then like a pile of crumbs surrounded by a giant amoeba. Every year the Tuttles threw a B.Y.O.B. Christmas party, and you could see how little of his income Rollie devoted to his home compared to what he spent on trout flies and Gore-Tex hunting togs. The furniture was all stapled-together and the knickknacks looked like they came out of a K-Mart discontinued merchandise bin. You felt sorry for *her*.

So, I was filling out my weekly expense sheet when Merle barged into the newsroom like a rampaging elephant, carrying on about the Landfill Murder and waving his notepad in the air.

"This is hot. This is juicy," he blabbered as he struggled to remove his imitation harris tweed polyester sports jacket and settle in behind his desk, which was on a dogleg to my right. As usual, I tried to ignore him. Pretty soon, though, his number one groupie, Ginny Unger, the "editorial assistant" *(i.e.,* gofer), bustled over to our area. She was the person, incidentally, who had given my address to Rebecca over the phone, a blunder that I had brought to her attention in no uncertain terms. She now officially hated my guts. Anyway, she stood behind his chair looking on as he rolled a sheet of copy paper into his IBM and started banging out his story. I was almost finished with my expense sheet.

"Wow!" Ginny exclaimed, reading over his shoulder, " '. . . the son of a prominent area physician, retired chief of surgery at Capital Med, Dr. Arthur Hurlbett . . .' "

That got my attention.

"How about this for a headline?" Merle stopped typing for a moment. "Surgeon's Son Is Country Cut Up."

"This isn't the *Enquirer,* Merle," Ginny joked back.

Meanwhile, I had stood up and was reaching over to his desk for his notebook.

"Hey, Graff, whaddaya doing . . . ?"

But I grabbed it away. And there it was in blue smudgy ink: *James F. Hurlbett—28 yrs—L. Placid, N.Y.* As I began to understand his connection to the Landfill Murder, the bottom dropped out of my stomach.

"Aw, Jesus . . ."

"Graff! Hey, what's the matter with him?"

I just stood there groaning and reading Jamie's name, over and over.

"He's kidding, right? Very funny. Gimme back my notes, will ya!"

He tried to grab it back from me. Of course he didn't know that I knew Jamie, but seeing his fat fingers in my face made me so mad that I slapped him several times with his crummy pad. "You'll get it back when I'm done with it, goddamn you," I told him.

"Hey, you two, break it up!" Rollie said. His desk was off a dogleg to my left.

By that time, though, Merle had squirmed out of my range. I flung his pad at him and bolted out of the newsroom, down the hall, and into the lobby. It was a big lobby, very stark-looking, with glass walls on three sides and a receptionist at a little desk in one corner and an enormous blue and red lucite sculpture that was supposed to represent "the spirit of the Kaiser Corporation" in the center of the room. I sat on this chrome and naugahyde sofa in the corner opposite the receptionist and tried to stop shaking.

The day they told me about my brother Philip's death, ten years earlier, I had been in my European history class at the Forrest School in Warren, Connecticut, on a gloomy November afternoon. I remember that one of the assistant headmasters came in to get me, and I knew from the way he conferred with the teacher, who nodded gravely and pointed to me, that it was something very bad. You were expected to be stolid and manly in the face of disaster, and not fall apart, and I didn't on the outside, but inside I was crumbling. They didn't give a whole lot in the way of details—only that he was killed overseas, meaning Vietnam—and that I had to go home. Then they drove me down to the train station in one of the official school station wagons and put me on the train by myself to New York, which is where I really went to pieces and cried until the train entered the tunnel under Park Avenue.

Now when I sat down in the lobby I was in shock. My mind had switched off like an overloaded circuit breaker, and my emotions had temporarily shut down. All I knew was that I had to get away from those clowns in the newsroom. So, I just sat there staring out the plate-glass walls at the cars coming in and going out of the gas station across the street.

Several years earlier, before I got hired, the Kaiser Korp had moved the newspaper's offices way the hell out into the suburbs, about eight miles from downtown, to this wasteland of shopping malls and parking lots and freeways. The interstate to Montreal ran right next to our building, though from the lobby side you couldn't see it. But I didn't care what I watched. And I'm not sure how long I sat there before Rollie came out and found me.

"You okay, kid?" he asked.

I don't think I replied. I may have grunted or something.

"What was that all about? Hey, Grover?"

"Leave me alone."

"Hey, are you crying?"

I must have been, though I don't remember it.

"No," I said.

"Hey, tell me what's going on. What were you two fighting about?"

"We weren't fighting."

"It sure looked like fighting to me."

"That guy was my best friend."

"Who . . . ? Merle?"

"No! Not that stupid motherfucker! The one who was murdered."

"Oh gosh . . ." Rollie said and started backpedaling away from me out of the lobby. I don't think he was prepared to deal with anything beyond a simple personality clash. Anyway, I left the building at that point so nobody else would bother me and headed for this little grass-covered mound with funnels sticking out of it beyond the end of the parking lot where the building's air-conditioning units were buried. After a while the *T-H* desk people started leaving for the day, trooping into the parking lot toward their cars. None of them seemed to notice me. I stayed out there a long time. It was still light out because it was just a week before the summer solstice. I'd completely forgotten about driving down to Fire Island for the weekend. Finally I got up off the grass and trudged back into the building. A new receptionist, the night girl, had come on duty. She said, "Hi," or something, but I walked past her as if she wasn't there.

The newsroom was practically deserted. Rollie and Merle were gone. Since it was Friday night, there were no reporters around. A few might have been out on assignment, but none of them was hanging around the office. The only people there at all were the night copy editor, Jerry Pumphrey, and his assistant, Rasman Chooghly, an American-educated Bengali immigrant. Rasman was a naturalized citizen and spoke English very well, but he did have an Indian accent. They were sitting up at the copy desk, which is this long, horseshoe-shaped table near the wire-service printers, eating their dinners—sandwiches out of brown paper bags. We all knew each other, of course, though I didn't see them that often. My desk was about seventy-five feet across the room from where they sat.

"What are you doing here, Grrrover Grrraff?" Rasman asked. He loved saying my name because it gave him an opportunity to really roll his "r's." It was all done in a friendly, joshing spirit, though.

"Nothing," I muttered.

"You should be out chasing poosy, my boy." He meant *pussy,* of course. That was another thing about Rasman: he was a sex maniac. It preoccupied him totally.

"I don't feel like it," I muttered again, trying to make it obvious that I wasn't in the mood for the usual badinage. I must have succeeded because Rasman quit asking me questions.

I picked up the New York *Times* at the same place where I had left off hours before. But I didn't really read it. I just held it up to my face to seem as though I was occupied. And then I entered the next psychological stage you go through when somebody dies: the dreadful realization that you will never, *ever* see them again. It's a pretty terrible concept, *never,* and the closer you think you are to wrapping your mind around it, the more truly elusive and impossible the idea becomes—until the word *never* starts ringing in your ears and the chills run down your spine.

But the strange thing was, while I was dwelling on the word *never,* I started to realize how long it had been since I had seen Jamie, or talked to him, or gotten a postcard from him, or even thought about him. And when I realized that I hadn't even *thought* about him once in weeks and weeks, I saw how he had become part of my past, in death as well as in life.

And that's what got me out of the *never* stage to the final stage: that combination of sadness and nostalgia where you remember all sorts of specific things about a person, and when you were together in college—like the acne medicine he put on at night, and some old sweater you borrowed from him that you liked to wear so much you never gave it back, and he never asked you for it, or the way he looked throwing a Frisbee on the quadrangle in the fall, with all the beautiful trees around, or finding out he had a date with a certain girl that you were secretly mad about but too shy to talk to, or all of us, him and me and Lisa, driving through the orchards on a snowy night out to the Farm, or the times when you got so stoned smoking together that even the furniture seemed funny.

I must have sat there thinking about all that stuff for an hour or more, rolling the memories around in my mind, because the next time I looked out the windows the sky above the interstate was pink and purple and the sun had finally gone down. I'm not sure what impelled me to do it, but the next moment I closed up the *Times,* walked over to the copy desk, and said to Rasman and Jerry, "Let me see Lyons's story about the Landfill Murder."

They asked what I wanted it for. It was a little irregular for one reporter to ask for another's story when it had reached the copy-editing stage. They probably also had observed that I was acting a little strange in general. Actually, just my being there at nine o'clock on a Friday night was quite strange. But I told them I wanted to read it and they gave it to me. This is what that asshole wrote:

> STOWE—In a case that has struck terror in the hearts of a half-dozen Vermont communities, authorities today identified the remains of a murder and dismemberment victim as James F. Hurlbett, son of a prominent area physician. . . .

That got me, right there: the word *area* as an adjective. You see it all the time in third-rate newspapers with bush-league reporters. It really pissed me off.

The next paragraph described how the pieces had been found in plastic garbage bags at various dumps, and the circumstances under which they were discovered. And then there

was a ridiculous part about how "area residents" were freaking
out over "a fiend on the loose."

Finally, there was this:

> Hurlbett, 28, described as "a part-time artist and
> full-time dropout," was the son of Dr. and Mrs. Ar-
> thur Hurlbett of Minerva Park. Dr. Hurlbett is retired
> chief of surgery at the Capital Medical Center, where
> he served in that capacity from 1964 to 1978. The
> deceased is survived by a sister. Dr. and Mrs. Hurlbett
> have declined comment.

Well, as you can see for yourself, Merle's story was a combination of the cheapest sensationalism and the most incredibly
stupid, tactless obituary writing. He obviously didn't know the
difference between a crime story and an obituary. And I don't
know where he got the part about Jamie being a "part-time
artist and a full-time dropout," but as far as I was concerned, it
was close to being libel, not just tactless and stupid. Of course
the dead can't sue for libel, but that's beside the point. And the
part about "Dr. and Mrs. Hurlbett have declined comment"
really burned me up because knowing what a lazy motherfucker Merle was, not to mention a chickenshit, I'm sure he
didn't *try* to reach them for a comment. He wouldn't have
known how to even go about it. So, he must have made it up.

By the time I finished reading that piece of shit, I was really
angry. I stuck a sheet of paper in my typewriter and rewrote
the whole story, reducing it to three quick professional-look-
ing paragraphs and expunging all of Merle's sensationalistic
stupidity. Then I handed it back in to Rasman and Jerry.

"What is this, Grover?"

"This is a rewrite of Merle Lyons's garbage."

"That isn't your job, Grover. Where's the original?" Jerry
asked. His tone of voice was quite calm, not angry. It must have
been apparent to him that I was in a turbulent state of mind,
but he nevertheless felt it necessary to point out that I was
bending the rules. Anyway I didn't give them the original. I
went back to my desk, held it up, ripped it into little pieces, and
let them flutter down into the garbage pail.

"You shouldn't have done that, Grrrover Grrraff," Rasman said. You could tell that he got a kick out of the gesture, though, because he was still playfully rolling those "r's" and smiling. He may have hated Merle's guts more than I did, because he had to deal with the egotistical sonofabitch as an editor and *knew* what a lousy reporter he really was. I was being overly generous before when I described Merle as "mediocre." In point of fact, he was incompetent.

But I didn't care to discuss the matter anymore, one way or the other, so I put on my jacket and started walking to the door when one of the phones rang up at the copy desk. I was right *at* the door when Rasman called across the room, saying, "Grrrover Grrraff, it's for you."

I couldn't imagine who would call me at this hour at the office on a Friday night. Or why.

"Who is it?" I asked Rasman. My hand was still on the door. I could see Rasman talk into the phone and nod his head.

"He says it's a surprise."

"Oh, for godsake . . ."

I walked all the way back to my desk and waited while Rasman had the call transferred to my phone through the switchboard.

"Hello . . . ?"

"Mr. Graff?"

"Yeah. Who is this?"

"Isaac."

It was a surprise, all right. About the last thing in the world I was in the mood for was hassling with him, and I couldn't imagine why else he would call except to give me a hard time.

"What can I do for you, Isaac?" I attempted to be business-like.

There was an eerie silence at his end of the line. I could hear him breathing and pictured him, all flushed and flaky-faced, pumping himself up for a display of outrage.

"We want a retraction," he said.

"Oh, you must have seen the story, then?"

"Yes, we saw it. It was all lies and distortions."

"It couldn't have been *that* bad. Maybe in a few parts—"

"You said you wouldn't twist what I said!"

"I did my best, Isaac."

"No you didn't, you godless punk. You did it on purpose."

"Well, what part is it that you object to, Issac?"

"The whole devilish thing!" he screamed in my ear. "Especially those lies about our finances. I thought I made it clear to you. Where did you get that . . . that *shit!*"

"From somebody I know in the attorney general's office, if you really want to know."

"From a horse's ass, you mean."

"Oh, I don't know about that—"

"Because none of it is true."

"According to him it is."

"It's horseshit."

"Whatever you say. I just don't feel like arguing about it right now, Isaac, if you don't mind. In fact, I was on my way out the door when you called. Now if—"

"Listen to me, you godless piece of shit. You print a retraction. You print it in Monday's paper at the latest. But you print it or—"

"Now you're going to threaten me, right?"

"Just see that you print it."

"I hate to disappoint you, Isaac, but there isn't going to be any retraction. You're really barking up the wrong tree."

"Do you think this is a game? This isn't a game, shitball. This is your life—"

"Oh, go fuck yourself."

I hung up. Just then I realized he probably got the whole thing on tape.

* * *

This kind of thing happens all the time. Not whether or not they taped it—which, frankly, I barely gave a second thought to—but just threatening phone calls in general. In fact, I can't think of one instance when I did a story about cultists where they *didn't* call up and demand a retraction.

What these idiots don't realize is that no newspaper will issue retractions on demand, particularly on any matter of substance. Libel is an extremely difficult and costly thing to prove. First of all, you've got to demonstrate not only that the material was untrue, but you've got to show damages, and on top of it you've got to prove that it was written out of malice. Since I was merely reporting the allegations of state officials, they'd never prove malice. In short, they didn't have a case. Isaac was wasting his breath, and I knew it.

"Who was that, Grrrover?" Rasman called over from his pool of light at the copy desk.

"My Uncle Theodore from Scarsdale."

"Is that any way to talk to your Uncle Theodore?" He and Jerry laughed and continued a game of gin rummy.

I sat there staring at the phone, developing an intense desire to not be alone that night. Disturbing images of Rebecca flashed through my head in disjointed bits and pieces, her legs, her breasts, her voice, all those words, like a fever dream. Finally I decided to call Barbara Frye, since she was the only person in the whole city I felt I could talk to. I just didn't want to go home to my crummy apartment in Heritage Hills.

Barbara was the arts editor of our evening paper, the *Tribune*. They gave her about fourteen column inches a day. A couple of times a week she'd write a review of something. Basically the Capital is considered a large hick town and even the giant shopping-mall cinemas with eight theaters don't show anything but space movies. Up until the seventies a couple of old theaters downtown showed foreign films, Barbara said, but now they only show porn. Once in a while she would review plays done by community theater groups, i.e., amateur productions in the suburbs. These were generally Neil Simon comedies or Paul Zindel melodramas performed in church basements, and often acted by people she knew, so her reviews tended to be cream-puff jobs. She was actually sort of a minor celebrity around the city and did a little five-minute "what's happening in the arts" spot on the local news every Friday night. People would recognize her when we went out.

The basic problem was that she was about ten years older than me. She had been divorced since her mid-twenties, didn't have any kids, lived in a really nicely renovated farmhouse out of town, and rather relished her role as a provincial arts maven. She was quite good-looking, small and slender, but in great shape for someone pushing forty. She worked out at a health club five days a week and ran in six-mile road races.

The big mistake I made was to suggest that we might live together. I said it one night in bed, in the dark, and she immediately set me straight on the subject. Since I lived in a jive-plastic apartment complex, she said, it obviously meant me moving into her house, and she had no intention of "compromising" her "hard-won freedom." She was an organized and determined person and she proceeded to edge me out of her life in a very systematic fashion. Every week she made herself a little bit less available, until she wasn't there for me at all. Then, one night around Thanksgiving, I showed up at her house plastered and asked her to marry me. That in itself wouldn't have been so terrible, except it was three o'clock in the morning, and she was in bed with the weatherman from the local NBC affiliate station, and I wouldn't leave, and he threatened to punch me, and finally Barbara threw both of us out.

After that she became extremely snooty and refused to even speak to me. Since we worked out of different newsrooms I didn't see her very often, sometimes for weeks, and then only in the parking lot. When you really get down to it she was a bush-league journalist going nowhere, but she was still more intelligent than any of the other bozos on either paper and I missed her.

Anyway, I called her at home, but there was no answer. I shouldn't have even bothered, since it was after ten o'clock on a Friday night, and she was probably off at some movie or art opening or fund-raiser for the Capital Symphony. So, I said good night to Rasman and Jerry, who were still playing cards, and finally left the goddamn office.

* * *

As I told you, our building was located in this consumer wasteland out in the suburbs. We were at the end of an enormous commercial strip about four miles long called Plaza Boulevard. All the way down on either side was one shopping establishment after another, including a couple of colossal malls. The area was developed entirely since the sixties. Before that it was just farms.

Mixed in along the way, between the malls and the muffler shops, were about a half-dozen singles bars. None of these places catered to a clientele more sophisticated than your average carpet salesman. If you grew up in New York City, like I did, the social life available in the Capital could be pretty depressing. Besides, I'm not much of a drinker, despite what I told you about the episode at Barbara Frye's house. I hardly ever drink during the day or even at lunch. It puts me to sleep. About twice a year I manage to get really plastered, but I pay a terrible price.

The problem is that I get brutal hangovers. I get so psychologically maimed that I have to spend the next twenty-four hours in bed in a dark room with no stimulation whatsoever. Even the sound of a truck going by will give me tachycardia. I guess my body doesn't metabolize alcohol very well. Or maybe I don't get enough of the right vitamins. But whatever the cause, I'm simply not willing to put myself through it very often. So, when I do go out, I usually just have a little white wine.

I certainly didn't intend to get blitzed when I pulled into the first nightspot along the strip. It was a large place called Jasmine East—there wasn't any Jasmine West as far as I knew—and it had a mixed crowd of adult singles, college students, and proletarian slobs. The decor was sort of South Seas Sleaze, with giant tiki gods here and there holding up the ceiling and a big dance floor made out of translucent plastic with colored lights flashing underneath. The music was unbelievably loud, a tremendous din.

I fought my way up to the bar and ordered a white wine. It turned out to be some California garbage as sweet as cough medicine, and it was served on the rocks, which is how upstaters like to drink their wine. I took the ice cubes out and put them in the ashtray and just tried to force the shit down. A few minutes later I decided to switch to red wine, which turned out to be some horrible rotgut Chianti, also served on the rocks, but at least not as sweet.

After a while I managed to strike up a conversation with two young women sitting next to where I was standing. One was tall and willowy with a big nose and a very impressive chest. Her friend was black-haired and quite small, not a midget or anything, but a slip of a girl about five feet tall with the cutest little Peter Pan haircut. It turned out that they were both clerks at Doheny's Department Store in Century Plaza, where the mobile-home crowd does its shopping. I bought them each a drink (apricot sour and sombrero) and started devoting most of my attention to the little dark-haired one, Donna. I made a few attempts to include her friend, Grace, in the conversation, but the din was so overpowering that you had to practically shout in the ear of the person you were talking to, and I loved the way Donna's hair smelled when I leaned close to her, so unfortunately Grace got kind of frozen out.

I kept the rounds of drinks coming, ordering two wines at a time for myself. Then for some crazy reason I switched to straight brandy, and by midnight I was getting bombed. Donna asked me to dance so we went out on the floor and she turned out to be a great dancer. I can do all those fifties jitterbug moves, and she followed right along perfectly, though she hadn't even been born back then. For a while a small crowd gathered around us and watched. I decided that I was madly in love with her. When we finally returned to the bar her friend was gone.

The trouble was that they had both arrived in Donna's car. I tried to convince her that I had seen Grace leave the club on the arm of a fabulously well-dressed guy, but she didn't buy it and struck off into the crowd looking for her. She finally located her in the bathroom, throwing up all those apricot sours. I made one last-ditch effort to get her to spend the night with me, suggesting that she lend Grace her car, but by this time she was starting to resent my tactics. It was all I could do to get her to write her phone number down on the inside of a matchbook and then I watched her help Grace wobble off into the crowd toward the exit.

I didn't stick around that ridiculous place more than five minutes after they left. The noise and smoke were making me sick too. Back in my car, driving down the strip, I started to realize how loaded I was and grew apprehensive about waking up hung over the next day. Also, for the first time in a couple of hours, I started thinking about Jamie again. So, instead of stopping at another stupid club, I headed home. I got on the expressway and crawled along at about twenty-five miles per hour while other drivers, possibly even drunker than I was, honked angrily and swerved to pass me. When I got home I lurched straight into the bedroom and fell asleep with my clothes on.

* * *

I woke up at 6:30 the next morning on the verge of a total metabolic breakdown. I felt as desiccated as a mummy, my head was splitting, my heart was racing like a gerbil's, and I knew it was only going to get worse because I was actually still a little drunk. The short-term plan of action was to take a shower and four aspirins, drink a large glass of milk, and return to bed with the curtains drawn and the covers pulled up over my head for at least another twelve hours.

But I wasn't able to go back to sleep, of course, so I just lay there in a little cocoon of despair, shivering—even though it was about seventy-five degrees out—and trying not to think about Jamie being chopped into pieces. For a while I thought I was losing my mind, I was so bent out of shape with anxiety. Once I actually came close to getting up and driving to the hospital emergency room, but I knew they'd just make me sit in the waiting area until Tuesday, and besides, I didn't think I could make it out to my car. It's hard for me to explain why I didn't just gulp down a few drinks. After all, alcohol is one of the best anxiety-relievers known to man. I suppose my father drummed the idea into my head that anybody who drinks in the morning, or to get rid of a hangover, is in danger of becoming an alcoholic. It was silly to worry about it in my case because, as you know, I don't drink that much on a regular basis. So, I made myself sweat it out instead.

Around three o'clock I managed to crawl into the kitchen and make myself a bowl of tomato soup with milk instead of water. I whistled for Babe at the sliding glass door but she was off on a ramble and wouldn't come home. My appetite was zero and it was all I could do to force down the soup. It depressed me even more to see what a beautiful day it was outside, so I went back to bed and tried to read old magazines. That's how bad my hangovers are. I can't even read a *new* magazine. They have to be old ones. New ones are too close to reality and seem to feed that horrible sense of incipient doom that engulfs me. When I'm strung out like this I prefer something more detached from the real world. Old *National Geographics* are the best.

I read the goddamn things until about eight o'clock, then tuned in the Red Sox–Yankee game on my clock radio. They were playing in Fenway and the broadcast was so crackly you could hardly hear it, which was a good thing in a way, because it took all my concentration to follow the action. By the third inning, I managed to fall asleep.

I slept more than twelve hours and woke up again after ten o'clock on Sunday morning, definitely on the road to recovery. After a shower I put on my jeans and an old polo shirt and my sunglasses and drove down to the little shopping plaza where the "Family Center" sign is to get the papers and a bag of jelly doughnuts.

I'm a Sunday newspaper junkie. I get the *Times,* the Boston *Globe,* and our own rag, and I read them straight through from cover to cover. During the baseball season I've been known to linger over the *Globe* sports section for an hour in itself, poring over all the Red Sox gossip, over every single box score, all the batting averages and pitchers' ERA's. It used to drive Barbara Frye up a tree. She thought sports, particularly baseball, was the select domain of imbeciles.

As for our own rag, the Sunday *Times-Herald,* you could get through the whole goddamn thing from end to end in under thirty minutes. I used to time myself at it. My personal record was fourteen minutes, and I'm no speed reader either. That one had been the Easter Sunday edition and skimpier than hell because about half the staff had called in sick that Friday. The front-page headline that day was one of the all-time gems of my career there: MILLIONS CELEBRATE EASTER!

So, I took the papers and doughnuts back home, and made a cup of Sanka, and started wallowing in all that gray newsprint. It was just after twelve o'clock when my phone rang.

"Darling! Where are you?"

"Obviously I'm here, in my apartment. Hi, Mom."

"Well, where *were* you? I've been worried sick. We expected to see you here on Friday evening and then your telephone was busy all day and all night Saturday—"

"I took it off the hook."

"Whatever for?"

"I was sick."

"Are you all right? I waited for two boats down at the ferry landing."

"Sorry I made you wait for nothing, Mom. I'm all right now. I was sick yesterday."

"With what?"

"One of those twenty-four-hour viruses."

"Oh. But, why didn't you call, Grover?"

"I'm sorry. I just forgot."

"I imagined you lying there strangled with the telephone cord, for godsake."

"Actually, Mom, something very unpleasant has happened up here." I struggled to phrase it. "Do you remember Jamie Hurlbett, my college roommate?"

"Of course I remember Jamie. He came to the beach. He did those lovely paintings."

"He was killed last week."

I could hear my mother draw in her breath sharply.

"In a car?"

"No. He was murdered."

"Oh, that poor boy! Why? Was it drugs, Grover?"

"I honestly don't know, Mom. I don't think anyone knows. Anyway, I found out about it on Friday, and I was too upset to come down."

"Poor baby. I'm so sorry. Did you go to his funeral?"

The question jolted me so completely that I thought I felt the whole room shift.

"I have to get off now, Mom. Excuse me. I'll call you back later."

I hung up, frantically searched for the Lifestyle section of the *Times-Herald*, and opened to the obituary page. Sure enough, there was a funeral notice for James F. Hurlbett. It said the memorial service would begin at noon at the Grace Episcopal Church in Minerva Park and that he would be laid to rest in Highland Cemetery immediately following the service.

The amazing thing was that, for some stupid reason, in the thirty-six hours since I'd learned of his death, it simply hadn't occurred to me that they would have a funeral for him. Obviously it was a neurotic way of coping with the fact of his death —just blocking it out of my mind. And seeing the notice there in the paper, with his name in black Gothic letters, staggered me all over again.

But I didn't have another moment to indulge in feeling bewildered or guilty because I'd already missed the memorial service and, unless I put some speed on, I'd barely have time to get to the cemetery. I changed into my dark gray suit in about five minutes. Outside, it was a gorgeous spring day. I felt like an utter stranger in the world, and strangely doomed.

*   *   *

The burial was taking place in a grove of maple trees about a hundred yards from the gravel drive. A couple of limousines were parked there along the little roadway, as well as a few Mercedes-Benzes. The Hurlbetts were quite wealthy, though you might not have realized it if you'd known Jamie. He was very unconcerned about possessions.

At an equal distance, off to the right of the grave site, the backhoe was parked waiting to do its work. In case you don't know it, most cemeteries use heavy equipment to dig graves these days. The operator and his crew were sort of lollygagging on the grass in their work clothes. From a distance it looked like they were telling jokes. I suppose you can't blame them. To them it's just another job. But it made me angry. The whole scene reminded me of Philip's funeral, except that day it had been cold with snow flurries.

After I parked I waited at the edge of the gravel drive for an opportune moment to cross the grass without being conspicuous and drawing everyone's attention. I was too far away to hear the minister. But soon I realized that no such opportunity would present itself, so I decided to start walking. I was about halfway across the grass when a woman dressed in black bent down and threw a handful of dirt into the hole. Then a tall, white-haired man did the same. A moment later the whole group of about two dozen people started breaking up and walking toward their waiting cars. I had missed the burial too.

Last to leave the site were Jamie's mother and father. I had only met them twice, briefly. The first time was one evening in our sophomore year when Jamie and I made a pit stop on our way to a weekend of rock concerts in New York City. The next time was graduation. I remembered very little about them except that they were a strikingly handsome couple. Jamie's mother was one of those suburban matrons who manage to keep their looks very much together well into their late fifties. When they had come up for graduation I couldn't help noticing how much Mrs. Hurlbett looked like Lisa, who had left the Farm by that time. Dr. Hurlbett was six foot four, with thick white hair and the kind of good looks you associate with Hollywood's elder statesmen—the Jimmy Stewarts and Cary Grants.

We were headed in each other's direction and eventually converged, but I don't think they recognized me. I apologized for being late and told them how shocked and sorry I was. Mrs. Hurlbett had on a hat with a black veil. Underneath, she appeared quite drawn. The years since that graduation ceremony had apparently caught up with her and she now looked her age —though the events of the past several days must have taken a toll of their own. She asked how I knew her son. I explained who I was and how, in fact, we'd all met before under much pleasanter circumstances.

"Oh, of course." Mrs. Hurlbett remembered and attempted a smile, but her mouth only quavered.

"I see you've shorn those long locks you used to wear," Dr. Hurlbett said. But whether he truly knew who I was, or was just using an all-purpose remark for anyone my age, I couldn't tell.

"Yes," I said. "I had to clean up my act and go out into the world and make a living, I guess."

"Do you live in town?"

"Yes. I moved here about a year and a half ago."

"Where do you work?"

"Just a corporate job," I hedged, not wanting to say I was a reporter for the *Times-Herald*, lest they think I was there for any reason other than Jamie being my friend. "I don't see Lisa," I remarked to change the subject. I immediately regretted it, since I didn't want to embarrass them. It was very awkward.

"We haven't been able to get in touch with her," Dr. Hurlbett said. "It's a terrible thing, her not being able to be here."

"Where is she?"

Dr. Hurlbett glanced at his wife, who made a little sound as if she were going to start crying again.

"Frankly, we're not sure," he said.

"Not sure . . . ?" I started to echo him, then stopped myself. I had understood, through Jamie, that over the years since college his sister had followed rather a vagabond existence. There had been various attempts to settle down in California, Sun Valley, and Oregon, all with different men.

"Maybe she's out West," I suggested stupidly, as if we might establish her whereabouts right then and there by a little brainstorming. Boy, I was saying one awkward, stupid goddamn thing after another. I couldn't believe myself. Meanwhile, you could tell that Jamie's parents were tired of chatting with me and wanted to go home. So, I just dropped it and didn't initiate any more small talk.

"Since you're in town, you must come over and see us some time," Jamie's father said. "It would be . . . nice to talk to one of my boy's . . . friends. Perhaps for dinner."

"Love to," I agreed, a little too enthusiastically. Now they were going to think that not only was I a moron but that I liked to mooch free meals. It was terrible. "Well . . ." I stuck out my hand to shake and saw that Dr. Hurlbett's was all red and knobby and gnarly-looking, with his fingers all bent up and deformed. Just then I recalled how he had had to retire from practicing surgery because of arthritis. I took his hand very gently and just touched it, then took his wife's gloved hand. "If you don't mind, I think I'll go say good-bye to Jamie myself now." We went our separate ways, they to their car, and myself to the grave.

By the time I got there most of the cars and limousines had peeled off and the rest were about to. The grave-digging crew was already disassembling the chromium apparatus that they used to help lower the casket into the hole. I peered down into it. You could see the brown polished wood right down in there with a few handfuls of dirt and a white lily scattered on it.

For a moment I tried to imagine Jamie lying down there peacefully with his hands across his chest. Just as I tried to picture it I remembered that they had found him all cut up in six different pieces and I didn't want to think about it anymore. I did want to spend a few quiet moments there, though. But before I knew it they were bringing up the backhoe to cover him up. I'll tell you one thing: they sure don't like to waste time in our society.

When I asked the driver if he would mind holding off and shutting down the machine for five minutes, he started grousing about how he and the crew were supposed to get off at four o'clock, and how they had another job after this one, and how they weren't getting paid to wait around. Then it was my turn to get mad. I called him a "stupid motherfucker" and a "disrespectful oaf" and told him he'd have to knock me into the hole to fill it in. So, it was a Mexican standoff. I stood there gazing down into the hole with the diesel engine ringing in my ears and said good-bye to Jamie.

And then I went home.

CHAPTER 4

By Monday morning my physical condition had returned to normal, and I was making a real effort to keep my emotions stabilized. I found myself wondering what Philip would have thought in my situation. I even caught myself talking to him, asking him how he felt about this or that. It might seem morbid to you, but I found it comforting. If I'd heard his voice talking back, I really would have had reason to worry about my mental health, but I didn't.

What I wanted, desperately, was to get back into the regular humdrum routine of my job and my life and forget about everything that happened over the whole miserable weekend. So, I got up bright and early and arrived at the newsroom before 8:30—which was quite unusual for me, since I didn't have to report to the city desk. In fact, I operated so independently that I rarely had dealings with any of the editors. That was why I knew I was in for the business when Ginny Unger came over to my desk and told me that Charlie Boland wanted to see me.

Charlie Boland, the fiery managing editor of a great metropolitan newspaper! Is that the image your mind dredges up? Well, forget it, because Charlie Boland was a company man all the way. Nobody even really knew what he did in his glass-walled office in the corner of the newsroom. Most of the routine day-to-day stuff, the assignments and everything, was handled by Steve Traczewski, the city editor, who sat at a sort of nerve-center desk in the middle of the newsroom. Charlie didn't write the editorials, either, because they had this old guy, Henry Bloch, whose whole job that was. About the only thing I could tell you for sure that Charlie ever did was hire reporters. And since only two new people had come on board in the time I was there, he sure didn't have much to do.

He was also the worst dresser for a supposedly important executive that I ever met. I think he got his entire wardrobe at the K-Mart. For one thing, his shirt collars had the uncanny tendency to fly up at the points instead of lying down flat like they're supposed to. Even though they were obviously cheap shirts, I think the collars would have lain down flat if he had known how to tie his tie properly. But he tied some kind of double Windsor knot that ended up the size of an apple turn-over. And so little material was left over from the knot that the tie barely hung down past the third button of his shirt. You'd think *his* boss, Dan LaMott, the publisher of both papers, would've mentioned it to him. LaMott was a graduate of the Dale Carnegie course and a pretty snappy dresser. But if he mentioned anything, it was apparently to no avail. Personally, if I'd been in charge around there, I would've forced him to do something about his personal appearance. He looked like a clown.

I wasn't the only one around the office who noticed Charlie's rather nebulous position or his personal peculiarities. Among the reporters, for instance, he had a nickname: "the Laughing Hyena." He happened to have a very disconcerting high-pitched laugh that erupted out of his office every time the door opened. The reason you heard it every time the door opened was because it was Charlie's all-purpose device for ending troublesome conversations. For example, if you went in to ask for a raise, he'd give you the company line on the old budget squeeze, and just as you were about to tell him how full of shit he was, his face would go into these contortions and he'd erupt in the hyena laugh.

The odd thing was how well it worked for him. People would think that they said something terrifically humorous, that they were superb comedians. And the next moment he'd be ushering them out his door. They wouldn't realize until ten minutes later that their business was left hanging. It was a great device for handling people, I guess, but that laugh could really get on your nerves.

Anyway, that morning I went over to his cubicle and knocked on the glass and he motioned me to come in. He looked upset and started playing with all the papers on his desk when I sat down.

"What's this I hear about you and Merle?" he began without looking up at me.

"I don't know," I said. "What *is* it you hear?"

"Something about a fistfight."

"There wasn't any fistfight."

"I heard there was."

"Who'd you hear that from?"

"A number of people."

"They must have misinterpreted something they saw."

"Oh? What was it they saw?"

"I was trying to read something on Merle's notepad and he was being difficult about it."

"It seems to me that it's his privilege. It's his notepad."

"It's not his privilege to be an obnoxious asshole about a serious homicide he's supposed to be reporting."

Charlie looked at me for the first time. His face muscles twitched and he started laughing.

"Hee hee hee hee hee hee . . ."

I didn't even smile. Charlie cut it short and shuffled the papers lying on his desk. I could see that they were just a bunch of press releases from the state government.

"Okay then," he began all over again, "what's this I hear about you rewriting Merle's story on Friday?"

"I don't know what you hear when I'm not in your presence,

Charlie. You're the best judge of what you hear, so why don't you just tell me?"

"Okay—you rewrote Merle's story."

"Indeed I did."

"Why?"

"Because it was a slovenly piece of shit."

"Well, Grover, don't you think that's our job, the editors, to decide the merits of a particular story?"

"Yes. Most of the time."

"But not in this case?"

"No."

"Why not?"

"Do you know what the story was?" I asked him.

"That murder in Vermont, the guy in the garbage bags, right?"

"That's right."

"So, what's the big deal?"

"The guy in the garbage bags was my college roommate."

"Oh . . ." Charlie said, his eyes darting all around the cubicle except at me. The muscles in his face twitched, but he managed to refrain from laughing.

"If that's what you wanted to talk about, I'll move along," I said and got up and made for the door.

"Actually, there is something else, Grover."

I stopped and turned around.

"Sit down."

I did. He opened up one of his desk drawers and fumbled with something clunky. It was a cassette recorder, one of the older, larger models they kept around the office.

Here we go, I thought.

"At eight o'clock this morning I had a visitor," Charlie said. "Claimed he was a representative of that outfit you wrote about last week—which, incidentally, was a heckuva story, Grover."

"It wasn't that great."

"It was solid, Grover. Good and solid," Charlie disagreed. He didn't know what he was talking about, I assure you. "But this fellow had a few complaints about it," Charlie went on.

"Now, I realize that it's not unusual with these kinds of stories to ruffle a few feathers. I've learned to expect it. Sometimes I even enjoy it myself . . ." At this point Charlie scrunched up his face and tittered briefly. I didn't join in and he stopped pretty quickly. "But the problem this time, Grover, is that he said you were very rude to him. And what's worse, he had it on tape."

But of course.

"You've got it in there, I take it?"

"Yup. But obviously they've got another copy. In fact, he said as much."

We sat there for a minute not saying anything.

"Well, are you going to play the tape for me, Charlie?"

"Oh, yes . . ." He seemed to wake up from a daze and pushed the "play" button. This was the conversation:

ME: "Hello . . . ?"

ISAAC: "Mr. Graff?"

ME: "Who is this?"

ISAAC: "Isaac at the Christopher Foundation."

ME: "What can I do for you, Isaac?"

ISAAC: "We would appreciate a retraction."

ME: "Oh, you must have seen the story, then?"

ISAAC: "Yes, we did. We feel that there are a number of inaccuracies in it."

ME: "It couldn't have been that bad. Maybe in a few parts—"

ISAAC: "Don't you think a few inaccurate parts are too much, Mr. Graff? You're a reporter. You should be accurate in all parts, or not have included them in your story."

ME: "Oh, I don't know about that."

ISAAC: "We think that in light of this, our organization has been misrepresented and deserves a retraction."

ME: "If you don't mind, Isaac, I was on my way out the door."

ISAAC: "Mr. Graff, in the name of fairness—"

ME: "I hate to disappoint you, Isaac, but you're really barking up the wrong tree."

ISAAC: "Mr. Graff, please—"

ME: "Go fuck yourself. There isn't going to be any retraction."

Charlie pushed the "stop" button. He rewound it while I sat there trying to reconstitute the original conversation in my head.

"Well, Grover?" he finally said.

"It's a doctored tape," I told him as though there shouldn't have been any question. "It's edited and overdubbed all over the place."

He just sat there nodding at me.

"Don't tell me you think this is real," I said a little shrilly.

"That *was* your voice, wasn't it, Grover?"

"Yeah, it was my—"

"So then you *did* tell the guy to go fuck himself."

"Yes, I did. But not until after he threatened me. A great deal of the actual conversation is missing, Charlie. And the things he appears to be saying to me are not what he said over the phone. It's manufactured."

"All right. What did he say to you?"

"Well, he called me a bunch of names. A 'godless punk.' A 'piece of shit.' "

"He used foul language?"

"Liberally. These aren't exactly a bunch of Cabbage Patch Kids. He also made a number of explicit threats."

Charlie leaned back in his reclining chair and squinted at me.

"Okay," he said. "What do we do about it?"

"We do nothing about it."

He shifted his weight uneasily.

"What's *he* going to do?" I asked rhetorically. "Take this tape down to Channel 8 so they can play it on the six o'clock news and let everyone in the city hear me say 'go fuck yourself'? I don't think there's anything he *can* do with the damn thing, except try to intimidate you. If they had a case, you'd have been speaking to their attorney, not to some joker with a tape cassette."

"Okay, Grover, then we forget it, right?"

"Right."

"Okay?"

"Okay," I reassured him. "Is that all, Charlie?"

His face muscles went berserk and he exploded in his hyena laugh. Obviously that was going to be all. I got up to leave.

"Oh, Grover, do me a favor, will you?"

"Sure, Charlie. What?"

"Lay off this religious stuff for a while, huh? Go find someone on the governor's staff who's embezzling the taxpayers' money, will you? But cool it with the religious kooks."

"You bet, Charlie," I said, and I meant it too. It was getting to be a complete drag.

"And hey, I'm sorry about that friend of yours."

* * *

Old Merle was at his desk when I returned to mine. He was enjoying his midmorning snack: two Hostess Snowballs, those pink gummy marshmallow-covered cupcakes with the coconut on top, and a cup of hot chocolate. There was a Nestlé's Crunch bar next to his typewriter, but it looked like he was going to save it as an hors d'oeuvre before lunch.

"Thanks for the rewrite job, pal," he said facetiously when I sat down.

"You're welcome," I told him.

"It needed a little polishing, huh?"

"It needed a lot of polishing, Merle."

"Well, it's a good thing you're around to make these decisions. Only do me a favor, Grover. Next time you think one of my stories needs polishing, at least clear it with me before you rush ahead with the job, okay?"

"Merle, that story was unworthy of your talent."

"Oh?"

"I just didn't want you to embarrass yourself."

"You're too kind."

"Think of me as your guardian angel."

His phone rang. It was Steve Traczewski at the city desk handing down an assignment.

"Sure, Steve. Right away," Merle said and got up. He jammed his notepad and the Crunch bar into one jacket pocket, the unfinished Snowball, crumbs, crème, and all, into the other and gulped down the rest of his cocoa.

"You and I will finish this later," he said.

"I can hardly wait."

He departed in a roar, as usual.

*   *   *

The first thing on my agenda, before I decided where to start looking for my next story, was to crack open the New York *Times*. I got a cup of Sanka out of the machine in the hall and had just turned to the weekend baseball scores when my phone rang.

Philip, should I answer it?

I picked it up on the fourth ring.

"Hello . . . ?"

"Is this Grover Graff, the reporter?"

"Well, it's not Grover Graff, the potato farmer. Sorry," I apologized. "Just joking. This is Graff."

"Uh, you don't know me, Mr. Graff. I read your story in the paper on Friday."

Right here I figured I was in for the business—another citizen calling in to say what a godless piece of shit I was.

"Oh . . . ?" I said.

"My name is Andrew Clothier. My wife and I thought you might be able to help us out."

"I don't know, Mr. Clothier."

"We have a daughter, Debbie. She's sixteen. Three months ago she ran away from home. It's not important why. You know how kids are. In May we received a letter from Debbie. She was in California—don't ask me how she got out there, hitched I guess—and in this letter she said she'd joined the same group you wrote about, these Children of Abraham."

"Uh-huh . . . ?"

"She said she was filled with the, quote, Holy Spirit, and so forth. We wrote back saying if that's what made her happy, then she had our blessing, thinking if we didn't criticize her decision or play the heavy-handed parent role that she'd come around in a while, maybe call home for air fare."

"Uh-huh . . . ?"

"Well, she never answered."

"Have you tried contacting the police?"

"As a matter of fact, yes. We spoke to the Marin County Sheriff's Department—"

"Marin County?"

"It's across the Bay from San Francisco."

"What town?"

"We're not sure."

"I see," I said and made a note.

"Well, apparently half the population up there are runaways. The officer we spoke to wasn't very helpful."

"Did he check the place out?"

"He told us there was no such organization."

"I don't think they looked very hard, Mr. Clothier."

"Maybe you can help us then?" he said.

For a moment I didn't reply.

"Will you come see us?" he asked.

I took his address. He suggested we meet in the evening because he was calling from his office, so we made it for seven o'clock at his home. He thanked me and hung up. I felt bad about him thanking me, though, because I didn't really think there was much I could do for him.

* * *

I was still staring at the phone when the goddamn thing rang again.

"Hello . . . ?"

"Hello, infidel."

My stomach tightened up.

"Hello, Isaac. I hope you're getting all this on tape."

"Oh, don't worry."

"I never worry," I said. Actually, I worry more than most of the people I ever met. If I worried any more than I do, I'd have to take drugs just to function properly.

"Where's the retraction?"

"You mean you didn't see it?"

"No, we didn't see it."

"Well, gosh, we ran a banner headline in a special edition. Which edition did you get?"

"Today's paper. Monday, shitball."

"Nice talk, Isaac. You know, we run four editions a day. There's the metro edition, the suburban edition—you probably know all this, since you were here this morning. Didn't they explain it to you?"

"They said there was no retraction," he fumed.

"Oh, wait a minute. I see what happened. After you left, my boss, Charlie Boland, was so upset that he stopped all the presses and had a whole new front page pasted up with this big banner headline—GROVER GRAFF GETS DOWN ON HANDS AND KNEES. The delivery trucks are probably on their way downtown, Isaac, even as we speak. Maybe if you went down to the corner drugstore—"

"You're full of the devil's own black shit."

"Hey, nobody's perfect, Isaac. By the way, that was a fabulous engineering job you did on the tape. Really first-rate. You ought to go down to Columbia Records and ask for a job in the studio. You could help Bruce Springsteen on his next album."

"Very funny."

"You think so? People have been laughing at my jokes all morning. Apparently I'm a natural comedian. I may even moonlight down in the Catskills if I can find an agent—"

"I don't think you'll have time for that, my little lamb."

"What's that supposed to mean."

"Think about it. Maybe you'll figure it out."

"I'll do that, Isaac. And in the meantime, think about this: if you or any of your buddies come near me or the place I live, I'll have the police down on your scurvy ass so hard it'll make your problems with the attorney general seem like a Sunday picnic."

"Good-bye, Mr. Graff."

"Good-bye, handsome."

* * *

Actually, I kind of hoped he would give me the opportunity to sic the police on them because I had a feeling they weren't going to quit pestering me otherwise. A night in the Elk Street lockup, with the rapists and the muggers, for example, might mellow Isaac out in a hurry.

Anyway, rather than stick around my desk and accept any more crazy phone calls, I decided to split for downtown. I'd come across some information, even before the Children of Abraham thing, linking Mayor Gulliver Peavy to a kickback scheme in a toxic-waste dumping racket and I wanted to check it out. Peavy, one of the longest-sitting elected officials in the country, was also "widely regarded as the crookedest mayor in America"—according to *Time* magazine. Our pusillanimous rag had hardly laid a glove on him in thirty years, and I had an idea about breaking that tradition, or at least forcing the issue.

So I spent most of the afternoon in the clammy basement of City Hall, reading microfilmed records of deed transfers—really exhilarating work—and around four o'clock I stopped at home to feed Babe and to move my motorcycle away from the front of my building.

To tell you the truth, I was getting a little paranoid. I didn't know if the Children knew that the bike belonged to me, but I didn't want them doing any volunteer mechanical work on it, like disconnecting the brake cables, or loosening the axle nuts, or replacing the hydraulic fluid in the master cylinder with Kool-Aid.

I whistled for Babe, but she wasn't around anywhere. Then I drove the bike way over to the other side of the complex and chained it to a lamppost there in front of somebody else's apartment. Finally I took a long shower and changed my shirt. By that time it was after five, and I was starving, so I set out on the depressing task of finding someplace to eat dinner.

There was only one decent restaurant in the entire Capital, a Chinese place attached to a motel way over on the opposite side of town. I could live on Chinese food. Barbara and I used to eat there all the time. But it was too far to drive, so I went to this wormy-wood-paneled steak pub attached to Century Mall instead. It was called the Porter House. Get it? What imagination.

Anyway, I ordered a white wine and a "junior filet." The waiter looked down his nose at me as though I were some kind of anorexic wimp for not ordering the "super sirloin." Unlike many of my fellow citizens, I find it difficult to snork down a pound and a half of prime beef at one sitting. They also had a salad bar where you could stuff your face and ruin your appetite before your dinner arrived. Since I eat out a lot, I took it easy on the salad bar myself, but it was fascinating to sit there and watch all the overweight middle-agers line up and pig out. Unless you happen to have sat next to Merle Lyons, you never saw such a terrific display of gluttony.

* * *

The Clothiers lived in the suburb of Steubenville, once a Dutch farming village, now carved up into housing developments with names that seemed derived from motels: Northwood Manor, Pine Tree Valley, Edgewood Knolls. Their house was the kind of white Colonial in Edgewood Knolls (no woods, no knolls) that Beaver Cleaver might have grown up in. It was after dinnertime but kids were out riding their bikes in the evening sunlight.

Mrs. Clothier answered the door. She was an athletic-looking woman with short, frosted curly hair, wearing a khaki skirt and a man-tailored pinstriped shirt, but with a lot of gold costume jewelry that feminized her appearance. Her husband soon strode out of the interior with a glass of whiskey on the rocks. He also had the lean look of an athlete, but was slightly stooped, as if he was habituated to some invisible burden. He wore a gray business suit, the tie unknotted and hanging loose from each side of his button-down collar.

"Won't you please come in, Mr. Graff," she said rather effusively. The house was full of good cooking smells, pot roast or something. It gave you a comfortable, homey feeling. You could tell that Mrs. Clothier wasn't a superlative housekeeper, but not in a way that was dirty. They just left a lot of junk out where you could see it—tennis rackets, magazines, a kid's baseball mitt, seed catalogs. She asked me several times if I wanted a "beverage," and so I asked for a cup of Sanka. About a minute after I arrived this little boy came halfway down the stairs and was introduced as their eight-year-old son, Andrew, Jr.

"Are you going to find my big sister, Debbie?" he asked me.

"I don't know."

"Why don't you go back upstairs and watch a little TV, Andy," Mr. Clothier told the boy. Then he showed me into the living room. His wife came in shortly with a tray.

"Cream?"

"Please."

It was real cream, too, not that plastic bullshit they make out of soybean oil that you get everywhere. There was an awkward interval while they watched me stir my coffee. I don't think they knew where to start, so finally I took the initiative.

"I'm not sure there's anything I can actually do for you," I told them frankly. "I want you to know that from the outset, because otherwise you might end up disappointed."

"We realize you're not a detective," Mr. Clothier said. His wife nodded in agreement. "We've just reached the point where we don't know what to do. You seem to know quite a bit about these people."

"Not much more than what I wrote in the story," I said, which was obviously not strictly the truth, since in the past week they'd revealed some pretty interesting new facets—like the ability to make me pretty goddamn paranoid, for one. But I didn't want to upset the Clothiers any more than they already were. "Would you mind showing me the letter she wrote you?"

"Not at all. We have it right here."

Mr. Clothier handed it to me and got up to freshen his drink while I looked it over. The stationery was yellow with blue flowers along the border, the kind a teenage girl might like. The handwriting was very neat, but tiny and cramped. The letter included that business about finding the "Holy Spirit" that he told me about over the phone. But there was also a lot of personal family stuff about not feeling loved or wanted and being criticized by her mother all the time, and how she hated school and her whole home life. I felt like a Peeping Tom reading it. It was signed simply "your daughter, Deborah," not "love, Deborah."

"You mentioned something about private detectives, Mr. Clothier," I said, handing back the letter. "You know, they do exist. And I understand some of them are damn good at tracking down missing persons. In fact, that's about ninety percent of what they do—divorce cases, runaway children. It's not like TV, where all they do is go around shooting crooks."

The Clothiers glanced at each other apprehensively for a moment. Mr. Clothier swirled the whiskey and ice cubes in his glass and drained it.

"We can't afford a private detective just now," Mrs. Clothier told me as her husband went into the kitchen again. I could hear him cracking an ice-cube tray. "We spoke to several of them, as a matter of fact, just inquiries, but their fee was really out of this world—$1,500 a week. *Plus* expenses."

"I know they're not cheap."

Mr. Clothier appeared once again, looming in the entrance to the dining room.

"Mr. Graff, I told you a lie this afternoon on the telephone."

"Oh . . . ?"

"I wasn't at the office. The fact is, I'm unemployed at the moment. At the present time, that is. I called you from a booth downtown."

"I'm sorry," I said. "I understand."

"I had an interview in town today."

"How'd it work out?"

"I don't know. Fine, I guess. It's not important. But the—"

"We just don't have the money for a detective," Mrs. Clothier began to sob. "I mean, we have to live, we have bills." Though distraught, she managed to maintain a certain dignity. Still, it made me pretty uncomfortable. In a little while she blew her nose and composed herself. Only then did her husband rejoin her on the sofa. "I'm sorry," she said, more to him than to me.

"You said over the phone that you had some snapshots, Mr. Clothier."

"Yes, yes, I do. I have them right here if you'd like to take them with you."

"May I see them?" Stupid question.

"Yes, here. Take them." He reached into his suit jacket and pulled out an envelope.

There were four photos, to be exact. I looked them over. The first was taken on a tennis court in rather harsh light. She had braces on her teeth. But even so you could tell that she was an unusually good-looking girl. Her body was willowy and athletic, like her mother's, and you sensed from the way she held her racket that she could play a wicked game. The second was a shot of Debbie with a backpack on. Fall in the woods.

"Paradox Pond," Mr. Clothier said proudly. "The whole family went up last October."

"No braces," I observed.

"She had the most pigheaded attitude about them," Mrs. Clothier said. "She insisted on having them taken off as soon as school began. I suppose it turned into a 'big issue' between us," she said, indicating the quotes with her index fingers. The gesture made her seem both sensitive to the predicament and yet also stubborn about her point of view. "I wanted her to keep them on. The *orthodontist* wanted her to keep them on. Do you have any idea what braces cost, Mr. Graff?"

"I think so."

"Thousands," she said. "Anyway, one night she partially pried them off herself, with a Swiss army knife. I could've killed her. After that they had to be taken off entirely." Mrs. Clothier sighed deeply. "She was very headstrong about it."

"I see," I said and looked back at the snapshots.

The third photo showed Debbie and a teenage boy, a Nordic lifeguard type, tall and blond. He was dressed in one of those gray and pink tuxedos with the frilly shirt and oversized bow tie that upstaters think of as formal wear. She was wearing a blue satin gown. Her shoulders were bare and some cleavage was visible. The way she smiled, with her lips closed, you couldn't see her teeth. The boy stood slightly behind her with his hands sort of girdling her belly. All in all, she must have been one of the more attractive girls in her school. You couldn't help wondering what kept her from being happy.

"Who's the guy?"

"His name is Larry Dobermann."

"Is he still around?"

"Yes. He's a senior. But he doesn't know anything. That was taken around Christmas. They stopped dating right after that. Nice kid. We liked him."

"Would you say he was a religious enthusiast?"

"Larry?" Mrs. Clothier scoffed. "No way."

"I see."

The last shot was a three-by-five studio portrait taken by a professional. It gave me an eerie feeling. I couldn't put my finger on it, though, and I didn't mention it to them.

"When was this taken?"

"In January."

"May I borrow these?"

"Please."

I got up. It seemed better for me to try to make a graceful exit before they asked me to do something I wasn't able to do —like find their daughter.

We shook hands and said good-bye. While his wife remained in the house, Mr. Clothier walked me across the lawn to my car. He didn't seem altogether steady on his feet.

"I guess I'll be in touch with you if something develops," I said, fiddling with my car keys.

"Mr. Graff. Uh, can I call you Grover?"

"Of course, Mr. . . ."

"It's Andrew. Do you have a family, Grover?"

"I have a mother and father."

"Married?"

"No, sir."

"Wait until you have a little girl. It's . . ." He closed his eyes and heaved a sigh. His breath was full of the smoky smell of bourbon. Across the street a mother called her child to come inside. It was twilight and the green taillights of fireflies flashed against the dark grass. "Would you be interested in going to California?" he asked.

I should have known it was coming. Actually, I did know. What I *should* have known was what to say. But I didn't. Meanwhile, he took another envelope out of his jacket pocket.

"There's $775 in here. The round-trip fare is four and a quarter. Maybe this weekend you could fly out and look around—"

"Mr. Clothier—Andrew—I'm just a reporter."

"I know."

"I can't take this money."

"Just hold on to it until the weekend and think it over. I trust you."

He proffered the envelope, practically foisted it on me, but I refused.

"Please, Andrew. If I took this, it would be misleading. I just can't."

"Just to hold on to?"

"I'm sorry," I said. I had to sort of edge around him to open the door to my Datsun. "Maybe something will turn up. You never know. Maybe you'll hear from her this week."

"Maybe," he said, breathing hard through his nose and not sounding very hopeful about it.

"I'll call you if any information turns up."

"Thank you."

"I'm sorry, really."

I climbed in and fired up the engine. Mrs. Clothier appeared in the front door and stepped down the lawn to her husband. I said good-bye again and took off. When I glanced back in the rearview mirror, they were holding on to each other in the twilight.

*   *   *

It wasn't until I was back on the highway and my mind started wandering that I realized what it was about the last photo, the studio portrait of Debbie Clothier, that I had found so eerie and unsettling. And when I realized what it was, I *really* got paranoid.

It was the feeling you get, sometimes, when you flip through old family albums of generations gone by—the knowledge that the subjects of the photographs are dead.

* * *

Babe still wasn't around when I got back to my apartment, but there was some interesting mail and a parcel-post box about the size of a liquor carton on my doorstep. It was quite light for its size. I let myself in and immediately turned on the Red Sox game. They were playing Baltimore at home. It was 9 to 7 Baltimore in the bottom of the sixth inning, a real slugfest. Dwight Evans was up with a guy on. He'd already pounded a solo shot in the first inning, the announcer said. I popped a beer, brought it over to the sofa, and started going through the mail.

The first letter I opened was from *Yankee* magazine, accepting a didactic little article (about 2,000 words) that I had cooked up about the Shakers, who had been very active around the Capital in the nineteenth century but who are now known for little besides the simple wooden furniture they made famous. A check for $250 was enclosed, a pleasant surprise indeed. The next letter was from an old Boston colleague of mine, Bob Raymond, who had just landed a job as managing editor on the Bergen (New Jersey) *Record*, a paper with a circulation over 150,000. He was "casting his net for talent," he said. I was flattered, but I knew at once that I could never stand to live in the Jersey suburbs—the Capital was bad enough—and that I'd have to turn him down.

The parcel-post package had "Macy's" printed on it and had my name and address written on yellow paper with blue carbon ink, so I figured it wasn't a bomb from Isaac and would be safe to open. Inside the big box was a smaller box, gift-wrapped and packed in a nest of those white Styrofoam peanuts. A card was taped to the box. I opened it. It was a condolence card signed "Love, Mom." I figured she'd gone out and bought something to help me get over the Jamie business. The box was a six-inch cube, the right size for, say, a paperweight. I pulled off the ribbon and carefully undid the paper. The smaller box also said "Macy's." I took off the lid and foraged through the tissue paper inside. Oddly enough, I thought at first that it *was* a paperweight. It wasn't until I touched it and took a closer look that I realized it was Babe's head.

I didn't fling the box across the room in horror or anything. I simply set it ever so carefully on the coffee table, got off the sofa, and sort of backed over to the door—like the way Rollie backpedaled away from me in the lobby when I told him who the murder victim was. I remember reaching for the dead bolt and locking it, and putting on the chain. Then I just cowered in the corner, hyperventilating.

What I did next makes sense only within the strange logic of paranoia. I immediately developed a kind of siege mentality and got it into my head that "they" could enter the apartment very easily by way of the sliding glass patio door. So I shoved the sofa over in front of it and piled a bunch of chairs on top of the sofa. In fact, by the time I was done I had every piece of furniture in the room stacked against it. But if you think that was strange, you should've seen what I did next: I took all the drinking glasses I owned out of the kitchen cabinet, set them up in a line on the carpet in front of the piled-up furniture, and smashed them with a hammer. Then I took a whole box of tacks and spread them among the glass shards. The idea was to create a security zone, right? But then I realized that all the broken stuff wouldn't do any good if the intruders had shoes on—which they almost certainly would—so I got the dustpan and scooped up panfuls of broken glass and tacks and poured it over the sofa and piled-up furniture, the idea being that in order to bust through they'd have to clamber over the furniture and, theoretically, cut the shit out of themselves in the process.

When I was done I was thoroughly disgusted with both the situation and myself. My nerves needed steadying so I took a shot of this Grand Marnier that Barbara Frye gave me for my birthday back in October, the only liquor I had on hand besides beer. Soon my paranoia subsided, only to be replaced by rage. It was all I could do to keep from driving downtown and trying to beat the shit out of Isaac—or even Rebecca. Somehow I managed to restrain myself.

I considered going to the police—making good *my* threat to Isaac—but in this state the laws against hurting pets are fairly lame and wouldn't even land the motherfuckers in jail for the night. There were some memorable cases of really serious cruelty to animals around the Capital during my time there—a man who starved and neglected a whole barnful of ponies, and a gang of bikers who tortured dogs for the sheer fun of it—and the perpetrators got off with dinky little fines. So, calling the cops was out at this point. Besides, after they saw what I'd done to my living room, they'd probably think I was nuts and did it myself.

For a while I just stood there in a daze sipping the Grand Marnier out of the bottle and staring at all the heaped-up crap in front of the patio door. I thought about checking into a motel, but I didn't want to give them the satisfaction of chasing me out. In a perverse way I secretly wished they'd send some of their members creepy-crawling into my apartment and give me the chance to bash their fucking heads in with my aluminum baseball bat. So what I finally did was turn out the lights, go into my bedroom, jam a chair under the doorknob for security, and lie down to wait.

I lay awake for hours listening in the darkness to the muffled noise of the nearby expressway, and thinking about the first time I saw Babe, all wet and scraggly, on Newberry Street in Boston, and missing her, and hating myself for letting them hurt her, and wondering what kind of sick motherfucker could do a thing like that to a helpless animal. Before too long I decided there was only one way I could realistically take on the Children of Abraham. That meant heading for California the next day to try to find Debbie Clothier out there, and to hang a load of indictments around their fucking necks.

CHAPTER 5

As far as I was concerned there was never any question but that the Kaiser Corporation was going to pay for my trip to the Coast, not the Clothiers. It was one way of maintaining the illusion that there was still nothing personal involved. At 7:30 in the morning Charlie Boland was already in his office. Actually, he always came in at 6:30, when the late edition was rolling off the presses, but you shouldn't get the idea that he was overworked and feel sorry for him, because he used to leave the place around 2:30 every afternoon.

I knocked on the glass wall of his cubicle and he motioned me to come in. The usual pile of press releases from the Department of Canal Inspection and other vital state agencies lay in piles across his desk. I think they were glued down as a permanent exhibit.

"Hi, Grover. Gosh, what brings you in so bright—"

"I need to go to California," I told him without beating around the bush.

"So do we all, my boy, so do we all."

"I need to go today."

"When are you up for vacation, Grover?"

"This won't be a vacation, Charlie. I'll need four and a

quarter for round-trip airfare, maybe a hundred for a car, and a couple hundred more for the hotel and everything else, meals, gas, whatever. I'd like you to make a voucher out for it right now, because I want to be on the plane this afternoon and I know it'll take them a few hours to get their act together upstairs. So, let's get the ball rolling right away, okay."

Charlie didn't say a word for at least ten seconds. He just sat there behind his exhibit of press releases, with his shirt collar standing up on one side, and stared at me. Then he burst out laughing in his most explosive hyena style.

"Cut that out, goddammit!"

I'm afraid I really blew my stack. To my amazement, though, Charlie didn't throw me out of his office. Maybe no one had ever blown up at him before and this was his first opportunity to realize how irritating his act was. He looked more hurt and embarrassed than indignant, to tell you the truth. At any rate, he composed himself after a while, cleared his throat, and then said sardonically:

"Would it be too much to inquire exactly what the purpose of this trip might be?"

I hated to tell him, but there was no way around it.

"Remember that outfit I did the story on last week?"

"The cult group," he said, all his facial muscles collapsing downward in dismay. "Didn't I tell you to lay off that stuff?"

"There have been some developments," was all I said. I didn't feel at this point that I could afford to tell him that the motherfuckers had cut off my cat's head and mailed it to me in a box. No matter how deplorable it was, he'd just accuse me of making it a personal thing, and to a certain degree he'd be right, and he'd never approve of the trip to California. So I took out the snapshots of Debbie Clothier and told him about my meeting with her parents—the whole business, including the father's pathetic attempt to "hire" me. He glanced at the photos and handed them back to me.

"Pretty young thing," he remarked. "But, Grover, what happens out in California is for the California papers. This is the Capital."

"But, Charlie, the girl's *from* here."

"So what?"

He could be so thick sometimes you wondered how he ever became part of the management, but I guess he was perfect by Kaiser Korp standards.

"Don't you get the story, Charlie? MISSING AREA GIRL FOUND IN CALIFORNIA COMMUNE. The girl's a missing person. Has been for more than a month. All of a sudden, *ding,* she's discovered in a West Coast branch of the same screwball outfit we've been looking into—an outfit that the attorney general's office is about to indict any day now."

I hoped he'd get turned on by the "area girl" angle. The word *area,* as an adjective, is the big buzz word of the bush leagues. AREA MAN STRANGLES WIFE, AREA TEEN ACCUSED OF SEX WITH GOAT, AREA CHILD SODOMY VICTIM. The word probably appeared in the *T-H* fifty times a day. It used to drive me crazy. Anyway, I was right. It did get him going.

"Missing area girl, huh?"

"That's what I'm trying to tell you."

"Where'd you say the parents are from?"

"Steubenville."

He leaned back in his chair with his hands folded in his lap.

"Give me an hour to think it over," he said.

"There's no time for that. If you don't get the ball rolling right now, they won't have the check ready in time. I know how they operate up there. It's like ancient Mesopotamia. I think they still add up columns of figures on clay tablets—"

"Grover, Stan Shapiro doesn't even get to the building until nine o'clock. There's nobody up there yet."

Stan Shapiro was the chief money guy. Ultimately, he had to sign any check issued on a voucher.

"Aw, hell . . ."

"So, get lost for an hour and then we'll see about it."

"Okay."

I got ahold of the New York *Times,* and a copy of our own rag, and some Sanka from the machine in the hall, and tried to keep occupied. At least the Red Sox had won in Detroit the night before. But it was hard to keep my mind off the shock of finding Babe's head in that box. It was the feel of it that I couldn't stop thinking about: the tissue paper and then the blood-matted fur. I had some crazy idea that maybe Philip would take care of her now. It was probably a stupid thought for someone who doesn't believe in the standard idea of heaven as a sort of country club in the sky, but that's what I imagined.

At ten after nine my phone rang. It was Ginny Unger telling me to come to Charlie's office. That's how they did things at the *T-H:* instead of walking twenty-seven steps over to your desk, they'd call you on the phone.

Charlie didn't even look up at me. He just handed over the green slip of paper, the voucher, as if by not looking at me he wouldn't have to take responsibility for authorizing it. It was made out for $800. I thanked him and took it upstairs to Stan Shapiro.

Four and a half hours later the check came down. I don't know what took them so long. I called about six times to find out what the hell they were doing up there, and the last time Stan Shapiro's secretary slammed the phone down in my ear. In the meantime I reserved a seat on the 4:15 flight to San Francisco. It was so late when I got to the bank to cash the check that the guard was just that moment bolting the doors. I had to scream my head off pleading to be let in. If I hadn't been wearing a tie and jacket, he probably would've pulled his gun on me, I was being such an obstreperous asshole. But he let me in and, after a bank officer called Shapiro to verify it, I managed to cash the goddamn check.

* * *

I'm not exactly what you would call a flying enthusiast. I'd flown before, plenty of times. Once, when I was eight, and my parents weren't getting along, they farmed Philip and me out for the summer to an aunt and uncle and cousins in Los Angeles, instead of the whole family going out to Fire Island as usual. On the plane back at the end of August, one of the engines caught on fire. You could see it right outside the window: this fireball on the wing. Philip was fascinated by it, but I was scared to death. He loved danger. Of the two of us, I think I was also more freaked out about the possibility of our parents splitting up. We didn't crash or anything. They made an emergency landing in Denver and loaded us on another plane for New York. But the experience certainly made an impression on me.

Years later I flew home from college a few times, because otherwise it would have been a seven-hour bus ride, but I would have to get absolutely bombed just to drag myself aboard the plane, and even that wouldn't really stifle the terror. I used to get so scared that I would reach for the hand of the person sitting next to me, whether it was a college coed, or somebody's grandmother, or a 250-pound businessman, and start whimpering like a gerbil. Luckily, when I was a junior, my father helped me out with some money to buy an old car. I hadn't set foot on a plane since then.

The odd thing is, this time I didn't give a moment's consideration to my fear of flying until I actually pulled into the airport parking lot—I had so many other things on my mind— and then I *really* started to get nervous.

In the terminal I picked up my boarding pass and made a beeline for the cocktail lounge, where I ordered a manhattan. I drank it in two swallows and ordered another. The bartender gave me one of those looks you see in the drunk-driver commercials on TV. It didn't help that one whole wall of the lounge was a big plate-glass window where you had to watch the planes taking off and taxiing around on the runways. Meanwhile, a string of terrifying thoughts raced around and around in my head: *Don't get on the plane . . . it's going to crash . . . don't get on. . . .* It was amazing how rapidly I was becoming a basket case. What saved me from chickening out was that thirty seconds after my second cocktail arrived they told everybody over the public address system that it was time to board the 4:15 flight to San Francisco. I knocked back the drink, lurched out of the lounge shaking like a little kid's windup toy, and made myself get on the plane.

Maybe I shouldn't have told you all this, because by now you're probably thinking I'm more unbalanced than some of the nuts I'd been writing newspaper stories about. But a lot of people are terrified by much sillier things—snakes, water, the dark. At least it's halfway logical to be afraid of flying. Airplanes *do* crash now and again. What amazes me is the number of people who aren't the least bit bothered by being 30,000 feet up in the air encased in a steel tube. Don't they ever read the papers? Probably not, come to think of it.

It was an underbooked flight. There was nobody in the seat beside me, which was both a relief and a further source of anxiety, because I wouldn't have to make an idiot out of myself in front of a total stranger, but then there'd be no one's hand to reach for either. I was getting high rapidly from inhaling those manhattans, but it didn't blot out my awareness of mortal danger any more than it would have blocked out the pain of a dentist's drill. The jet engines were whining in the background. From up front came the *thunk* of the cabin door being shut. The stewardess stood at the head of the aisle and showed us how to use the oxygen masks. The lights flashed on that say "Fasten Seat Belts" and "No Smoking." Then the engines revved up to a high-pitched scream that practically split my eardrums, and we were rolling down the runway. I entered that familiar state of utter helpless despair. The plane shot up off the runway as though it had been hurled out of a giant slingshot. Those new jets don't fool around about climbing, boy. All the familiar buildings and shopping-mall wastelands of the Capital wheeled by outside at a weird angle and rapidly shrank in size. Finally the plane punctured a cloud and the window went gray. Then we rose above it to a meadow full of sunshine and fluffy cotton. Only then did I allow myself to close the window shade.

After we leveled off at cruising altitude I tried to read the airline magazine in the seat pocket but I could barely comprehend the pictures, let alone concentrate on the stories. I was hyperventilating and sweating and squirming around in the seat, hating myself for getting on the goddamn plane in the first place and worrying about how I was ever going to make myself fly back from California. (The irony escaped me that in order to fly back it would have to be logically assumed that we'd land there safely.) In a little while the stewardess rolled by with her cocktail cart full of those miniature bottles and asked if I'd like a drink.

"Yes, a triple scotch on the rocks, please," I said. Unfortunately, that was against the rules, so I made do with a single. But before she rolled away I just happened to mention that I was terrified to the point of having a nervous breakdown. She sat down in the empty seat next to me for about ten minutes and held my sweaty hand and talked to me in a smooth, quiet voice, saying everything was going to be fine, and how *she* flew all the time—which was obvious, since she was a stewardess, for godsake—while I kept apologizing for being such a childish asshole.

The amazing thing is, she actually managed to calm me down. Before long I began to notice that she was quite a good-looking girl—short sandy brown hair with bangs, cute smile, perfect teeth. Her nameplate said, "Jan." Just before she left I asked if she happened to have a date that night in San Francisco. I don't consider myself a smooth operator with women and I rather surprised myself by acting on impulse, but she responded, to my even greater surprise, by writing down her phone number and sticking it in the handkerchief pocket of my sports jacket. It gave me something a lot more pleasant to think about than imagining the plane ditching in a Kansas wheat field.

By the time she was gone I was feeling almost like a normal human being again. I think partly it was also a matter of time. After all, having anxiety attacks is a tremendous energy drain, and you eventually run out of gas. In a little while Jan brought me dinner, which was not half bad if you're used to the kind of garbage I eat all the time in the *T-H* cafeteria. The entrée was stuffed roast of veal with a brown sauce, asparagus (over-microwaved), pilaf, and a half carafe of some real nice California Zinfandel. So, I started feeling pretty good, until they showed the movie.

It was *On Golden Pond* with Henry Fonda and Katharine Hepburn and it was all about death. This old married couple goes up to the family summer place in New Hampshire for what is obviously the last time. To me it was worse than a horror movie, because the *monster* in this movie was death, which everyone knows is real, lurking just off camera in your own life, and it got me thinking about Jamie again, and Philip, of course, and poor Babe, and that photograph of Debbie Clothier, and by the time it was over I was incredibly depressed. Then, before you knew it, we were getting ready to land. I barely had time to get frantic and overwrought again when the wheels touched down on the runway.

As we were leaving the plane I asked Jan, the stewardess, if she could recommend a decent hotel in town. She told me to try the St. Francis.

"Do you like Chinese food, by any chance?" I asked. "I understand the city's renowned for it."

"Crazy about it."

"I'll call when I get checked in."

"Great," she said with a smile.

At the car rental place all they had left were Ford Fiestas, not my idea of a hot set of wheels, but the one they gave me had hardly a thousand miles on it. It even had that new car *smell.* This was quite a treat after what I'm used to: an eight-year-old Datsun 310-B with mildew in the upholstery. Soon I was tooling up the Bayshore Freeway toward the city, past rugged brown hills and palm trees and Candlestick Park, where the Giants play. For some reason everything about California looked familiar, and it took me a while to realize why: I'd seen it all before on TV.

* * *

When I tell you what happened next you're really going to think that I have a few loose screws in my head. I got to the St. Francis Hotel, right in the center of town, and they gave me a room on the twenty-second floor. Now it just so happens that I am not delighted about being up high in tall buildings. No doubt it is related to my fear of flying—of heights in general. When I was a kid I grew up in an apartment that was on the twelfth floor, and I supposed I'd established twelve floors, in my mind, as the upper limit of my comfort range. But notwithstanding the origin of this neurosis, I simply do not feel safe any farther than twelve floors above the sidewalk. In fact, I can't stand it. Especially in a place like the St. Francis Hotel in San Francisco, where the elevators are these little Plexiglas torpedoes that move up and down on the *outside* of the building like a goddamn carnival thrill ride. Besides, it's one thing being stuck up in a tall building in New York, but in San Francisco they could have a tremendous earthquake at any moment—and wouldn't *that* be groovy, up on the twenty-second goddamn floor?

Not that I'm obsessed with earthquakes, you understand, but any reasonable person the least bit acquainted with U.S. history would have to agree that it could happen there again, just like it did in 1906. So, to me, it was a justifiable concern, even if the desk clerk thought I was being an asshole.

I suppose you think it's a little peculiar that somebody who worries as much as I do about flying, and going up in tall buildings, would own a motorcycle. I admit that it seems inconsistent. But it just doesn't frighten me to drive a bike, at least at a prudent speed. Granted, you could still crash, but at least you're not going to *plummet* out of the goddamn sky. You might not appreciate the distinction, but it makes a difference to me.

Anyway, I made the clerk change my room to one much lower down, on the fourth floor. By the time I got upstairs, and showered, and put on a clean shirt, it was after eight o'clock Pacific time, which meant it was after eleven o'clock my time. I was starving. It took me a few minutes to screw up my nerve, but I called the number that Jan, the stewardess, had stuck in my pocket.

On the first ring an answering machine clicked on. I was about to hang up and not leave any message when I realized that it wasn't her voice on the tape. It was a woman with a black ghetto accent. At first I thought that maybe it was Jan's roommate, but she was saying some really surprising things—how "hot" she was, and telling me to take my dick out of my pants. It got crude real fast. Pretty soon it penetrated my little walnut brain that it was one of those "dial-a-porn" numbers. I hung up and called the number again to make sure I dialed it right. The answering machine clicked on again and this time a different girl—also not Jan—came on with another sexy taped message.

Naturally I felt like a chump, but to tell you the truth I also thought it was a pretty funny gag. After all, a good-looking stewardess like Jan is probably hit on by some guy every time she leaves the ground, and it must have been a big pain in the ass to her. So you had to admire her sense of humor.

I left the hotel and wandered a few blocks over to Grant Avenue, the main drag of Chinatown. There were dozens of restaurants there and almost every one looked like a good place to eat. I picked a Hunan-style joint. They cook with a lot of chili peppers in Hunan. It's sort of the Mexico of China. I didn't get depressed about being alone until they seated me at a table by myself. To get my mind off it I took out the photos of Debbie Clothier and looked at them over and over and over again.

CHAPTER 6

The San Francisco *Evening Star* was old Frank Kaiser's first newspaper, and though he is long gone (d. 1944), the paper remains the flagship of the Kaiser chain—like a leaky old freighter leading a fleet of garbage scows. After a huge breakfast at the hotel—eggs, pancakes, *and* hash browns *and* a corn muffin!—I headed over to the *Evening Star* building at Mission and Third, right in the heart of downtown. It was an old building in the beaux arts style (you could still see a big patched-up crack on one wall from the 1906 earthquake) joined to a much newer, really disgusting industrial-looking addition, an aluminum and glass monstrosity with turquoise panels beneath each window, all grimy from car exhaust. The security at the main entrance was a lot tighter than at the *T-H* (where there isn't any security to speak of), but my credentials got me inside with no problem.

Up in the newsroom, I told an editorial assistant who I was and everything, and she showed me into the managing editor's office with no unnecessary formalities. His name was Earl Mowbry, a rangy, good-looking Southerner, younger than Charlie Boland and a hell of a better dresser. I don't know if he had any more real duties to occupy him than Charlie did, but at least he struck me as being halfway intelligent and didn't laugh like a jackass every time I opened my mouth. I explained what I was doing out there and asked if any of his reporters had a bead on the cult scene in the Bay Area.

"You bet," he said, being perfectly accommodating, and reached for his phone. Not a minute later a very attractive woman came into his office.

Not that I'm a monomaniac or anything, but you couldn't help noticing what a knockout this lady was. She was older than me, in her mid-thirties, I guessed. Her height was deceptive because she had on high-heeled leather boots, so without them she was probably about five foot four. She was the kind of female professional who has learned how to dress conservatively but still look sexy at the same time. She had on a belted gray sweater-dress that was not necessarily revealing but gave the impression of softness and warmth. Her honey-colored hair was cut in a kind of feathery shag. There were quite a few gray strands in it that she left undyed. I liked that. Her face was pretty, but not in the classical Hollywood sense. Her nose was slightly flattened. But she had a wonderfully wry expression because she smiled more on one side of her mouth than the other. Earl introduced us.

"Grover Graff, Jeanie Goldstone."

I suggested that we go grab some coffee and talk, and she said "fine." It all happened rather quickly and I sensed that Earl might have been a little miffed. I even wondered if she was his girlfriend, or something. Those things do happen between people working closely together. There's no use fighting it, or making it into a political issue.

*   *   *

Up in the cafeteria, Jeanie had a cup of Kaiser Koffee while I stuck to my usual Sanka—caffeine puts me right through the roof. It turned out that just three weeks earlier she had done a feature updating the religious fringe scene in the Bay Area. Remember, San Francisco had been the spawning ground of a lot of spiritual movements, weird and otherwise, in the past decade, Jim Jones's People's Temple and Werner Erhardt's est, to name a couple of widely divergent examples. Her story wasn't *on* the Children of Abraham, per se, but the group was included in it as being relatively new to the scene. In fact, she had been to their "Holy Spirit Center" herself and could tell me exactly how to get there. It was up in Marin County, all right, across the Golden Gate Bridge from the city.

"How did you find it?" I asked her. "The Marin County sheriff doesn't seem to know where it is."

"Some people at the Unification Church turned me onto them. I think they disapprove," she said, wrinkling her nose and flashing the wry smile that showed her appreciation for the ridiculous. "It's very much a sex thing, you know," she added. "And they were all such extraordinarily good-looking people. It was a little eerie."

I took out the pictures of Debbie Clothier and she scrutinized them closely.

"I don't recognize the face, but I was only up at their holy establishment for an hour. People came and went. I'm sorry."

"Hmmm . . ."

"There's a kid you ought to talk to, though," she suggested, brightening. "His name is Steven Strunk and he's a veteran of about six different groups—the Moonies, a Krishna organization called Bhakshivedanta, The Christian Overlord Brotherhood—real kooks!—and a bunch of others. He's from Lodi, the pits, left home at about fifteen and bounced in and out of these groups like a rubber ball. He was absolutely one of my best sources."

"Is he actively involved still?"

"Well, he's not living with them up there. He's got an apartment in the city, and he works nights at a gas station on Lombard. I'm pretty sure you could get hold of him during the day."

She wrote down his address.

"That's very helpful. Thanks."

We chatted a few more minutes while we finished our coffee. Jeanie had first gotten interested in religious nuts back in the Watergate era when she was assigned to investigate the Moonies' rabid support of Nixon in the Final Days.

"God, it must've been great to have been a reporter during Watergate."

"It was, Grover," she agreed with that trademark smile and a wistful, faraway look in her eyes. "It was the best."

We left the cafeteria. Jeanie took me down to the "morgue" —that room where they keep back issues of the paper, these days on microfilm—and dug up her recent story for me. My plan was to look this kid Strunk up and then head up to Marin County around dinnertime, when all the Children were likely to be back from their peregrinations, selling Abe-grams, or whatever, and see if Debbie Clothier was among them.

Before she left me in the morgue, though, Jeanie asked if I had any dinner plans of my own that night. It certainly took me by surprise, especially after the practical joke that Jan, the stewardess, played on me the night before. In fact, I told Jeanie about it because I thought it might appeal to her sense of humor.

"I'll have to remember that one," she said with a dry chuckle. "Do you like Mexican food?"

"They don't have much of it where I come from, except a taco at the Burger Barn."

"Great. I'll introduce you to some of the real thing."

"I'm liable to be late getting back into the city," I said.

"I'm a late eater," she said, then turned serious again. "I'd like to talk to you about what you dig up. You mind?"

"Not at all. You've been so helpful, it'd be a way to thank you. To share the information, I mean." I can be so awkward somtimes it's beyond belief.

"Meet me at the Puerto Verde on Polk and Union. Nine o'clock sound okay?"

I said fine. She wrote the name of the restaurant down and explained how to get there, said, "Happy hunting, Grover," and left me in the morgue.

Her story was sort of a *Guide Michelin* to the gourmet religions of San Francisco and its environs, done with a nice ironic touch. There were only two short paragraphs about the Children of Abraham, and they didn't tell me anything I didn't already know—except this: apparently one of their beliefs was that they were "in contact with a race of metal-headed people who lived at the center of the earth."

* * *

Steven Strunk's apartment was in a run-down wood-frame Victorian house on Page Street in a no-man's-land between the Haight-Ashbury neighborhood and the Fillmore district, San Francisco's black ghetto. Though it was midday at the height of June, it was cool out without a sweater. A stiff breeze that smelled like the ocean blew bits of paper trash through the vacant street. I climbed the rickety steps to the entrance of Strunk's building. A sign over a row of six rusty buzzers said, "BROKEN—COME IN." A mailbox inside had "STRUNK 2-B" taped neatly across it. I went upstairs, found the door, and knocked. There were footsteps within. A voice asked through the door, "Who is it?" When I said I was a reporter and that Jeanie Goldstone sent me over, he opened up.

"Let me see your press card," he said. I took it out and handed it to him. "You're a long way from home. What do you want from me?"

"Little talk. That's all."

He looked at me askance, then slowly swung the door open and stood out of the way so I could enter. He was about twenty years old, shorter than me, about five six, but with all-American good looks, and very neat-looking. His dusty-blond hair was cut in the new post-punk style. He wore khaki pants that still showed crease marks where they'd been ironed and a bright yellow promotional T-shirt from a local radio station that said "KBQK—ROCK THE WAY YOU LIKE IT—ALL NIGHT LONG." He wore a pair of flesh-toned eyeglasses that made him seem both earnest and rather off center, like the science whiz in your junior high school class.

His apartment, also, was surprisingly tidy for a young guy living alone. It was just two rooms: a bedroom and living room/kitchen type space, with a wooden porch off the kitchen which, on closer inspection, proved to be the landing of an outside fire stairway. The place was furnished with a couple of wicker chairs newly painted in pastel purple enamel and a cast-off-looking sofa with a Navajo blanket draped over the back-rest. A modest-size portable stereo box sat on a purple-painted cable spool that he used as an end table. You could tell that he'd made an effort to create a livable environment for himself, probably against rather heavy odds, and it made you want to root for him to succeed in getting his life together. Finally, there were plants all over the place—ferns hanging in the windows, a rubber tree in a big pot on the floor, a sunny windowsill holding many varieties of those little cacti you get at the five-and-ten store. Over the sink he had about a dozen avocados in various stages of cultivation, some just pits sprouting in water with toothpicks holding them up and some already planted. There were more that I didn't know the names of. I mentioned that they were nice plants.

"I like to grow things," he said. "This friend of mine has about sixty acres up on Bodega Bay. He might sell me ten of them. It's at least a year away, but I'm going to try to do it."

"Every time I get a plant, I forget to water it and it dies," I told him.

"Really? Well, you got to water them. You got to do that, at least."

"I always forget."

"God, I hope you don't have pets."

The feeling of Babe's matted fur in the tissue paper flashed back to me. The one glassy eye. It made me shudder.

"No," I told him. "No pets. Chilly here on the Coast."

"Weather's crazy in this town. It's hotter at Christmas than on the Fourth of July."

Pretty soon we got down to talking about the Children of Abraham. He'd been involved in the group for about eight months, he said. The way he described the experience it all sounded like sunshine and fresh air and good fellowship.

"If it was such a positive experience, then why did you drop out?"

"I don't know." He shrugged his shoulders. "Got bored with it, I guess."

"I understand that there's quite an emphasis on sex in the group."

He smiled uncomfortably. "It played a part."

"A big part or a lesser part?"

"It was important."

"And you got bored with it?"

"Are you really a reporter? Or a cop? Or what?"

"I'm exactly what I said I am. Steve, why did you leave the Children?"

He drew his knees up and wrapped his arms around them, gazing abstractedly into the plain wooden floor.

"It got a little too intense for me."

"The sex?"

He glanced up and puffed out his cheeks, a look of deep gloom and vulnerability clouding his face.

"There were things they wanted me to do, that"—he sighed —"that I wouldn't do."

"Like what?"

"Hey, you didn't come all the way out here from back East to ask me this," he said in an angry tone of voice.

"No," I admitted, flustered by his sudden vehemence.

"Then what did you come here for?"

I took out the photos of Debbie Clothier and handed them to him.

"Do you know this girl?" I asked. He looked through the shots and then back up at me with a vacant expression. "This girl's hometown is where I come from. She's why I'm here."

"You really are some kind of cop."

"No, Steve. I'm a reporter. Honest. Do you recognize her?"

"Yeah," he said, electrifying me, though I tried not to show any reaction. "Only her hair's different in these pictures."

"Do you know her name?" I asked.

"She was called Leah. We all had Holy Spirit names up there. You know, Bible names."

"I know. What was yours, by the way?"

"Bezaleel," he said. "What was her regular name back home?"

"Debbie Clothier."

"Debbie . . ." he echoed the word as if trying to make it fit the image in the photographs.

"Pretty girl," I remarked.

"Real sweet," he said, chewing nervously on the inside of his cheek. "*Real* sweet."

"Was she still up there when you left?"

He bristled. "You know, I don't have to answer these questions—"

"Tell me, Steve. Was she up there? Yes or no?"

"Yes," he said so low I wasn't sure I heard him right.

"I beg your pardon. Did you say yes?"

He glanced back up at me and nodded his head. Little droplets of sweat glistened on his upper lip. His eyebrows scrunched together as though he was trying intensely to remember something. Then he looked back down at the photographs in his hand, turning them over and over. "I can't talk to you about this anymore," he finally said.

"All right," I said, careful not to push him too far this time, since there was a possibility I'd need to talk to him again before I was finished in California. "May I have the photos?" He handed them back as if they might blow up in his hands. We both stood up at the same time. "By the way, where's that gas station you work at?"

"What gas station?"

"Don't you work at one?"

"Who says I do?"

"Jeanie Goldstone mentioned it."

"Oh." He seemed to relax just a little. "Well, yeah, I do work at one."

"Which one?"

He studied my face a moment. His Adam's apple bobbed up and down as though he had trouble swallowing. "The Gulf on Lombard and Fillmore."

"You must work nights, huh?"

"She tell you that too?"

"I believe she did."

"My life's an open book," he said ruefully and shook his head. I sensed that he had quite a bit more to tell me but that it would take some doing to gain his confidence and drag it out of him.

"It looks like you've made a very good start for yourself here." I attempted to buck him up. "Maybe you'll move on to bigger and better things."

"Bodega Bay," he said, brightening for the first time since we began our conversation. Or perhaps he was just happy to be getting rid of me. He opened the door. "Don't forget to water your plants."

"I don't have any."

"Get some. They sure cheer a place up."

"I will," I said, and started down the stairway, but his voice stopped me.

"Hey, mister," he said. "If you happen to go up there, do me a favor, will you?"

"Sure. What?"

"Don't tell them you talked to me. Or that you even came here."

"Okay."

"No, really."

"Depend on it, Steve. From now on, as far as I'm concerned, you don't even exist."

* * *

It was two o'clock when I left his apartment. I stopped off for a bite of lunch in the first Chinese place I spotted. It was on Sacramento Street, nowhere near Chinatown, and all I had was some fried dumplings, but it still made the *T-H* cafeteria look like a hog trough.

After that I had some time to kill, so I got into the Fiesta and headed up to Marin County. From the center of the Golden Gate Bridge you could see an enormous fog bank, literally a wall of clouds, moving ominously from the ocean into the Bay. To my right the city still stood in sunlight, its white stucco buildings shining against the rugged brown hills. It was such a beautiful sight that I didn't even remember how nervous I always get on big suspension bridges—let alone imagine what would happen if an earthquake struck—until I reached the other side.

I got off the freeway a few exits past Sausalito and followed a county road past a strip of suburban shopping bullshit. In a little while the split-levels became fewer and fewer. The road grew steeper and began winding up around Mount Tamalpais. Eventually it led to the John Muir Woods National Monument, a tract of redwood trees preserved by the federal government. I paid two bucks to get in and wandered around the nature trails for a couple of hours, looking down from a footbridge at huge trout finning in a brook, and feeling the rough bark of the gigantic trees, and wondering what I was going to say to Debbie Clothier when we ended up face-to-face. I certainly wouldn't be in a position to influence her. Even if she was homesick, the other members would exert plenty of psychological pressure to keep her in line. In the end I figured the best I could do was get the story of her teenage spiritual odyssey and tell her that her parents loved her and were worried about her.

* * *

Jeanie Goldstone's directions led me to a dusty driveway on the eastern slope of Mount Tamalpais. From the road there was a magnificent view of San Pablo Bay and the distant city. A magnum-size mailbox, painted white, simply bore the number 9080. I pulled up the long drive. Soon a house came into view, one of those rambling, hacienda-style affairs, two stories, with white stucco walls and red-tile roof. There were quite a few cars parked around a circular driveway in front of the house: a couple of Toyotas, a van, a pink 1957 Chevy Bel Aire in cherry condition, a much newer and cruddier-looking Chevy station wagon, and a Black Porsche 911-T. I parked behind it and walked up to the front door.

The guy who answered the bell was the complete antithesis of Isaac back home. He was a handsome, dark-haired bloke who looked as if he came straight out of the leisure-wear pages of *Gentleman's Quarterly*. He was wearing a pair of Calvin Klein army-green baggy pants and a stylish gray sweater flecked with purple and aqua and with the sleeves rolled up to show his tan forearms. He was barefoot. A pair of tinted glasses rested out of the way up on his brow. He smiled pleasantly when he answered the door and said, "Hi," in a rather breathy voice. Altogether, he gave the impression of someone who had assiduously studied every Warren Beatty movie ever made.

I told him exactly who I was and where I was from. I planned to keep things ethical and aboveboard on my part—until I nailed the motherfuckers for harboring runaway children for the purpose of sexual exploitation, or something like that. Also, I kind of liked the idea that news of my western sojourn would flash back East. I felt it was my turn to make *them* a little paranoid. With some luck the attorney generals of *two* states would soon be breathing down their necks. Anyway, I played it perfectly straight and showed the guy my credentials.

"You're a long way from home, pardner," he said in an appealing, easygoing manner. I could just picture him in a TV series: "Buck and his Bible"—the rollicking adventures of an earnest young frontier preacher who is catnip to the ladies of Gopher Gulch. "Please, come in."

Cooking smells wafted through the house, something organic, redolent of cabbage and soy sauce, plus the yeasty aroma of bread baking. Female voices rang in some far-off room. The difference in furnishings between this place and their house in the Capital was striking. Here, everything was plushy, modern, and colorful. There were no antiques. From the entranceway I could see well into the living room. It was spacious in the style you typically associate with California, and in the center of it was a sunken conversation pit. It was strewn with colorful batik-covered pillows—just the place for a group grope. Instead of paintings they had large woolly hangings on the wall. They reminded me of a similar monstrosity in the *T-H* lobby. Big potted plants were everywhere, palms and ferns, and I wondered if Steve Strunk had taken care of them during his time there.

I asked my host what his name was, and he said Ishmael.

"Like in Moby Dick?" I asked.

"No, like in the Bible," he replied with his winning smile. I took a small notepad out of my inside jacket pocket and made a note, brushing past him in the meantime and moving a little deeper inside the house. Carpeted hallways led off from the left and right. It was becoming obvious to me that Ishmael was not about to take me on a guided tour. Rather, he was genially waiting for me to state my business. I was hoping to catch a glimpse of some of the other people in the house, specifically Debbie Clothier.

"What brings you all the way out here, Mr. Graff?" he finally asked, crossing his arms. I clicked my pen closed and took out the snapshots.

"Do you recognize this girl?"

He took the photographs from me as if they were slightly radioactive and studied them, shuffling through the whole series three times. My stomach squinched up, wondering what was going through his head, whether he was going to lie or not. But then he looked up, and in a voice rather timid for such a brawny guy, he said, "No."

"Take another look at the photos."

He did and looked up again at me with a blank expression.

"I believe she was given the name Leah here," I coached him.

He leafed through the shots one more time and slowly began nodding his head.

"Yes," he said, handing back the shots. "I didn't catch the resemblance."

"Has she changed that much?"

Ishmael shrugged.

"Is she here now? I'd like to talk to her."

"No."

" 'No' she isn't here? Or 'no' I can't talk to her?"

"She isn't here."

"Is she out selling pamphlets or something?"

"No."

"Well, when do you expect her back?"

"We don't. She's not here."

"Do you mean she doesn't reside here anymore?"

"That's right."

"She just up an left?"

"We transferred her."

"Where?"

Ishmael licked his lips, thrust his hands in his pockets, and fluttered his eyelids.

"To Vermont," he said with some hesitation and a lame smile.

"Vermont!"

"Yes. Vermont."

"What's in Vermont?"

"We maintain a farm there."

That's when I remembered Isaac telling me about their "place in the country" that he was being so coy about.

"I see," I said, writing it down on the notepad, not that I needed to, but to think for a moment.

"Whose decision was that?" I asked.

"All of us."

"Was she included in it?"

"Oh, certainly."

"When did this transfer take place?"

"Hmmm. It's kind of hard to remember. At least a month ago."

"Do you recall when, exactly."

"Around the first week in May."

"I see."

"Yes, I'm sure it was then because—"

Just then somebody else entered the foyer from the hall behind me, only I didn't hear his footsteps because the place was so plushly carpeted. As Ishmael halted in mid-sentence, he also looked apprehensively over my shoulders, and when I turned around to see what had stolen his attention, there was that pale, blond-haired character with the sunglasses and the dark clothes from the house on Union Street back in the Capital, the one they called Shitfingers.

"Hello, Isaac," Ishmael said nervously.

I clicked my pen closed.

"So, you're Isaac now," I said, completely unprepared for this neat switch.

"Maybe," he said. "You're a little out of your range, aren't you, Mr. Reporter." I realized that it was the first time I'd heard him speak. His voice was husky and strangely melodic.

What he did next was really bizarre. He stepped up to me and pointed with his index finger at a shirt button down by my stomach. When I looked down to see what he was pointing at, he zipped his finger right up across my face. It was a stunt that hadn't been pulled on me since the sixth grade. He thought it was hilarious, and his braying laugh was on a par with Charlie Boland's. He stopped almost at once. "Really," he said in a sincere tone. "What can we do for you?"

If his act was designed to intimidate me, I've got to admit that he had succeeded.

"I'm looking for someone," I told him, attempting to re-compose myself. "A girl."

"Are you?" he said, then pussyfooted over to one of those woolly wall hangings, and peeked behind it. "She's not there. We might have to turn this whole place upside down." He cracked up at his own joke again and returned to face me.

Determined to keep playing it straight as long as possible, I took the photos out one more time and handed them to him.

"Ooo, what a tender little morsel," he remarked, flipping up the next one. "Yummy. I could eat her up."

"Maybe you did," I cracked, unable to resist.

He looked up and grinned. Those sunglasses of his were really unsettling. "We're vegetarians," he said.

"I understand you shipped her to Vermont?"

"Who told you that?"

"Ishmael."

"Ishmael told you that? Did you tell him that, Ish?"

Ishmael nodded his head, obviously upset.

"Then it's true," the new Isaac said.

"For some reason I'm skeptical."

"Are you?" he replied in a mocking tone. "Well, what's your theory?"

"I don't have a theory. I have a missing sixteen-year-old girl."

"You can't miss what you never had," he said impishly.

"Did you ever have her—"

He bent down as though he was going to pick something off the carpet, and a moment later he swung upward with both his hands clasped together and clobbered me on the jaw. It happened so quickly I never had a chance to duck it. I literally saw stars for a moment. The next thing I knew I was lying on the floor looking up. My mouth was numb and some warm liquid was running down my cheek. Shitfingers/Isaac was standing over me with his hands braced on his knees.

"You have to leave now, Mr. Hot Dog Reporter," he said. "Help him up, Ish."

Ishmael grabbed the lapels of my sports jacket and pretty much hoisted me back on my feet by main force. I was still stunned. You might think I was being a coward, but frankly I didn't see anything to gain at this point by a show of bravado. If it came down to it, I'd press assault charges on the motherfucker, even if I had to lead the Marin County sheriff up to the house personally. Anyway, I didn't resist.

"Show him out, Ish."

Ishmael steered me out the front door by my elbow and escorted me to my rent-a-car. I spit a few gobs of blood out on the driveway. I could feel a cut on the inside of my lower lip, and one of my bottom back molars was loose. It really demoralized me because I'd just had a root canal done in it. The display of gore left them unimpressed.

After I got in behind the wheel, Shitfingers/Isaac came down and leaned down by my window.

"Go back where you came from," he advised me calmly, dumping the photos in my lap.

"What if I choose to stick around?"

"Don't. It's not worth it."

"Excuse me, will you," I said, and spit more blood out in the dust. I started the engine.

"Have a nice day," he said before I backed out of the driveway.

CHAPTER 7

So, I didn't find Debbie Clothier up there after all. On my way down the mountain, though, I started worrying more about coming home without a story than about where Debbie Clothier might really be, or even about being roughed up. I kept imagining one lame headline after another: AREA GIRL NOT FOUND . . . AREA GIRL STILL MISSING. . . . I could just picture Dan LaMott, our publisher, calling Charlie Boland onto the carpet for giving me all that dough to fly to California for nothing.

It was still light out as I headed back down the twisting road. On the side of Mount Tamalpais that faced the Pacific, I started encountering patches of fog, so I switched on the headlights, not that it did any good. I am an extremely cautious driver under ordinary circumstances, and on this particular mountain road, in the fog, with no guard rails or anything, and places where the shoulder just dropped off into the canyons below, I was driving like somebody's grandmother. I must have crept along like this for a quarter of an hour when I noticed two headlights come up through the fog behind me. Before much longer the lights were right on my rear, tailgating in a serious way. I would have pulled over and let the guy pass, except it was so foggy now that you could barely see five feet past the edge of the road to tell if it dropped off at any given stretch or not. So I really couldn't pull over. And I wasn't about to speed up, either, for his convenience. If I'm on an unfamiliar road in bad conditions, I don't care how many cars I'm holding up, I'm not going to put my own life in jeopardy just so some asshole can make it down to the health club on time for his goddamn squash match.

Obviously I should have been more suspicious, but I was so preoccupied by other things, including just keeping my eyes on the road, that I didn't make the connection until the car started bumping my rear bumper. And then I really flipped.

It was impossible to tell what kind of car it was from looking in the rearview mirror. All I could make out were the two fuzzy headlights. At first the car just jostled me, like a few love taps on the back end, but soon I was getting rammed pretty hard. Even though I was in a state of panic, some thoughts and ideas did filter through the hysteria. First of all, I told myself that whoever was doing this—Isaac/Shitfingers, Ishmael, or some flunky of theirs—couldn't be so stupid as to try to actually kill me because they must have realized that other people knew where I was and what I was doing there, and that they'd never get away with it. Of course this wasn't very reassuring because, for all I knew, they *were* stupid enough to try it, and even supposedly brilliant people can be crazy enough to do stupid, reckless things. Just look at Napoleon or Adolf Hitler.

After giving up on that I tried to figure out some way to make them stop it, or fuck them up, like speeding up suddenly, or slamming on the brakes. But that seemed just as dangerous as letting them keep bumping me. Another idea I had was to carefully stop the Fiesta, get out, walk back to the car on my tail, yank out whoever was behind the wheel of it, and try to beat the living shit out of him. But that idea had certain draw-backs too: like what if they beat the shit out of me instead, and tossed me into a goddamn canyon? Or what if they locked their doors and tried to run me over?

So, basically, I just let them keep bumping me all the way down the goddamn mountain, past the Muir Woods National

Monument, until we arrived near the bottom and entered that fringe of suburbia I passed through on the way up. And at the first opportunity I pulled into the parking lot of a convenience store. At last I could see that the car behind me was a cruddy Chevy station wagon, the same one that had been in the Children's driveway. It didn't turn into the 7-Eleven lot but stayed on the road headed toward the freeway and vanished into the fog. There were two heads in the car. I couldn't make out their features, but I had a pretty good idea who they were.

* * *

For quite a while I just sat there slumped in the Fiesta, hyperventilating, listening to my heart thud, and watching to see if the old Chevy might come back or not, but it didn't. Finally I decided I really needed a drink to calm my nerves, so I went into the 7-Eleven store to buy a six-pack. The back end of the rent-a-car was pretty banged up—the passenger-side taillight was bashed in, for one thing—and I was glad that I paid an extra five bucks for the optional insurance.

As things turned out, you could buy hard liquor and wine in the store as well as beer—the liquor laws are different out there—so I bought a pint of scotch instead of a six-pack because I needed a stiffer drink than beer. I was still shaking badly when I paid the cashier. She must have thought I was the new neighborhood alcoholic, the way she looked at me.

I took the bottle out to the car and happened to notice my face in the rearview mirror. There was a big smudge of dried blood running from my mouth to down behind my ear, and my lower lip was quite swollen and purplish. I went back inside the store and asked to use the bathroom, but the cashier said they didn't have one (which was bullshit, of course). But I didn't want to argue about it, so I bought a packet of Kleenex and a small bottle of club soda and took them back out to the car to clean up my face. I drank a few swallows of scotch right out of the paper bag, like a goddamn wino. It really stung the cut on the inside of my lip. I probed around the loose molar with my tongue and could feel it wobble back and forth. I'd read about teeth that are knocked loose growing back tightly into the socket again, but since this tooth had had a root-canal treatment it was actually dead, which meant it'd probably fall out after all, which really depressed the shit out of me. Anyway, in a little while I was calm enough to drive again, so I fired up the engine and left the stupid parking lot.

It was a quarter to seven. Once my mental faculties returned to near normal, I decided to drive back into the city and drop in on Steven Strunk at the gas station where he worked. Before all the nastiness erupted, Ishmael said that they had sent Debbie Clothier back East to their Vermont farm in the first week of May, roughly six weeks ago. If Strunk had still been there at that time, he might know whether this was true or not. His reaction to those photos of Debbie Clothier earlier in the day had been obviously emotional. Maybe he had been in love with her and the leaders sent her away to break them up. I knew that they frowned upon members forming couples within the group. Maybe that was the real reason Strunk had dropped out.

Second, I thought Strunk might be able to shed some light on the identity of Mr. Shitfingers. Apparently they had tried to run some kind of number on me (and probably the attorney general's people as well) by swapping names. Strunk might even know if there actually was a Prophet Abraham who was running the group and profiting from their activities and who he was. I had a few hunches of my own, and they pointed to that spooky blond-haired motherfucker with the dark glasses and the quick hands.

Anyway, I drove back across the Golden Gate into the city. It was so foggy on the bridge that you couldn't even see the lights of San Francisco from the middle of it, and you couldn't see the water way down below, either, which was a good thing for my nerves because I wasn't in the mood for another anxiety attack.

The exit ramp emptied directly onto Lombard Street. All I had to do was stay on it and drive across town to Fillmore. With the stoplights and evening traffic, it took about fifteen minutes, and sure enough, there was the orange Gulf sign over on the right. A heavyset, middle-aged guy in sports clothes was manning the pumps, but there was no sign of the kid. I pulled up to the "full service" island.

"Does a young man named Steve Strunk work here?" I asked.

"He's supposed to!" the guy said angrily. "Sonofabitch is twenty minutes late for work. Who are you? A cop?"

"No."

"I don't need any trouble," the guy said. "What do you want him for? You a parole officer or something?"

"I'm his psychiatrist," I attempted to reassure the guy.

"Psychiatrist! What is he, a nut or something?"

"No, it's nothing. I just need to talk to him. To change an appointment."

"Oh . . ." the guy said, obviously disturbed.

Meanwhile, a big wine-colored Mercedes pulled up behind me. I drove the Fiesta around to the side of the station and parked it. Don't ask me why I told him I was Strunk's psychiatrist. I just figured it would cause less of a problem than if I said I was a reporter. And I couldn't have said I was his brother because we didn't resemble each other in the slightest. It was the best thing I could come up with on a moment's notice. It's funny, though: how many psychiatrists do you know who would drive to the place where you work to change an appointment? Most of them won't even return a goddamn phone call.

Anyway, I asked the man if he minded if I waited around the premises for a while in case Steve did show up. He wasn't exactly cordial about it, but he didn't say no, so I stuck around. Apparently he owned the establishment, and he started grousing to me about how his wife had supper on the table down in Daly City, and how you couldn't depend on anybody these days, and went on to deplore the condition of society as a whole. It occurred to me that he actually believed I was a psychiatrist. Finally, at 8:15, when Strunk still hadn't appeared, the owner said, "Fuck it," he was closing up and going home. He disappeared into the office and started switching off all the station's lights.

I had a very unsettled feeling about Strunk's not showing up, and decided to drive over to his apartment to see what was going on. Maybe something I had said during our interview had prompted him to blow off his job. I guess I felt responsible. But even more important, I needed that information about exactly when he had left the Children of Abraham.

It's quite easy to find your way around that part of the city. While it's terribly hilly, and the streets go up and down these hills like a roller coaster, they're still laid out on a regular grid, in blocks. Actually, the Capital is a much more incoherent sprawl than San Francisco proper. When I got over to Page Street, though, I knew at once that something bad had happened. It was a scene I'd visited a hundred times as a reporter.

Police cars stood blocking off both ends of the street. Their revolving gum-ball lights sent eerie blue shafts cutting through the fog. An ambulance waited in front of Strunk's building, its red light blinking wanly on and off in the fog like a heartbeat. I left the Fiesta double-parked on Turk Street and ran up the steep hill to Strunk's building. Several policemen in blue service uniforms waited on the sidewalk. The sound of their crackling two-way radios echoed emptily off the slum buildings. I approached one of the officers and flashed him the press card in my wallet. He didn't ask to take a close look at it, but apparently accepted me as a reporter at face value. Besides, I was wearing a tie and jacket, and these days I guess you can impress anybody just by not being a slob. It was a good thing I'd cleaned the blood off my face.

"What happened here, Officer?" I asked, taking out my notepad for the sake of appearances.

"Homicide," he said tersely. "A real mess."

My heart dropped into my stomach, like when you get on a real fast elevator going down. At the same time I remembered the cartoon on the cover of that Abe-gram the first Isaac had shown me: the one of "Godless Society" crashing in an elevator.

"Have you got any details?" I asked automatically, acting on reflexes.

"Kid had his throat cut. Ear-to-ear job. He made it out to the second-floor landing, then fell down the stairs. Buckets of blood . . ."

A moment later the ambulance attendants struggled down the stairs with the stretcher. The body was trussed up and completely covered. Blood had seeped brightly through the sheets. Three more uniformed policemen and a plainclothesman followed behind the stretcher.

"Do you have an ID on the victim?" I asked the plainclothesman as the others loaded the body into the ambulance without any particular haste.

"Who the fuck are you?" he snarled back at me.

"It's all right," the first officer said. "He's a reporter."

"*Chronicle?*"

"*Star,*" I said.

"You new?"

"Fairly."

He made a face and took a breath. "It's a white male. Name —Strunk, Steven, twenty-two years old. Next of kin, hometown, the rest we don't know yet. Ditto suspects and motive. Maybe drug-related. End of press conference."

He sort of shoved past me then. Not belligerently, but as though he was weary and disgusted with life in general.

At this point I had a difficult decision to make. It was possible that I was the last person, besides his murderer, to see Steven Strunk alive. I might also be in a position to put the finger on a suspect. But there were other considerations, some of them urgent. First of all, Strunk was dead, and telling the police what I knew wasn't going to help him in any way. What's more, once I started talking, they might detain me in San Francisco as a material witness for days, if not longer. And I realized now that I had to be out of San Francisco on a morning flight back East before that little motherfucker Isaac/Shitfingers knew I was gone.

I thought about poor Strunk, and his tidy little apartment, and about how nobody would water his plants now, and how they would die soon too, and it all just convinced me to keep my mouth shut and not say anything to the cops. Instead, I walked back down the steep block to the car and drove over to the Puerto Verde restaurant to meet Jeanie Goldstone.

* * *

I was a half hour early. Actually, I was tempted to drive out
to the airport, ditch the car, and try to catch a night flight back
East. But I wanted to inform Jeanie about what had happened
and, to be honest, I really needed someone to talk to. So I
ordered a white wine spritzer at the bar and sat down to wait. It
was quite a posh place. They charged you $3.25 just for a
simple cocktail, if that gives you any idea. It was amazing,
though, how attractive and well-dressed the customers were,
by and large, compared to the overweight geeks you encounter
in the average so-called good restaurant back in the Capital. I
tried to imagine Charlie Boland entering the dining room in
one of his K-Mart shirts with the collar askew, and his tie knot
the size of a cherry turnover and I could picture every head in
the room turning to watch him as though he had been born
without a nose.

To my surprise, Jeanie came in the door at nine o'clock on
the dot. Most of the people I've ever known are simply incapa-
ble of showing up for anything on time. It drives me crazy. I
doubt that I've been late for half a dozen appointments in my
whole life. In fact, I'm usually five minutes early. I'm not brag-
ging, just trying to point out what a simple goddamn thing it is
to show up when you're supposed to. Anyway, I sure was glad
to see her.

She was wearing a long, jade-green skirt, reddish leather
boots, a cream-colored low-cut blouse, and a forest-green velvet blazer. She saw me sitting up at the bar as soon as she came
in, but the captain intercepted her and asked her if she wanted
a table. She held up two fingers. I left the bar and joined her.

"Hi."

"This way, please," the captain said, menus tucked militarily
under his arm. We followed him.

"What happened to you?" she leaned over and whispered
when she'd gotten a closer look at my swollen lip.

"I got punched in the mouth."

"Oh dear . . ." Jeanie said. The expression seemed so old-
fashioned coming from someone so sophisticated. For a mo-

ment I imagined a rural Minnesota girlhood. Pigtails in the inkwell, pies cooling on Grandma's windowsill, county fairs.

We were seated. A waiter took our drink order: margarita and another wine spritzer. "Who did it?" she asked when the waiter disappeared. "Not Steven."

"I'm afraid something quite nasty has happened to him." I tried to prepare her for the news, though not very adeptly, I suppose.

"What?"

"He's dead."

This time she didn't say "Oh dear" or anything else. Her jaw dropped and she gaped at me. While anyone who's worked as a newspaper reporter gets to see more of life's ugliness and the aftermaths of mayhem than the average citizen, you don't completely lose the capacity to be shocked. In my time I'd covered several murder scenes where the bodies were still in place. I'd covered traffic accidents that were even more gruesome than the murders. But you still get sick and shaky every time you see it. It's still death. And Jeanie had felt for Strunk, empathized with his struggle to lead a dignified independent life, in much the same way I had.

"That poor boy," she finally mumbled, shaking her head. About the same time the waiter arrived and set down our drinks. Jeanie downed hers in a few swallows, put the glass back on his tray, and ordered another one. He withdrew.

"What happened?" she asked with a shudder.

"Somebody cut his throat."

"Oh, God. When?"

"Sometime between when I left him this afternoon and about eight o'clock tonight. The cops found him in the hallway."

"Then, you did see him alive today?"

"I might have been the last person to see him in that condition."

"Have you told the police?"

"No."

"Oh dear . . . Why not?"

"Because I have to get back East tomorrow before the others do."

"What others?"

"There's this one particular guy in the group. Sometimes they call him Isaac, sometimes they call him something else. Did you meet him by any chance? A spooky blond-haired guy who looks like a young Andy Warhol and dresses in black outfits and wears sunglasses all the time?"

"No."

"Well, he was at their headquarters back East, pretending to be someone else. And he turned up at the house in Marin County this afternoon. In fact, he's the one who punched me in the mouth."

"What did you do?"

"Me? Nothing. I certainly didn't punch him back."

"No, what did you do that provoked him to punch you?"

"They're somewhat unhappy with me in general. The punch was nothing, really. Back home they cut off my cat's head and mailed it to me in a box."

This time Jeanie more or less recoiled into the padded leather banquette with her eyes bugging out. The waiter reappeared with her second drink and set it down. She groped for it without taking her eyes off me.

"Why?" she asked in a small, timid voice.

"They took exception to that story I wrote about their problems with the law."

"Why didn't you tell me this morning?"

"I didn't want you to think there was anything personal in it."

She winced.

"And now you think they've killed Steven Strunk?"

I nodded.

"Do you know whether he was a junkie, by any chance?" I asked.

"A junkie? No, I don't think he was a junkie. Why?"

"The police mentioned something about drugs. Maybe they found some works in his apartment."

"I didn't think he was a junkie, Grover."

"I didn't think so either," I said.

She pulled the lapels of her velvet jacket together as though it was chilly in the restaurant. For quite a while neither of us said anything. I just swirled the ice cubes around in my glass while Jeanie morosely sipped her drink. I kept imagining Strunk's parents, in Lodi or wherever they were from. I pictured a sort of semi-crummy bungalow on a hot dusty lawn with a few scrawny, wilted trees in the yard. And inside, his mother crying softly over her dinette table.

"I'm sorry to dump all this on you," I finally said.

"For goodness sake, you don't have to apologize. I just had no idea."

"They're rough customers."

"What about the girl?"

"That's the thing. Strunk positively identified her from the photos. So, at some point she was definitely up there. In fact, I suspect they had a thing going. Anyway, there's a chance that she may be back in Vermont now. The group's got a farm there. Before I got punched one of the other guys in charge told me that they had sent her back East to it."

"What makes you believe him?"

"He told it to me before that blond-haired bastard showed up and the situation got nasty. I think he might have let something slip. Anyway, what I have to do is get back East and see if the girl is there now, in Vermont, or ever was, before Isaac goes back and gets all his little ducks in a row. If I get there and she's not there, and nobody ever heard of her, then we'll know she never left California in the first place."

Jeanie stared across the table at me with a very grim face.

"I think you ought to go to the police."

"No." I shook my head.

"You really ought to."

"I can't. If I went to them now, I could be stuck here for I don't know how long. I have to get out of here first thing in the morning."

* * *

Somehow after that we were able to talk about a few things besides the Children of Abraham, and people they'd hurt. Maybe it was the drinks. We chatted about working for the Kaiser Korp. She told me about the jerks in her office, and I told her about Merle Lyons and Rollie Tuttle and Charlie Boland, and about Charlie's wardrobe, and in spite of everything else that had happened, we managed to laugh a little.

Earl Mowbry, the managing editor of the *Evening Star*, was not her boyfriend, as things turned out. As a matter of fact, Jeanie said with that lopsided smile of hers, he was gay. This was San Francisco. Jeanie herself was divorced. Her ex-husband was the metro editor of the Los Angeles *Times*. That Minnesota girlhood I had dreamed up for her was totally off the mark. She was born and raised in Anaheim, in the shadow of Walt Disney's Magic Kingdom, where her dad was director of public relations. I told her a little about Barbara Frye and about growing up in Manhattan. I didn't mention Philip, my dead brother, or Jamie, because I knew it would only cast a further pall on things.

We'd brushed off the waiter so many times that when we finally felt ready to order some actual food, the kitchen had closed. Jeanie suggested that we could go back to her apartment and she would make us a couple of sandwiches. I said I'd love to with the same kind of stupid eagerness I showed when I met Jamie's parents at the cemetery and they idly suggested I drop by for dinner. Now, with Jeanie, it was pretty obvious that something else was going to develop. Single women in their thirties do not invite you to their apartments just for a sandwich, especially when you're registered at a hotel that has twenty-four-hour room service. To be honest with you, I felt guilty about being thrilled by the idea of sleeping with her. With people getting killed all over the place, it seemed indecent.

Anyway, I paid the drink bill with Kaiser Kash and we left the restaurant in her Fiat Spyder. The Fiesta we left in the parking lot.

Her apartment was in the Pacific Heights district, a neighborhood of beautiful three- to five-story town houses in an amazing array of architectural styles from Early Mission to High Victorian to Faux Rustic. She lived on the third floor of a gorgeous brown-shingled building loaded with dormers and turrets that had been the mansion of a timber baron in the 1920s. We went up.

"In the fall you can see the Golden Gate from here," she said, standing behind me as I peered out a window. I could feel her breasts lightly against my back. The fog was so thick that you could barely see down the block.

She told me to make myself comfortable while she fixed a couple of sandwiches. Her apartment was very attractive, but I couldn't help noticing how different her taste was from Barbara Frye's. The furniture was dark, Victorian, with a lot of lace on the arms of chairs and on tabletops. It was also rather cluttered with little objets d'art—nice things, like ivory letter openers and silver boxes and an agate egg—nothing like Barbara's bleached-oak-and-fruit-bowl look.

In a little while she came back with a platter of avocado and cheese sandwiches and a liter of wine. The bread, which was very crusty, irritated the cut inside my mouth, so I just ate the soft stuff inside. Afterward we sat together on the sofa with our shoulders touching. I ached to kiss her, and when I finally did she said I was welcome to stay the night.

In the bedroom she lit an oil lamp on her dresser and sat at a dressing table to take down her hair while I watched from the edge of her bed, feeling like a customer in a Barbary Coast bordello. Way off in the distance, a foghorn was lowing.

"They really have foghorns out here," I remarked out of nervousness.

"Yes, they really do, Grover," she said, turning, a silver hairbrush in her hand.

"I thought it was something they played up for the movies."

She stood up and unbuttoned her blouse. Her skin was very pale in the lamplight and the flesh seemed to pour out of her clothing like batter. Then she came to me.

She made love like someone accustomed to and comfortable with her own desires. Afterward she asked what happened to my foot, and I told her about the winter camping accident. I asked her to set the alarm for quarter to six in the morning. Then she lay pressed warmly against me in the darkness until her breathing modulated into the rhythm of sleep. The foghorns blew all night long.

* * *

She was somewhat less enthusiastic about getting up at the crack of dawn than she'd led me to expect, but I went into the kitchen and made her a pot of fresh coffee, and we were out of her apartment by quarter to seven. The plan was to first go to the hotel and retrieve my belongings, and then pick up the rented Fiesta for the drive to the airport. She waited in her Fiat in front of the St. Francis's entrance while I checked out because the only place to park anywhere nearby was the underground garage at Union Square.

I had just finished paying the hotel bill at the main desk, and was picking up my bag to leave, when the clerk said, "Oh, Mr. Graff, you have a message."

It was a plain envelope with my name on it, but no stamp or anything else—obviously hand-delivered. Inside was a sheet of plain white paper with this concise message typed all in upper-case letters right in the center of the page:

SERVE THE LORD WITH FEAR

"Excuse me," I asked the desk clerk. "Did you happen to see the guy who delivered this note?"

"No, sir," he said. "But I just came on at seven o'clock."

"I see." I read it over to myself a few more times and folded it up. "Look, I know this is a little irregular, but I'd like to check back into my room again."

"Did you say 'check *in*'?"

"That's right. Can I have the same room back?"

"If that's what you'd like, sir."

"Some last-minute things have come up," I explained, holding up the folded note.

"Certainly, sir."

Of course I had no intention of staying there another night, but since the motherfuckers found out what hotel I was in, I might as well let them think I was still in town. Anyway, I picked up my bag and made to leave the desk.

"Uh, Mr. Graff," the clerk stopped me. "Someone will take your bag—"

"That's okay," I assured him. "It's just samples. You know, software. Well, got to head down to the old Silicon Valley and make hay while the sun shines, huh? See you later."

Jeanie had gotten a copy of the *Chronicle* out of a sidewalk vending box and was reading the short item about the man who had had his throat cut in a Page Street apartment the night before. The police had no suspects yet in the case, she read the part to me out loud.

"I got a message from the mountain," I told her and handed her the note. She read it in about a second, handed it back, and stared at me for ten more seconds.

"You can still take it to the police, Grover," she said. "You really ought to."

"Come on. We'd better go now."

"To the police?"

"No, to pick up the other car."

"I don't think you should fool around with these people anymore."

"I'm not fooling around. Please, Jeanie. My plane leaves in less than an hour."

She made a face and jammed the gearshift into first, not saying a word as we drove through Chinatown. They were delivering fresh produce to the groceries and the restaurants at this hour and the air smelled of wet greens. Otherwise there was very little traffic and we got to the restaurant parking lot in a few minutes. Jeanie parked her Fiat and saw me over to the Fiesta. I chucked my bag in the passenger seat and got in.

"Please don't call the cops, even after I'm gone," I implored her. "Give me a couple of days back home to see what I can work up."

She closed her eyes and nodded.

"I guess I'd better be going now. Do you get back East much?"

"No. Not much."

"If you do, will you look me up?"

"Sure."

"My number's unlisted, so hang on to this," I said, writing down my phone number in my notepad and ripping out the page for her. "Tell me yours." I wrote it inside the cover. "I don't get out here much either. But I'd like to see you again."

"The logistics aren't very promising," she said with a rueful smile.

"I suppose you're right. Well, thanks for everything." I couldn't believe I said that, and fired up the engine to hide my embarrassment.

"Good-bye, Grover. Be careful."

She leaned in the window and kissed me good-bye. Then she turned and started back to her car. I pulled out of the parking space and honked, but Jeanie just waved good-bye without looking back.

The trouble with people telling you to be careful is that it tends to remind you how easy it is to fuck yourself up. That's the part that scares me.

* * *

I made the 8:10 flight. It turned out that we were scheduled to change planes twice, in Chicago and Pittsburgh, meaning I would have to cope with three takeoffs and three landings in a single trip—not a happy prospect.

Oddly enough, though, I remained psychologically very much intact. I didn't hear any voices in my head telling me the plane was going to crash and not to get on. And I didn't even have any drinks. Instead, I had another lumberjack's breakfast —waffles, eggs, toast, sausages, bran muffins, and Sanka—I was famished after just nibbling on a little avocado and cheese the night before. My tooth was still wobbly and I had to chew on only one side of my mouth, but my lip felt better. Then, on the plane, I kept taking out that nasty little note and rereading it over and over, and it pissed me off so much that I hardly noticed when we were rolling down the runway. And when I realized that I had managed to get through the ordeal of a takeoff without acting like a mental patient, I knew that I'd be all right for the rest of the trip. I even looked out the windows at thirty thousand feet.

CHAPTER 8

With the time change and everything, I didn't arrive back in the Capital until nearly four o'clock Eastern time. Naturally I was concerned that I'd never even locate the farm, let alone get over to it in Vermont before dark. But it would be the summer solstice any day now, so I still had quite a few hours of daylight to work with.

During the long flight I'd pretty much made up my mind to drop the pretense of merely following a story lead; if the Clothier girl was up there in Vermont, I would try to persuade her to leave with me. If she wouldn't hear of it, then perhaps the news of Steven Strunk's murder would get her attention. And if she didn't believe me, I had the newspaper clip from the San Francisco *Chronicle* in my shirt pocket. What I mainly had to worry about was finding a way to talk to her alone, without the others horning in. That would be the hard part. If she was there.

Of course I had no intention of checking in at the office first. I didn't particularly want Charlie or anybody else to know I had returned from California so soon because even if I explained the situation, they'd never understand it, and would give me a lot of shit about coming back without a story, and wasting expense money.

On the plane I had racked my brain trying to think of some way to locate the farm without tipping off the gang down on Union Street that I was back in the area, but I hadn't come up with any inspirations. Then, when we arrived at the Capital terminal, I simply went over to a pay phone, called Vermont information, and asked for a listing for the Lyman Foundation. It took three separate calls because they have this stupid policy that the operator will only search three localities for a number at a time, and I needed to check nine separate localities—Rutland, Burlington, Brattleboro, Bennington, Manchester, and a bunch of others—but on the third call they came up with a listing in Dorset township. That's all there was to it. I even got my quarter back.

What I did next was a little more creative. I called the number and put on a thick, crusty accent, like the Pepperidge Farm man in the old bread commercials on TV. It so happens that I'm quite a good mimic. I can do a lot of accents really well—French waiter, German Nazi, Black ghetto, Pakistani cab driver, you name it. Actually, Philip was the true master of this in our family. He did John F. Kennedy to perfection. He could also do Donald Duck, which a lot of people *think* they can do, but which is hard to do right, so you can really understand the words. It used to keep me in stitches. Anyway, a young-sounding girl answered the phone. I told her in this crazy voice that I was the state poultry inspector from Montpelier and I needed to come out and inspect their chickens but wasn't sure how to get to the farm.

Now, not only do I *not* know if they *have* such a thing as poultry inspectors over in Vermont, or anywhere else for that matter, but I had no idea whether they had chickens out at their farm. For all I knew they really were vegetarians—though I did distinctly remember the first Isaac saying that they kept livestock there, and most vegetarians eat eggs at least. In any case, the girl I was talking to sure didn't ask any questions about it, so they must have had chickens, and maybe there is such a thing as a poultry inspector. She just accepted the idea at face value and rattled off the directions to their place without hesitating. I wrote them down in my notepad and told her I'd be out sometime that week. It was as simple as that. I was so nervous making the call that it wasn't until I got to my car out in the short-term parking lot that it even struck me: the voice at the end of the line might have belonged to Debbie Clothier.

*   *   *

The Vermont border is less than an hour's drive from the Capital and Dorset is no more than ten miles north of Manchester, the tourist town where Jamie had that one gallery show so many years earlier that I told you about. It was so strange driving out of the Capital into the New England countryside, just hours after I'd been among the palm trees and the redwood groves, that California seemed like it had been an hallucination. I made it up to Bennington by quarter after five and Manchester by six.

I drove up the main drag, past the defunct Equinox Hotel (where, it is alleged in offbeat legend, Abraham Lincoln's son, Robert Todd Lincoln, a Negrophobe, once beat a black doorman with his cane for trying to help him out of his limousine), past the Orvis Company, where Rollie Tuttle spent the bulk of his salary on fly rods and fishing accessories, and finally past all the "old-timey general stores," gift galleries, book nooks, basket barns, and gourmet food boutiques that comprised the center of that tourist town. Seven miles north of Manchester, following the directions given me over the phone, I turned onto a ragtag county road for a couple of miles, then hung a left onto an unpaved road which led to a T junction. I took the dirt road to the left, passed a "Dead End" sign, and followed it a mile down to the end.

A pair of whitewashed brick gateposts topped by flower boxes filled with pink and blue petunias flanked the road there. A sign bolted to one gatepost declared the property beyond to be "Private." For those in need of clarification, a sign on the opposite gatepost said "No Trespassing." But there were no actual gates, nor any other impediment, like a chain, so I simply drove through.

Two rows of wineglass elm trees, all in various stages of dying from the Dutch elm disease, formed an impressive avenue leading up to the house. Driving closer, I could see that the property, once rather grand, had not been kept up. Brush was creeping over what had been groomed plantings beyond the elms. Clumps of staghorn sumac, that ubiquitous trash tree of New England, had sprouted in front of blooming rhododendrons.

The house was a three-story Georgian-style brick building with unequal clapboard additions on each side. The whole thing was painted white. It had green shutters with little crescent moons cut out for ornamentation. One shutter on the second floor hung askew. Off to the right about two hundred feet was a smaller white clapboard cottage which looked as if it had been built as a guesthouse.

Altogether the place had the look of a retired stockbroker's country manor gone somewhat to seed. If several cars hadn't been parked in front of the house, I might have wondered if the place was really lived in. Now I didn't know exactly who I was liable to encounter there, but on the way over I'd cooked up a scheme to at least get my foot in the door, if they didn't punch me in the mouth and kick me out right from the start. It was a variation on playing it straight, with a little twist thrown in.

It took quite a while before anyone answered the doorbell. In fact, I'd given up waiting and had actually taken several steps on my way around the house, where I'd heard some music playing, when the door was thrown open and a voice said, "Can I help you?"

He was a merry-looking guy about my age with red hair, a bushy red beard, and upturned mustaches, sort of how you'd imagine Santa Claus in his prime as a hale young man. His cheekbones were red from the sun. He had on blue jeans, a green T-shirt, and work boots. Brown dirt spots stained the knees of his pants. He was wiping his hands on a dish towel. I walked up to him and said, "Hi," trying to size him up. Physically, it was a little hard to tell, because he was standing on the front steps, so he seemed bigger than he really was. But he was obviously brawny.

"What can I do for you?" he asked again, shifting his weight a little impatiently now.

"My name is Grover Graff," I told him. When he remained impassive I added, "I'm a reporter from the *Times-Herald*."

With that he finally nodded in comprehension, tilting his head a little bit as though he were trying to take me in better.

"You're quite well known around here," he remarked after a long pause.

"Am I thought of fondly?"

He shrugged his shoulders.

"I take it you read my newspaper story, though."

"Sure did."

"Well, the thing is—did I catch your name?"

"Jacob."

"The thing is, Jacob, over the past week I've been prompted to really search my heart, to ask myself, did I treat you people fairly in that story? Frankly, I began to have my doubts. So, I thought I'd come over here to Vermont, where it's so pretty, and have a look at your farming operation . . ."

He nodded his head and batted his eyelids in a dubious way.

". . . you know, try to find something more upbeat about the group to make up for any misunderstandings I might have caused . . ."

He crossed his arms and kept nodding.

". . . and also to find out if this girl is residing here."

He stopped all his nodding and uncrossed his arms. I thrust the photographs of Debbie Clothier at him.

"I believe she goes by the name Leah among you," I added.

Jacob glanced at the photographs and then at me, and back at the photos and back at me again. For a few moments he looked like someone trying very hard to think fast on his feet, and I began to hope that I'd finally lucked out, that she was here. If he didn't let me speak to her, I thought, I'd explain how she was underage, and what kind of legal trouble that might expose him to.

But after all that anticipation he just shook his head and handed back the photographs.

"I never laid eyes on her before," he said without blinking. "She's not here."

My brain sagged.

"I don't mean to be a hard-ass about it, Jacob, but would you let me look around myself, just to soothe my natural skepticism?"

I had another lecture ready for him about police and warrants, to soften him up for when he said no, but he surprised me by saying, "Come on, I'll show you around." He didn't sound thrilled about it, but I had to admit he didn't act like a person with something to hide. He pushed open the door and gestured for me to go inside.

* * *

He acted so guileless that there didn't seem to be much point in even inspecting the place, but I had to play the stupid bluff out, and besides, I was naturally curious how they arranged things there, how many individuals were on the premises, et cetera, even if Debbie Clothier wasn't there. As for my personal safety, I doubted that this guy Jacob had been alerted by the people in California about me; I was also fairly sure the California gang, including Isaac/Shitfingers, still thought I was in San Francisco. I imagined one of their minions hanging around the lobby of the St. Francis Hotel waiting for me to show up. He'd have a long goddamn wait. Anyway, Jacob took me on a guided tour.

To the left of the entrance foyer was a large living room with a fireplace and built-in bookshelves. It had the look of a college dorm. The furniture was scuffed up and scruffy-looking. The bookshelves were half empty, and the books on them were mostly paperback science fiction and fantasy, plus stacks of Abe-grams. On the mantelpiece, leaning against the white-painted chimney, was the original artwork of an Abe-gram done on illustration board with watercolors. It depicted a horde of pointy-headed aliens with lizard faces emerging from manhole covers on a busy city street, with all the ordinary citizens fleeing in every direction. The title was "They Come!" I hadn't noticed it on any of the printed versions, but this illustration was signed on the bottom by the artist. It said simply, "Lyman."

"This way, Mr. Graff," Jacob said.

He ushered me into a dining room with a long mahogany table, which had seen better days, surrounded by eighteen mismatched chairs (I counted). The house had the same smell of institutional cooking that I remembered from prep school.

"We eat here," Jacob informed me flatly.

"Ah-ha." I nodded to emphasize my comprehension.

He led me through a set of swinging doors into a large kitchen of early sixties vintage linoleum and cabinetwork. There were a couple of refrigerators and a six-burner stove. Two young women were washing and rinsing dinner dishes. They looked up at me from their sinks, with wet arms and tentative smiles on their faces. Neither of them was Debbie Clothier. They appeared to be college-aged. One was fair-haired with a single long yellow braid and wire-rimmed glasses. The other was shorter and had dark hair, cropped close, pixieish, you might say. Both were quite attractive, despite their rather plain attire—long skirts and T-shirts. Plunk them down on the average college campus and they would have turned a few heads.

"Timna, Rachel, this is Mr. Graff, the newspaper reporter."

They immediately scowled and returned to their dishwashing chores.

"A pleasure to meet you," I said.

"This way."

Jacob showed me out the far end of the kitchen to the sort of vestibule that Vermonters call a "mud room"—a place where you can leave your shoes in the spring when it's all gloppy outside.

About a hundred feet behind the house was a large, weathered gray barn and a number of smaller outbuildings. One of them, I was thrilled to see, was a henhouse, meaning they kept chickens after all, whether they ate them or just used the eggs. A gray-barred rooster was scratching in the gravel outside it.

"What we do here isn't farming, exactly," Jacob explained, as if the guided tour was a big pain in the ass for him. "It's more like large-scale gardening. This way."

Off to the right of the barn stood a small orchard of apple and pear trees, and on the far side of it was the garden. It was about an acre in size and surrounded by a rather flimsy wood and chicken-wire fence. As we approached the music grew louder and saw a number of people working among the rows. I counted thirteen, then two more heads appeared from behind a row of pole beans. Twelve were women and the rest were males. Two more women sat outside the fence on a bench made of a halved log with their backs to me. They seemed to be spectating, though one was brushing the hair of the other. The music was coming from a portable boogie box next to them on the bench. It was an uproar of heavy metal rock and roll, totally at odds with the peaceful, pastoral scene before me.

"Lovely evening out here," I observed.

"This is everybody." Jacob ignored my remark, gesturing with a sweep of his hand.

When they saw us the people all stopped what they were doing and stood up slowly or leaned on their implements.

"It's probably the jacket and tie, huh?" I said, indicating my attire. He continued to ignore me.

"This way," he said, leading me toward the garden gate, sort of a jury-rigged affair with hinges made of baling wire. "Go on, see for yourself."

I entered the garden, taking the photographs out of my pocket as a reference—though by now the image of Debbie Clothier was etched permanently onto my brain. None of the individuals in the garden was her, all right, and when I asked them about the girl in the pictures they just shook their heads.

"Are you a policeman?" one of the gardeners asked, sweeping a strand of breeze-blown hair out of her face.

"KGB," I said, somewhat maliciously. She recoiled from me as if she actually believed it, and I took a little perverse consolation from the stupid joke, I admit. But the depressing truth was that I was right back at square one again: no Debbie

Clothier and a sick feeling that I had been a prime chump to come back East so soon.

Frankly I was all set to drop the whole fucking business, and on my way back through the rows of peas and radishes was already thinking up excuses to mollify Charlie Boland when I happened to look at the two girls sitting on the bench beyond the wire fence. The dark-haired one, on the left, looked hauntingly familiar. As I stepped closer that awful plummeting sensation returned to me, as though someone had sprung a trapdoor under my feet. The dark-haired girl sitting twenty feet ahead of me was Lisa Hurlbett, Jamie's twin sister.

* * *

I mouthed her name, too shaken to say it out loud. But as I stepped nearer something even more bizarre than the sheer fact that she was there became apparent. She was staring right at me, and gave no hint whatsoever that she recognized me. My appearance hadn't changed much in seven years, since college. I was maybe five pounds heavier, my hair was cut a little shorter, but that was about it. There's no way she wouldn't have recognized me.

She herself looked quite a bit different from the old days. For one thing, she was noticeably heavier, by as much as maybe twenty pounds. She was wearing the group's regular garb, a long loose skirt with a T-shirt. Her breasts had fallen. Her face looked puffy and lifeless, and in spite of the fact that someone had just brushed her hair, she looked unkempt. There were food spots on her T-shirt, and her bare feet were dirty. Yet I was sure it was Lisa.

I walked through the garden gate, approached the bench, and kneeled down on the grass in front of Lisa and the girl beside her.

"Have you ever seen this person?" I asked Lisa, proffering the photos of Debbie Clothier. She took the four snapshots and turned them over and over in her lap, but didn't answer. After a while her companion took them out of Lisa's hands, glanced through them, shook her head, and handed them back. Lisa watched without apparent interest and scratched a mosquito bite on her arm. I stood up.

"Thanks for showing me around, Jacob," I said, and started back toward the house in a semidaze. He escorted me.

"We're going to have our Holy Spirit meeting in a little while," he said. "You're welcome to join us."

"I have to get back."

"There'll be cider and doughnuts after."

I glanced over my shoulder, back at Lisa.

"What's wrong with that girl on the bench?" I asked Jacob at the door to the mudroom.

"Which girl?" Jacob asked. I wasn't sure whether he was dissembling or really stupid.

"The one who didn't say anything."

"Oh, her. Nerves."

"Nerves? What's wrong with her nerves?"

He shrugged his shoulders. "I wish I knew."

"What's her name?"

"Tamar."

"Pretty name," I observed, wanting not to appear too interested, and went inside the house.

"Go ahead and check the living quarters too?" Jacob volunteered, clearly exhilarated at having nothing to hide.

"Some other time, maybe," I said, totally distracted at this point and quite anxious to get out of there. "But thanks."

"You see, she's not here," Jacob exulted, following me through the kitchen and the rest of the downstairs.

"Someone sure gave me a bum steer," I agreed, and walked out the front door.

"So don't go writing in that newspaper of yours that someone's here who's not."

"Don't worry, I won't," I assured him, hurrying past the other cars parked in the driveway to my Datsun. I climbed in behind the wheel and started the engine. Jacob stood beside my window nodding his head gravely, as if he'd gained sudden insight to one of the world's one hundred greatest thoughts.

"Just remember," he said. "This is a big country. The wayward are everywhere."

CHAPTER 9

Dr. Hurlbett and his wife lived in the suburb of Minerva Park, an exclusive bedroom community in the hills overlooking the river five miles north of the Capital. When I had left the farm the sun was hanging over the western horizon and I had to drive straight into it practically the whole way. It gave me a whale of a headache. In fact, it was so bad that I had to stop at a grocery store in the little village of Cedar Mills and buy aspirin, which I washed down with a swallow of that scotch I'd bought way back in Marin County the night before. It didn't help much that I hadn't had a moment's sleep in almost three days. But I felt I had to inform Dr. and Mrs. Hurlbett about Lisa right away, and it wasn't the sort of thing I wanted to do over the phone, especially after what they'd been through with Jamie.

I'd been to the Hurlbetts' house once, ages ago, and then only for a half an hour. It was in our junior year. Jamie and I were on our way down to a Bruce Springsteen concert at Madison Square Garden. Our visit amounted to little more than a pit stop so that Jamie could hit up his mom for some cash and for us to get some food. I stayed in the kitchen during most of it because Jamie and his father got into a quarrel, ostensibly about Jamie using the money to buy drugs. But it was one of those futile, false-front arguments that parents have with their children. The truth was, Jamie's father never forgave him for not even trying to follow in his professional footsteps as a medical man. He never paid any attention to Jamie's art or praised his paintings—even the ones Jamie gave them as Christmas presents—and so there was quite a lot of bitterness between them while he was in college, and no doubt afterward too. A psychiatrist could have had a field day with that family. So I hid out in the kitchen helping the maid make us a bunch of tuna-fish sandwiches while the two of them squabbled.

I didn't remember the exact location of the house, but I knew the address because I'd sent letters to Jamie there, care of his folks, when I wasn't sure where he was various times after college. So, when I got to Minerva Park, I asked a guy out walking his poodle to direct me to Larch Lane. It turned out to be two blocks away. But they were very long blocks. This wasn't just some ticky-tacky development of half-acre lots. It was designed, by the same architect who did the enormous Dakota apartments in New York, as one of the first totally planned suburbs.

The houses were substantial, Gothic, gloomy-looking affairs on large wooded lots, like mini-estates—which is precisely what they were. No two were alike, though the brick Gothic style was uniform throughout. Since they were built just after the turn of the century, they had matching carriage houses. Back then this had been the privileged preserve of the city's business elite, including old Claude Hillebrand, founder of the original capital *Times,* who later sold out to Frank Kaiser and who acquired the very first completed home in Minerva Park in exchange for a series of editorials promoting the extension of city sewer and water lines beyond the city limits (at the city taxpayers' expense). Today, Minerva Park is the nesting ground mainly of doctors, lawyers, periodontists, and state government bigwigs. It wasn't written down in any charter, but it is well known that Jews weren't allowed to buy property there until after World War II.

It was that luminous hour of a June night when the sun has

just gone down and everything is bathed in soft, rich light. I knew the house when I saw it, even though it was set back quite a way on the property and half concealed by mature shrubbery. Yellow electric lights glowed in a couple of downstairs windows with diamond-shaped, leaded panes, so I assumed they were at home.

Mrs. Hurlbett answered the doorbell herself. If they had a maid, it must have been her night off. For a moment Mrs. Hurlbett looked startled, as if the sight of me had stirred some deep emotion. I assumed it was my connection with her dead son. She had on a quilted robe, though it was a summery evening, and without makeup, she looked considerably worse than she had that day in the cemetery.

"How nice to see you," she said with an obviously forced smile. I could also tell that she had forgotten my name again. "Won't you come in, please? Arthur's in the library."

I followed her there, noticing that she turned off the lights as we left the foyer, and also as we passed through the formal living room. The Hurlbetts' library was larger than the living room in my parents' New York apartment, and I could tell that it was where they spent most of their time. There was a lot of that clubby red leather furniture, a fireplace, and a wall of bookshelves. Dr. Hurlbett had been watching television when I came in, something like "Dynasty," but he rose out of his leather easy chair and switched it off a moment after I entered.

"Dear, you remember . . ."

"Grover." I tried to help her out.

"Grover," she said.

"Yes, of course. Come in, my boy."

I was already in, but I stepped forward to shake hands. He didn't offer his, but held them up and apologized about his arthritis acting up. They were quite red and knobby. He gestured to the sofa and I took a seat there. Then he asked if I wanted something to drink. I asked for a scotch, since I could see a bottle of Dewar's on the lowboy they used as a bar and didn't want them to go to the trouble of opening a wine bottle, even if they happened to have one around. Dr. Hurlbett was working on a scotch himself. His wife took a seat in a wing chair to my left, lowering herself carefully, as if her pelvis might shatter with normal use. And she sat on the edge of it wringing a tissue that she took out of the pocket of her quilted robe. She seemed still rather distraught about things.

"How nice of you to stop by," Dr. Hurlbett said, delivering my drink, and then not sitting down himself, but rather standing in front of me, looming, you might say.

"I wish this was just a social call, Dr. Hurlbett, but I'm afraid I have something a little . . . well, peculiar to tell you."

They glanced at each other anxiously.

"I saw Lisa today."

Her father seemed to stagger backward a step, as though rocked by a blow. "Where?"

"In Vermont. A place up in Dorset, outside of Manchester. A sort of farm. The thing is . . . well, she looked . . . she behaved very strangely."

Dr. Hurlbett finally sat down in the club chair opposite the sofa where I was. "Did you talk to her?" he asked.

"No. Uh, that is, yes, I talked to her. She didn't talk to me." The Hurlbetts exchanged another alarmed glance. "Perhaps I ought to backtrack a little for you. You see, for the past two weeks I've been investigating a religious organization. Well, that's what they claim to be. It's a fringe group. You might call them a cult. I'm a newspaper reporter—did I mention that when I saw you?"

"No."

"I didn't think so. Anyway, the name of this group is the Children of Abraham. Don't ask me what they believe in. It'd sound like a crazy mishmash to you, I'm sure. But they're in some hot water with the state prosecutors over their finances and I've been looking into their affairs. I had a story about them in the *T-H* last Friday. Maybe you saw it—"

"We take the New York *Times.*"

"Oh. I don't blame you. Well, anyway, since my story came out there have been some additional developments. I don't want to bore you with it, but I was in California yesterday in connection with this thing—"

"California?" Dr. Hurlbett seemed to have trouble following.

"They have a kind of . . . well, a kind of commune there, too, north of San Francisco, and one here in the Capital, of course, and also this farm in Vermont, and—"

"You mean you were in California yesterday and Vermont today?"

"I left California this morning. It's not important. I'm a bit strung out physically, to tell you the truth, but that's neither here nor there. The thing is, I'm beginning to think that the people in this organization are a little more far out than I originally thought."

"And you saw Lisa among them?"

"That's right, sir."

He and his wife shared another glance, this an appalled one.

"When was the last time you were in contact with your daughter, Dr. Hurlbett?"

Mrs. Hurlbett began to answer, but her husband cut her off.

"About six months ago, Grover," he said.

"Was this on the phone, or by letter, or what?"

"On the phone," Mrs. Hurlbett said.

"In a letter," her husband said.

They said this at exactly the same time. Of course it seemed odd, but then Dr. Hurlbett explained that there was a letter followed by a phone call, both around Christmastime.

"Did Lisa sound okay to you then? Did she sound disoriented, like she didn't know who she was or anything?"

"Well, Grover, if she didn't know who *she* was, then she would have hardly known who *we* were, would she? Or have called us," Dr. Hurlbett said, his impatience beginning to boil over in the sarcasm that Jamie had described the few times he talked about his family. I got a very clear impression of how difficult it might have been to be the old guy's only son.

"Of course, sir." I granted that my question had been rather foolish. "But did she sound okay? Normal?"

"Normal," he said with a bitter little laugh. "It's not a word that would seem to apply to our daughter. You know, Lisa's always been kind of a gypsy. Not that we tried to interfere, mind you. We just felt that her behavior was somewhat, uh . . ."

"Adolescent," her mother said.

"Yes," Dr. Hurlbett agreed with a sigh. "But rather past the age when one expects that sort of thing, you know, traveling across the country repeatedly, the different men."

"One after another," her mother said.

"Each worse than the one before," her father said.

"To be honest with you, I don't know a thing about your daughter's life since college. Jamie never—"

"Well, we'd always been concerned, of course," Dr. Hurlbett went right on, "that her life-style—I believe that's the new word for it—was not exactly conducive to a young woman's happiness. Mind you, we never tried to clip her wings. How could we, really? We always hoped she'd eventually get tired of it."

"That's right," Mrs. Hurlbett said. "And settle down."

"But when we spoke to her at Christmastime, she sounded fine, very content. She was living with some fellow in the countryside, but he was working at least."

"They both were," Mrs. Hurlbett said.

"And it sounded like she had decided to drop her anchor for a while."

"And settle down."

"Where was this exactly?" I asked.

They glanced at each other again.

"Northern Canada," Mrs. Hurlbett said.

"British Columbia," Dr. Hurlbett explained.

"I see."

I swirled my ice cubes around trying to imagine this North Woods life of hers, and what might have caused her to leave it if it was the first state of contentment she'd ever found after so many years of restless roving. Dr. Hurlbett offered me another drink, but I told him no thank you. The first one, combined with the lack of sleep, had made me rather woozy.

"So, you had no idea she was back East?" I asked.

"No," Mrs. Hurlbett said.

"None whatsoever," her husband concurred.

"Well, that's kind of weird, isn't it?" I said, not meaning to be rude. If I'd been less exhausted, I wouldn't have blurted it out like that.

"It's very . . . weird," Dr. Hurlbett agreed. "Perhaps that explains why her behavior was so peculiar when you saw her. This is shocking, Grover, believe me."

Mrs. Hurlbett shifted even more to the edge of her seat, as if she could bear neither to get up or to continue sitting still. She was wringing the tissue in her hands more energetically, too, and chewing on her lower lip.

"You see, sir, these people I've been investigating, this group that operates the farm, well, I have reason to believe that it's not a good place for Lisa to be—"

Suddenly Mrs. Hurlbett left her seat and began pacing on the carpet in front of the fireplace. Her husband watched her with a kind of detached curiosity, as if he were studying a patient in his old hospital office. I was reluctant to keep badgering them, but there were still a few questions that I felt only they could answer.

"Dr. Hurlbett, how long ago was it that you last heard from Jamie before . . ." I couldn't bring myself to finish the sentence. I felt awful even having to raise the subject. Unfortunately, my hesitation must have forced them to complete the terrible thought in their own minds. Mrs. Hurlbett stopped pacing, grasped the edge of the mantelpiece as though trying to steady herself, and began to quietly cry. "I'm sorry," I apologized to both of them, "but it might be important."

"I believe we received a letter from him in May," Dr. Hurlbett said. "Just a few weeks . . . before the . . . uh . . ."

"Where was it mailed from. Do you know?"

"Why, Lake Placid."

"He was still in Lake Placid?"

"That's where he lived."

"Could he have maintained some ties in Vermont, maybe something secret that nobody knew about?"

"Grover," Dr. Hurlbett said gravely. "Do you suppose my son was involved in drug trafficking?"

"I doubt it, personally, but you certainly can't rule it out these days. Back in '79, when he was living over there for a while, do you know where he stayed, or who with?"

Dr. Hurlbett stared at me a moment before answering.

"You didn't visit him there?" he asked.

"No. I stopped to see his show at a gallery in Manchester, and then we went out to a restaurant. But I never got over to where he lived."

"Didn't the two of you correspond?"

"His address was a P. O. box in Manchester. He could be pretty mysterious about details."

"It was a chalet on the butt side of Snow Valley," Dr. Hurlbett said.

"Are you sure about that?"

"Of course I am. He rented it from an old colleague of mine who'd grown too frail to ski. I arranged it. But what's the point here, son?"

"I guess I'm wondering if Jamie might have been involved with the people on this farm I was telling you about, where Lisa is—"

"Call the police! Call the police!" Mrs. Hurlbett suddenly screamed, crumbling to one knee in front of the fireplace and sobbing wildly. She looked absolutely tortured. Dr. Hurlbett rushed to her side, stooped, and put his hands on her shoulders, as though trying to steady her mind by steadying her body. But she was racked with sobs.

"It's all right, sweetheart. It's all right—"

"It is *not* all right," she cried hoarsely, and then let out a shriek of despair that was astonishing in its volume and pitch. This led to another siege of hysterics, with Mrs. Hurlbett alternately wailing and repeating "Call the police" and "My babies" over and over until it was a slur of nonsense words. When she began to subside her husband put his arms under hers, helped her to her feet, and started escorting her from the room saying, "Don't worry, Kitty, don't worry." As they reached the door he glanced over his shoulder at me and said, "Wait here, son."

Once I was alone I realized that I was shivering, and not

from being cold, either. I crossed the room to the lowboy where the liquor was, poured myself a fresh drink, and—not even bothering with ice—downed it in about four gulps and poured myself another, reflecting on how recent events had affected my drinking habits. A minute later Dr. Hurlbett returned, gingerly closing the door behind him.

"She'll be all right," he said. "I gave her a little something. These past few weeks have been hell on her."

"I understand, sir."

He joined me at the bar and poured himself another scotch too. Merely unscrewing the bottle cap cost him an effort because of his arthritis.

"Just how was Lisa behaving?" he asked me in an even tone of voice that suggested a long experience with consultations on grave medical matters.

"It's hard to describe—"

"Don't try to spare my feelings. What'd she look like?"

"Disheveled. Overweight."

"Fat?" he made a face as though he disapproved. "She wasn't prone to that. None of us are."

"Well, perhaps bloated would be more accurate—"

"All right, son, but what did she do?"

"She didn't do anything. She didn't recognize me. I was as close to her as I am to you and she didn't know who I was. She just sat there."

"Perhaps she'd forgotten who you were."

"Out of the question," I said.

"Did she remember once you reminded her?"

"That's just it, Dr. Hurlbett. I couldn't really say anything like that. You see, these people don't like me very much. They're rather upset about that story I wrote in the newspaper. The reason I went over to Vermont in the first place was to search for another missing girl, a teenager, from Steubenville. Anyway, when Lisa didn't seem to recognize me, I thought it better to not let on that I knew her. They're real good at hiding people, this group, when you want to get somebody out of their clutches."

"For instance this teenager."

"Exactly. It just seemed to me that it would be a hell of a lot easier to eventually get Lisa out of there if I didn't let on that she meant anything to me."

"I think you did exactly the right thing, son. Perhaps Kitty's right too. We ought to call the police." He turned and strode over to a baize-topped writing table and reached for the telephone.

"Uh, Dr. Hurlbett, calling the police might not be the wisest approach in this situation. First of all, it's another jurisdiction. Second, despite the way she behaved, it's possible that she's there of her own free will. And third, unlike this girl from Steubenville, Lisa is of age."

Dr. Hurlbett put down the telephone.

"All right, then," he apparently agreed, "what about hiring one of these fellows I've read about to . . . to simply remove her from the premises, get her into a motel or something, and give us an opportunity to at least check her out medically and so forth, make sure she's not *on* something."

"I'm afraid it's become harder to do that, sir. You just can't go into that kind of situation and pluck someone out anymore, even your own flesh and blood. There have been a series of court decisions all over the country the past ten years involving so-called de-programmers who've done just what you described. Unfortunately, in the eyes of the law it's considered tantamount to kidnapping."

"That is bad law."

"I guess it's part of the price we pay for living in a free country. I don't think the founding fathers realized there would be so many dangerous assholes running around in two hundred years."

Dr. Hurlbett seemed to bristle a little at my language. I probably wouldn't have said it if I hadn't been so burned out and exhausted. But then, his shoulders slumped, he heaved a disheartened sigh and gazed into the carpet, looking defeated and old.

"Pardon me," I said.

"Don't worry about that," he said quietly.

"Do you have an attorney, sir?"

"Certainly."

"I suggest you call him tomorrow, or even tonight if possible. Perhaps he'll know a way that she can be placed legally under your supervision, if she's in psychological trouble. Then the three of us, you and me and your attorney, can put our heads together on this thing and find a way to bring her home without putting her in jeopardy."

"Jeopardy?" he said, a pained, abstracted look on his face.

"In jeopardy of disappearing. Will you do that, sir? Call your attorney."

"Yes," he replied gloomily, "I will."

"Good," I said and put my drink glass down on the table, signaling that it was time for me to move along. But as I was about to wish him good night he put a knobby red hand on my shoulder and looked plaintively into my eyes.

"Grover, would you consider going back to that farm? Try to talk to her and see if she might leave the place with you and come back here voluntarily, so we can avoid all this . . . all this unpleasantness?"

"I don't know, sir. She didn't seem to even know who I was."

"Perhaps she was pretending not to know you, and for precisely the same reason you gave—in order not to let on. To protect herself."

"I hadn't thought of that," I said. "It's been a while since I had any sleep, sir."

"I understand, Grover. But isn't it possible?"

"Yes, it's possible she pretended not to know me. You would have thought she'd have given me some sort of signal, though."

"Perhaps she did and you missed it."

"I might have," I admitted.

"Are you worried about your personal safety? Tell me, frankly. I won't think less of you."

I thought it over a minute.

"Only to a point," I finally answered him. "They've tried to intimidate me physically a few times, even gotten a little rough, but I don't think they'd go much further. I'm too well connected to the powers-that-be—the press, the police, the prose-cutors."

"Then you'll give it a try?"

"All right," I said after a moment's hesitation.

"I'm very grateful to you, son. And I know I speak for Lisa's mother too. I hope Jamie knew what a good friend he had in you."

"It's the least I can do," I told him, on the verge of getting weepy. "Well," I said with a deep breath, "I better be going."

He walked me back through the house to the front door.

"Good luck, tomorrow, Grover."

"Thanks. Oh, one more thing, Dr. Hurlbett—if you don't hear from me in person or otherwise by nine o'clock tomorrow night, call the state troopers."

"You can depend on me, son."

He took his hand off my shoulder and put it on my head, sort of halfway between patting it and anointing it like a priest. Then his hand wandered down the side of my head and he stroked my cheek. It was rather unsettling, but I assumed that he was remembering his son and using me as a substitute to express a range of feelings from grief to love to regret which he was simply unable to give voice to. I indulged him for a little while, not wanting to embarrass either of us. But then he did something really strange—he leaned forward and kissed me on the cheek. Of course I'd never been a father and lost a son, and while I could imagine the depth of emotion such a calamity would touch, and understood how he identified me with Jamie, his kissing me like that still gave me the creeps.

"I really must go, sir," was all I could say.

He finally removed his hand from my face and—very oddly, I thought—said, "You be a good boy now."

"Don't worry, I'll be all right," I assured him as though I were a kid again talking to my own father. Then I turned to go.

Night had fallen. The broad lawns and elaborate flower beds of Minerva Park resounded with keening insects. I stumbled on the flagstone stairs that led down to the driveway and almost fell into an azalea bush. Dr. Hurlbett remained in the doorway until after I got into my car and started the engine, his white hair gleaming in the edge of the hall light and his face obscured in the darkness.

* * *

I hadn't eaten a goddamn thing since breakfast in the coffee shop at San Francisco airport and I was so hungry when I left the Hurlbetts' that I did something I almost never do except under the most extreme circumstances: I stopped at the Burger Barn. On principle I try not to spend any money in the fast-food establishments of our republic for the same reason that some pacifists don't pay their taxes. But I just didn't feel that I could wait more than five minutes to get some simple nourishment, and I was afraid to eat anything but soft food because of my wobbly tooth.

So I sat there under the fluorescent lights, surrounded by teenagers talking about drugs, wolfing down two double cheeseburgers and wishing I had some other place to go than home. I even almost called Barbara Frye. But I did have to drop my stuff off, and change, and pick up my checkbook, because I was almost out of expense money, and I figured I probably would spend the night there, unless they had nailed a dead chicken to my door or something.

Besides, I'd pretty much made up my mind to move out of the goddamn place and find somewhere to live that was: (a) *not* some jive-plastic garden apartment, (b) out in the country, that is, away from the goddamn Capital, and (c) surrounded by enough property for a large dog. I kept thinking about poor Steve Strunk and how he asked if I had any pets, and about Babe and what they did to her, and that's where I got the idea that it might be nice to get a very large dog.

In the first place, a dog makes a great pet. I'd never had one, personally, growing up in Manhattan and everything, but I've known quite a few people who did, and they were crazy about their dogs. Secondly, if you have a very *large* dog, some motherfucker will think twice about messing with it, or even pussyfooting around your property. Anyway, I didn't have one yet, and I didn't have much choice, either, except to go back to my goddamn apartment.

I parked several buildings away from mine and snuck up the back stairway, tiptoed over to my door, and pressed my ear against it, trying to hear if maybe somebody was inside, but I didn't hear anything. Finally I just went in.

I turned the lights on only long enough to check the place out and lock the doors. No one was there, it turned out, but I was shocked to see what a disgusting mess I'd made out of the living room. The furniture was still piled against the patio door and covered with shards of broken glass and carpet tacks. There were no signs that anyone had broken in while I was away, though.

It was all right to keep the light on while I was in the bathroom, because it didn't have any windows, but once I returned to my bedroom I was afraid to turn anything on, even a flashlight, afraid someone might be outside watching to see if I was home. Even though I was exhausted, I had a lot of trouble falling asleep. Usually I have to read myself to sleep, and you couldn't very well read with no light, could you? So, I just lay there staring into the dark ceiling, trying to figure out what to do the next day.

What I told Dr. Hurlbett about not being afraid for my safety was not exactly the truth, but as far as returning to the farm to get Lisa was concerned, I was more worried about practical considerations than the danger. For instance, how could I even get her off alone, by herself, away from the others, just to speak to her confidentially? Then I had an inspiration. I didn't have to get her off alone. I could simply force the issue in front of the whole group. I'd wait until suppertime when they were all gathered together for the evening meal, and I'd go in and confront Lisa right there at the table, and tell her that her father and mother were worried about her and ask her if she would leave with me. Right in front of everybody. If Jacob and the others gave me any trouble, I'd tell them that my newspaper and the authorities knew where I was and that they'd better not interfere.

Actually, I didn't want to think about it anymore after that, not just because I was sick of the whole goddamn business, but because I knew if I dwelled on it I'd just think up a lot of reasons why the plan wouldn't work. Instead, I had another inspiration that did work: I switched on the clock radio next to my bed. The Red Sox were playing the Brewers out in Milwaukee and the game was only in the fifth inning. Unfortunately the Sox were getting clobbered 8 to 2, but I fell asleep before the top of the sixth.

CHAPTER 10

The next morning, which was Friday, I could no longer avoid going back into the office to report to Charlie Boland. He was in his glass cubicle presiding over his press releases when I got there around eleven o'clock in the morning. We exchanged pleasantries and bantered about how the East Coast really "has it over" the West Coast ("because you miss the seasons out there," Charlie said), and how my flight was, out and back, blah blah, but you could tell that Charlie was anxious to hear what I had accomplished.

So, I told him what happened: about my meeting with Steve Strunk, and about Isaac/Shitfingers suddenly turning up in Marin County and punching me in the mouth, and how they bashed the back end of my rent-a-car all the way down the mountain, and finally about Strunk's murder. I also told him about my quick trip to Vermont the day before. I didn't tell him about Lisa turning up there because I didn't want him to think that what started as an investigation of charity fraud was turning into some kind of personal vendetta. But in every other respect, I told him the truth.

In spite of it all it was pretty obvious to me that Charlie was hardly listening. And when I finished he just stared at me across his desk like someone who has suffered through an extremely tiresome joke and then missed the punch line.

"That's a lot of interesting new information you've got there, Grover," he said. "But where's the girl?"

"We don't know yet."

"Okay. Then what's the story angle now?"

"The same as before. It's still developing."

"How much longer is it going to take you to develop it to the point where we have something we can run with?"

"I don't know. I've got to go back there this evening—"

"To California!"

"No. Vermont. Relax, will you Charlie."

He exhaled, ballooning out his cheeks in the process, and started tapping the edge of his desk with one of those little pica rulers that newspaper editors always have around.

"Look, Grover, I don't feel you should spend too much more of your time on this thing. I don't really see where all this is leading. I mean, granted, there are some interesting elements—"

"Is that what you call it when somebody tries to run one of your reporters off the road in his car—an interesting element? Or when a source gets his throat cut six hours after an interview?"

"I don't mean to belittle these things—"

"I hope not—"

"—but, frankly, Grover, Dan the Man was not exactly tickled by your first installment, and he almost went through the roof when he found out about the trip to California. And to be perfectly honest with you, this seat of mine grew a little warm as a result."

By Dan the Man, he meant Dan LaMott, the publisher of both the *T-H* and the *Trib*. Everyone called him that. He was only thirty-eight years old and it was generally thought that he was on a rocket ride to the upper echelons of the Kaiser Korp. When the national management sent him to the Capital, both papers were hemorrhaging financially. In two years he got the *T-H* out of the red. It was quite a feat, except when you consider that he accomplished it by putting what little was left of the paper's integrity in third place behind advertising and circulation. He had a fourteen-year-old son who was a junior high school dope dealer with three youthful offender arrests (no convictions). His wife had passed out drinking at the annual company picnic the first summer I was there.

"I'm sorry I got you in hot water over the voucher, Charlie," I told him sincerely, "but if LaMott had it totally his way, this paper wouldn't run anything but photos of chimpanzees wearing party hats."

"Well, he just about shit a brick over the $800."

"It was a legitimate trip."

"I know it was, Grover. I approved it. And I told him that. You just need to know how he feels about it."

"I understand his concept of journalism, if that's what you mean, and it's for the birds, if you want my opinion."

I was getting a little shrill. Charlie's reflex response, of course, was to laugh hysterically. I realized that it was just his way of coping with the stress I was causing him, but it made me so mad I wanted to grab his Windsor knot and throttle him with it. I didn't, though. I just sort of hung my head and waited until he was finished. Then I said contritely, with a bashful little smile, "I guess you're right, Charlie. I should at least take the guy's attitude into account, as long as we both have to deal with the bastard."

"That's exactly the point, Grover."

"I mean, no sense tossing gasoline on the fire."

"Now you're talking. Look, you just play it cool for a while, wait until the smoke clears, and the whole thing'll blow away."

Something about the way he said that made me very nervous.

"Wait a minute, Charlie. I'm still going back to Vermont this afternoon."

"Fine," he said with an expansive wave of his hand. "Go."

"And I'm keeping on this story."

"Good. Keep on it."

"And when I finally *do* develop it, I expect you to run with it."

"We will," Charlie said. "You develop it to the point where

you have something really hard, and I'll back you all the way, Grover."

"Okay, Charlie," I said, holding out my hand to shake. "Thanks. I appreciate it." It was the truth. In fact, it made me feel kind of ashamed for underestimating his moral fiber.

* * *

I spent the next hour reading the New York *Times* and our own rag, trying to catch up on things that I'd missed. The Red Sox, by some miracle, had ended up winning that game in Milwaukee and were on their way to New York for a crucial four-game series with the Yankees starting that night. I used to root for them in the old days. Philip used to take me up to the stadium on the Lexington Avenue subway, back in days of Tom Tresh and Joe Pepitone, the years when they were steady losers. It was easy to root for them back then. You felt sorry for them. After living in Boston, though, I became a rabid Red Sox fan. And anyway, how can you like the Yankees these days with the front office the way it is? You can't even feel sorry for them anymore.

Around noon I went out to deposit my paycheck, and then, as sort of a reward for all the crap I'd been through, I took myself out to lunch at that Chinese place I told you about—the only decent restaurant in the Capital. It was full of bureaucrats from the State Department of Mental Retardation, whose building is across the street, so I had to wait for a table and didn't get back to the office until a quarter to two. While I waited, though, I called Dr. Hurlbett at home to see if he had contacted his attorney, but there was no answer.

Back at the office what I planned to do was check out the afternoon paper, the *Trib*, for country rental listings because I was serious about getting out of my apartment as soon as possible. Unfortunately, Merle Lyons was holding court at his desk. Whatever he and his groupies were talking about, though, they apparently didn't want me to hear, so as soon as I settled in, the group dispersed. Then Merle was able to turn the full wattage of his charm on me.

"I hear you went out to San Francisco," he said, leaning back in his chair like a pasha.

"You heard correctly," I said.

"How'd you manage that?"

"I was on a story."

"I bet."

"You can put money on it."

He sipped his cocoa, still gazing at me with a gleam in his eyes and a provocative smile.

"Maybe I can dream up some excuse to go out there and throw a little company cash around," he said.

"That would be asking an awful lot of yourself, don't you think, Merle? Incidentally, you've got a piece of glop on your tie."

It happened to be the truth. There was a big greasy glob of Kaiser Kafeteria gravy or something dribbled down his tie. When he looked down and saw that I wasn't kidding, he waddled off to the bathroom to rinse it out.

When he was gone Ginny Unger came over to my desk and handed me an envelope. She waited there, with a big grin on her face to watch me read it, but I just put it aside and eventually she got bored and flitted away. Then I opened the envelope. It was a memo from Charlie Boland, and this is what it said:

> In regard to our conversation of this morning, I'm afraid I am going to have to alter my decision for reasons that seem compelling to me now that I have had time to think about it. You are to desist from your current investigation and be available to the city desk for general assignment. I have informed Steve Traczewski of this and you will report to him on Monday morning at 8:00 A.M. I'm sorry to renege on this morning's discussion, but you have enjoyed a great deal of freedom in your time here and feel [sic] that a little more supervision of your activities might not be such a bad thing.
>
> [signed]
> Charles B.

When I looked over at his cubicle the lights were switched off and he was gone. I guess it turned out that I had *overesti-mated* his moral fiber. I should have known he would spring something like this on a Friday afternoon and then split for the whole weekend. In front of his darkened cubicle, Ginny Unger sat at her desk grinning at me across the newsroom, enjoying the hell out of my consternation. No doubt she knew the contents of the memo because she had typed it.

Well, after that, I was so pissed off that I got up, rammed my chair against the desk, and stalked out of the newsroom. Merle was on the other side of the swinging double doors, on his way back from the bathroom, and I accidentally flung them open in his face.

"Hey, Graff, you sonofa—" he started yelling at me, but I was already on my way down the hall. I couldn't bother waiting for the elevator, but bounded up the fire stairs to the fourth floor and marched into Dan LaMott's outer office. His secretary flinched when she looked up and saw me panting. She was a very stately-looking gray-haired woman in her fifties and her formidable personality was well known among the staff. Her name was Mrs. Blanchard, but they called her "the Steel Curtain," because that's how hard it was to get past her.

"I'd like to see Mr. LaMott," I told her.

She stared at me blankly for a moment.

"Mr. LaMott. I'd like to see him, please."

"I heard you. Do you have an appointment?"

"No."

"Well, you have to—"

"My name is Graff. I'm a reporter. I need to see him right away."

She looked straight at me and said, "I'm sorry, but Mr. LaMott isn't in right now."

I happened to notice the brass coatrack where Dan LaMott's legendary London Fog trench coat was hanging—the coat that he was known never to leave the office without because he was originally from Seattle where it rains practically every day—so I had a pretty strong feeling that he was still there. Mrs. Blanchard saw me notice it too. Instead of arguing with her some more, I just walked past her desk and opened the door to his inner sanctum. He was in there, all right, sitting behind his big desk with his feet up reading that afternoon's *Tribune*.

"I'm sorry, Mr. LaMott, but—"

"It's all right, Dorothy," he assured her. She stood her ground, the protective mother hen, but he repeated that it was all right, and wrinkled his nose, and motioned her to leave and close the door. Then he came out from behind his desk, put his hand on my shoulder, and shook my hand. It was a Dale Carnegie technique.

"What can I do for you, Grover?"

He knew my name, of course, though we hadn't spoken two times all year, and then just to say hello. As a matter of fact, he knew the name of everyone in the building, from the editorial staffs to the printers down to the lowliest janitor. It was another part of his Dale Carnegie training. For all its corniness, though, it did make you feel more at ease, I must admit.

"Charlie Boland just put me on the city desk," I said. "And I think you told him to."

"I did, Grover," he agreed.

"Would you mind if I asked when you told him that?"

"Not at all. I believe it was Wednesday."

"I see."

So, Charlie had gotten his marching orders long before our discussion that morning. He had been lying right to my face.

"I hear that you don't approve of the stories I've been doing, Mr. LaMott."

"Grover"—he removed his hand from my shoulder and strode purposefully over to his window, which had a really wonderful view of Plaza Boulevard—"we've been getting a lot of calls and letters from our readers."

"We've gotten quite a few calls down in the newsroom too," I told him. "And they're almost all from the members of the group I'm investigating. I suppose you received a tape too."

"Yes, I did," he said and turned back to face me. "You shouldn't have spoken that way, Grover. It was extremely rude, and stupid of you, I might add."

"Did Charlie tell you it was a phony tape?"

"We didn't do an in-depth analysis of it."

"Well, he might have at least mentioned that little detail. It was doctored through and through—edited and overdubbed all over the place. Charlie and I discussed it. He should have told you."

"It *was* your voice, telling this fellow to go screw himself, wasn't it?"

"Yes, it was my voice. But what they edited out were the threats they were making against me, threats of violence, which is why you heard me saying what I did at the end of the tape. But believe me, it was justified."

"Grover, it's never justified to say that. I don't care how much you're provoked. Part of your job is to take a certain amount of flak from the public and to keep your cool."

"All right," I agreed. "But the problem is that you've taken action against me on the basis of something you misunderstood."

"Grover, it's not a matter of the tape, whether it's fake or doctored or whatever—"

"Excuse me, Mr. LaMott, but it *is* important, because it obviously influenced your decision."

"Look, Grover, I was in the army and I've been around newspapermen for more than fifteen years. I'm not Miss Goody Two-shoes. What I'm concerned about is alienating our readers. Some of these complaints are coming from people I know personally, people who are important in our Capital community, who are, frankly, sick and tired of opening the *Times-Herald* every morning and seeing another attack on religion—which, whether you believe it or not, is a sensitive subject to a lot of people, and which you've got to respect."

"I suppose they're not sick of seeing chimpanzees and puppy dogs on page one."

"Now you're just being sarcastic."

"Pardon me. But I don't think it's fair of you to say that I'm attacking religion itself. I write about people, people who are often unbalanced individuals, people who are sometimes charlatans and crooks—"

"But that's just it, right there, Grover. That attitude of

yours. 'Charlatans! Crooks!' Organized religions around the world depend on contributions—all of them—and who's to say that people are getting their money's worth or not. I've never seen you attack the Catholics, and they've got more darn money than General Motors."

"It's hardly the same thing—"

"But it is, at the philosophical level we're discussing it. Who's to say which religion is legitimate and which isn't? The Romans? An Adolph Hitler? The Soviet Politburo? The Kaiser Corporation? Certainly not *you*, Grover Graff, who's just a tiny cog in this whole machine. I won't have it, Grover."

"How about the attorney general?"

"How about him?" LaMott echoed me.

"He's planning to hand down indictments against this particular group, in case Charlie hasn't mentioned that either."

"Fine. He's duly authorized. Let him do his job."

"And my job is to report his findings."

"Yes. To report his findings. But not to render judgment above and beyond his findings. Not to mock sincere people, however bizarre their beliefs seem to you."

"What if their bizarre beliefs extend to killing people?"

"Murder . . . ?"

"That's right."

"Are you referring to that girl? The one you went to California to search for?"

"She's only a maybe at this point. I'm pretty sure they killed another kid in San Francisco, one of their former members, for just talking to me."

"He was killed while you were out there?"

"A few hours after I interviewed him."

"Charlie told me you came back from California without the girl *and* without a story."

"Well, I guess he would say that."

"Have the police charged any of these people?"

"No. Not yet."

"Why not?"

"I don't think they know who did it."

"Ah, but you do."

"I have some very strong suspicions."

"What about the girl? You didn't find her out there."

"No, I didn't."

"Then she's a missing person."

"It's possible that she's a dead person."

"Do you have any evidence?"

"I have a lot of leads that don't quite jibe."

"Leads that 'don't quite jibe' are not hard facts."

"What do I have to do? Lug a corpse into the office and flop it across your desk to justify a story? I'm an investigative reporter."

"Not anymore, for the time being, because starting Monday you will be on general assignment. You will cover fires, and automobile accidents, and events which the police, whose job it is, have already investigated and come up with some gosh-darn facts about. And you will lay off religion from now on."

"I'm not laying off this story."

"Either do what we tell you, or find a job on another paper."

"I'm not going on general assignment."

"Look, why not at least take the weekend to mull it over, Grover? Give yourself a chance to calm down and relax. Reporting jobs aren't so easy to find these days."

"Mr. LaMott, I was nominated for a Pulitzer two years ago. I don't need your third-rate excuse for a newspaper."

"I'm sorry you feel that way."

"No you're not. That's just some more of your Dale Carnegie bullshit."

He walked around me all the way across his big office to the door, opened it, and with a smile on his face gestured with a broad sweep of his hand that I was welcome to depart.

"Best of luck out there, Grover," was his ever-genial farewell.

* * *

What with throwing my job out the window, and everything, I had tried to act a little more self-possessed than I really felt. Actually, I was in such a turbulent state of mind, I barely remember leaving LaMott's office.

Down in the newsroom Merle was back at his desk, typing away with his pudgy fingers. Rollie Tuttle had also returned from his rounds of the suburban town offices. He began asking me about my trip to the Coast, but I was quite unable to hold a friendly conversation and just started cleaning out my desk. There wasn't a whole lot to clean out—just a thesaurus, my Rolodex, a folder of my clippings, and a bunch of promotional record albums that Barbara Frye had turned over to me because she didn't want them—I didn't want them either, they were such garbage. Otherwise, I didn't have any philodendron plants or Smurfs or a complete goddamn dinner service for eight (you'd be amazed at what kind of junk some people keep in their office desks).

When Merle and Rollie saw me cleaning out my desk, they naturally deduced that something rather serious was going on, and Merle, for one, was unable to restrain his glee.

"Don't tell me he got fired," Merle said breathlessly. That's what chickenshit he was. He didn't dare gloat at you directly, but did it in the third person, as if you weren't really there.

"In case you're referring to me, Merle, no, I didn't get fired, I quit."

"Oh, for goodness' sake, Grover . . ." Rollie said. You could tell he wanted me to calm down and listen to some avuncular advice, but Merle was simply too overjoyed to keep his mouth shut.

"There is a God after all. Oh happy day! Hallelujah!"

"Hey, Merle," I said, "you interested in some records?"

"What . . . ? Yeah, sure. Whaddaya got there?"

I picked up the first one. "Quiet Riot," I said, and smashed it over his head. "Duran Duran." I hit him with that. "Def Leppard." Same thing. "Twisted Sister." Smash. Of course they didn't really break. They just sort of bent.

Merle tried to get up, but I kept him pinned down in his chair. For all his bulk, he was not a strong guy. Next, I shoved his face into the carriage of his electric typewriter with his nose right down against the roller.

"Okay, Merle, now I'm going to teach you how to write a record review. Ready?"

And I started hammering the keys. He hollered a bit and carried on, but there was hardly anybody left in the newsroom at this hour on a Friday, except Rollie and old Henry Bloch, the editorial writer, off in a distant glass-walled cubicle. And Rollie was too flabbergasted, at first, to come to Merle's rescue, until he thought I was strangling the fat motherfucker and then he pulled me off. Merle's nose and forehead were covered with black ink.

"I'm going to make a professional out of you yet," I said, and scooped up my stuff and headed for the door.

"Hey, Grover . . ." Rollie yelled after me. "Hey, Grover . . . uh, keep in touch. . . ."

And that, for the present time, was the end of a promising career in journalism.

CHAPTER 11

For a while I sat in my car in the parking lot wondering about what I had done, certainly disgusted with myself to some degree, but struck also by what now seemed the inevitability of it. I took that pint of scotch out of the glove compartment and drank a swallow of it while I stared at the building. The company insignia, a huge golden "K" surmounted by a crown and bolted to one of the walls, looked like it belonged over the entrance to an Italian restaurant. I couldn't stand to look at it another minute, so I turned over the ignition. Whether as a reporter or as a lone individual, I was still going to go to Vermont. It didn't change anything as far as Lisa Hurlbett and her parents were concerned. When I pulled out of the parking lot it was a quarter after four.

Once you got across the river and away from all the suburbanoid smarm around the Capital, the road ran through farm country. It was a particularly beautiful landscape of abrupt hills and quiet hollows leading into the more rugged Green Mountains. The corn was up, light green knee-high sprouts so pretty against the dark brown earth. Wild orange day lilies and black-eyed susans bloomed along the roadside.

Despite what had happened at the office, I began to feel

better and better—and it wasn't from drinking, either, because I hadn't touched a drop since the parking lot. I began to realize that bagging my job at the stupid rag was overdue anyway; that I'd wanted to leave since last winter but had unthinkingly allowed things to just slide along. True, I didn't have another job to turn to, but I was pretty confident about landing on my feet. I could sell a few more magazine stories. And there was always Bob Raymond's offer to come down and work for the New Jersey paper if my situation ever got desperate. If nothing else, you could have a field day down there writing about the Mafia.

By the time I made it up to the farm I was actually in an exuberant mood, perhaps too much so, because when Jacob answered the door I temporarily allowed myself to forget who and what I was dealing with and acted a little too frisky.

"Hi," I said. "It's me, the poultry inspector."

He nodded his head and smiled thinly.

"What's for din-din?" I asked.

He stopped smiling.

"Come on, Jacob, aren't you going to invite me in? I happened to be back in the old neighborhood and decided to stop by. Boy, something in there smells mighty good."

I couldn't quite tell whether Jacob was unamused by my antics or simply too dumb to figure out what the hell I was doing there. In either case, he invited me into the house.

"You wait here," he said in the living room, pointing to a comfortable easy chair. I assumed that he did not want me fraternizing with the others, some of whom were indeed busy setting the supper table in the adjoining dining room. Anyway, he excused himself and left me sitting there alone.

At first I just sat there. But then I stood up and sort of wandered over to the arched entranceway of the dining room and watched the girls laying out the flatware and napkins. None of the males took part in this task, by the way, nor did Lisa. You could tell I was making the girls nervous, though. A moment later Jacob returned, and when he saw me standing up he became rather upset.

"Didn't I tell you to sit in your chair?" he said.

"I didn't realize that this was my assigned chair."

"It's where I expect you to sit until we're ready for supper."

"All right," I said, sorry I'd acted playful with him in the first place and trying to size him up again physically. He seemed to be about two inches taller than me and perhaps ten pounds heavier. I was growing somewhat more apprehensive than when I'd first arrived. The plan didn't seem quite as clever as when I cooked it up the night before. To tell you the truth, I was beginning to regret coming back at all and wished I'd had a chance to speak to Dr. Hurlbett's attorney beforehand. Anyway, I returned to my designated seat without making any more fuss. And when Jacob saw me comply, he excused himself again.

On the table next to my chair were a number of books and pamphlets. One of these was a paperback book called *None Dare Call It Conspiracy,* which, in case you're not familiar with it, is one of the sacred texts of the John Birch Society. It didn't really surprise me to find it there, because religious nuts and political right-wingers are two of a kind. One of my all-time favorite assignments, as a matter of fact, had been to cover the annual John Birch Society convention in Boston. They held it at a big hotel there because the founder of the organization, the millionaire candy manufacturer Robert Welch (Junior Mints) lived in the Boston suburb of Belmont. The convention lasted for four days and I had a blast. You never saw so many unbalanced individuals in one place in your life, unless you've spent time in a mental hospital.

In a little while someone rang a bell outside. Evidently a lot of the others were still in the garden. It was only 6:30 and sunny out. I could hear them trooping inside through the mudroom and the sound of running water as they washed their hands. Then they entered the dining room and began to take seats around the table. It was eerie, because nobody was talking, and this was too large a group for that to happen naturally, unless they had some kind of rule about speaking during meals. Not that I'm an egotist, but I tended to believe they were doing it for my sake.

I didn't spot Lisa, but from my assigned seat in the living

room you could see less than half of the table. Finally Jacob
came down from upstairs and told me they were ready, and
that I could come in and join them. He gestured to an empty
chair at the middle of the far side of the table. As I looked
around at all the faces it became painfully apparent that Lisa
Hurlbett was not among them. My stomach turned at the futil-
ity of it all.

Jacob recited a litany of grace invoking their "Holy Spirit,"
while I tried desperately to figure out what to do next. When
he was done everybody started passing around huge serving
bowls and platters of food: some kind of vegetable mélange,
brown rice, vegetable fritters, black bread, and salad. Still,
nobody said anything. There was only the clatter of cutlery,
the creaking of old wooden chairs, and here and there a cough
or a throat being cleared, all accompanied by furtive glances
from one to the other, some of them unsettlingly mischievous.
Once more, the direct approach seemed to be the only work-
able way to proceed. I broke the strained silence.

"Uh, you people are probably wondering why I'm back here
again."

Some looked at each other blankly, as if they truly couldn't
imagine why. Others made smirky little faces. As I glanced
around the table I found myself making a mental note of where
the three males plus Jacob were sitting. Except for Jacob, they
weren't any bigger than me, and one was quite young, perhaps
eighteen, and physically underdeveloped.

"Uh, yesterday when I was here," I resumed, "there was a
woman sitting outside on that log bench next to the garden.
She had long black hair with some gray in it. Acted sort of
spaced-out. Where is she?"

Again, a lot of blank looks, some tittering.

"You told me her name was Tamar," I said to Jacob, then
turned my gaze on another girl across the table. "You were
sitting with her, combing her hair."

The girl just stared back at me.

"Don't tell me that wasn't you," I said.

"It wasn't me," she said without blinking.

"Horseshit," I said.

"Mr. Graff, you mind your tongue—"

"Well, pardon me, Jacob, but who do you think you're trying to fool here? You know goddamn well who I'm talking about. And I suggest you get her down here immediately."

At this point, one by one and in pairs, the female members of the group started leaving the table and disappearing into various parts of the house until I was left with Jacob and the three males. Finally I stood up myself, frankly a little concerned about how I was going to get out of there and wondering whether they might try and interfere.

"Okay," I said. "I'm leaving now, too, Jacob. But I'm coming back here with an attorney and with some officers of the law, and you jolly well better be ready to produce this girl when I do."

I made a move as if to walk around the table, but one of the other guys took a step so as to try and block me in a subtle way.

"Excuse me," I said to him.

He wouldn't move.

"Jacob," I tried to appeal to whatever sense he had, "I hope you realize that there are quite a few people who know exactly where I am tonight, and what I'm doing here, so if you're trying to give me the business, you'd better think twice about it."

Now Jacob stood up.

"Ishbak," he said, and the youngest of the three looked at him. "Go outside and pull the wires off Mr. Graff's distributor cap."

"Better not do it, kiddo," I told him.

He must have been none too bright, either, because he asked, "Which car is it?"

"The one that isn't one of ours," Jacob told him without seeming to lose his patience. The kid hesitated and then left the room.

As soon as he started through the living room, I tried to get out from behind the table and follow him. But the guy on my right kept blocking my way, and when I attempted to shove past him, he pushed me back.

"You're making a big mistake, Jacob," I said.

He shrugged his shoulders as if to say he was willing to take that chance. I, on the other hand, was not willing to fuck around with them for another minute. I glanced at the guy to my right, then grabbed a heavy glass pitcher full of milk that was in front of me on the table and swung it around by the handle so that it shattered against the side of his head. He screamed and reeled away. I saw a large blur moving toward me on the other side, grabbed the bentwood chair that I had been sitting in, and brought it down over the top of the moving blur, which was Jacob, who crumpled under it. Then I vaulted over the center of the table, getting sautéed vegetables all over my suit jacket, and rushed into the living room but was tackled there by the third young guy. He brought me down against a table that had a telephone on it. I managed to grab the handset and banged him repeatedly over the head with it until he let go of me and I was able to get back on my feet.

There was screaming from back in the dining-room area but I ran for the front door. Outside on the driveway that moron Ishbak was standing in front of my Datsun scratching his head. Apparently he hadn't yet figured out that in order to open the hood you had to spring the release latch from under the dashboard inside. When he saw me coming he took off running across the front lawn.

I jumped into the driver's seat, cranked the engine, and jammed the stick in reverse. I was driving down that long avenue of half-dead elm trees toward the gateposts when Jacob emerged from the front door with a rifle in his hands. I almost shit in my pants, but somehow managed to keep steering the car backward using the rearview mirror. Then I heard an explosion, and at the same moment a shower of glass flew up above the right side of the hood. Somehow I managed to make it out between the gateposts without smashing into either of the goddamn things. Beyond them the road was somewhat wider. I was able to turn the Datsun around, rammed it into first gear, and spun out in a big shower of gravel. Where the road came to a sideways T, I kept going straight ahead, thinking that they might not follow me that way.

I was too frightened to stop and get out of the car to check the damage. It seemed fairly certain that the weapon he'd used was a shotgun, and that from the way the glass flew he'd probably blown out the right headlight. What worried me more was that some pellets might have punctured the radiator. So I kept a very close eye on the idiot lights on the dashboard, but the engine didn't punk out on me.

The road was very winding. It climbed up and then twisted down a mountain and finally intersected with a lonely two-lane blacktop road. A sign there said "Hebron" with an arrow pointing left, so at least I knew where I was. I didn't go straight to the police from there for several reasons. I had crossed the border out of Vermont, and no cop from our side had any authority over there. I had no stomach for driving back to Manchester and risk running into a carload of the crazy motherfuckers on some back road. I'd return to the farm, all right, but in the company of the appropriate law officers and armed to the teeth with writs and warrants, which I felt Dr. Hurlbett could easily obtain through his attorney and their connections.

So I headed straight back toward the capital, specifically to Minerva Park. The yellow idiot light indicating that my engine was overheating started to flicker on and off about five miles shy of my destination, but I just ignored it and kept driving.

* * *

My hands were still shaking when Mrs. Hurlbett answered the door, though I had taken several swallows of that scotch to calm my nerves. Unlike the night before, she was wearing regular clothes—linen slacks and a print blouse—but she acted equally ill at ease. I interpreted that as her disappointment at seeing that Lisa was not with me. Without any formalities she led me into the library.

Dr. Hurlbett was standing in front of the fireplace straightening a painting above the mantel—not one of Jamie's by the way. There were three people seated on the sofa facing him, the backs of their heads to me. As I entered and rounded the sofa their faces came into view. In the middle, wearing his sunglasses, was Isaac/Shitfingers. To his right sat Rebecca. At his left sat Lisa. I heard the door close with a *thunk* and looked

up. Standing in front of it was the first Isaac. His skin condition
had cleared up considerably in two weeks. I glanced at Dr.
Hurlbett and the others, and back at Dr. Hurlbett. In one of
those transports of nausea and amazement, like a diver who
knows he is rising too fast out of the depths but can't help it, I
understood with sudden clarity how it all worked out.

"You're Abraham," I said.

Dr. Hurlbett didn't affirm or deny it, but just slowly moved
behind his club chair as if to touch something solid, gazing at
me as though he were trying arduously to work out some
intractable puzzle. His jaw moved like someone wearing uncomfortable dentures.

"You killed Jamie," I added.

Mrs. Hurlbett uttered a sort of yelp and lodged a knuckle
between her teeth as if to squelch a terror that had taken up
permanent residence somewhere between her heart and her
brain. Lisa didn't react at all. She behaved as impassively as she
had on the bench beside the garden in Vermont. Rebecca sat
on the sofa casually with her arms crossed and looked at me
with satisfaction and curiosity, as though I were an extremely
interesting specimen that someone had just pinned to the wall
in a museum. The blond Isaac with the sunglasses smiled the
whole time and finally erupted in a fit of his braying laughter.
Rebecca glanced down in her lap with a smile, as though
slightly embarrassed by her own amusement.

"Are you going to kill me too?" I asked.

"Oh, I think so," the blond Isaac said. "Esau!" he barked
over his shoulder, and the first Isaac, the one with the wormy
face, stepped forward to behind the sofa. "Show, Esau."

Esau reached under the wine-colored V-necked sweater he
was wearing without a shirt and produced a pistol from his
waistband, a small, nickel-plated automatic, and pointed it at
me. He did not seem comfortable in the role of henchman and
kept glancing at Isaac—the *true* Isaac, that is, since it was finally
apparent who was who—as if for reassurance. Meanwhile, I
backed away, as though that might make it harder for him to
shoot me. It's stupid, but one does tend to do that when
somebody pulls a gun on you. My blood felt suddenly carbon-

ated and I was afraid I might faint. It occurred to me that this room and these people would be the last things I would ever see in my life, forever. Then my shoulder blades bumped up against the mantelpiece.

On the floor to my right was one of those brass stands full of fireplace implements. I considered grabbing a poker and trying to bash somebody's head in as a farewell gesture. It was foolish and hopeless to even try it, but I did anyway. Unfortunately I grabbed the little broom they give you for sweeping the ashes out of your hearth. Esau dropped into a crouch and held the gun out straight with both hands. I waited for the bullet, but it didn't come.

"Put that down, you asshole," Isaac said. Rebecca held a hand in front of her face and laughed. I don't care what anybody says: even if someone has already promised to kill you, you still do whatever you can to prolong your life for a few more measly minutes. Anyway, I chucked the broom on the carpet. Then I sort of slouched in resignation against the mantelpiece, but I lost my balance and literally tumbled backward into it. There wasn't a fire, of course, because it was June, but I twisted my left thumb on one of the andirons and it hurt like hell. Isaac and Rebecca loved it. The way they were sitting on the sofa carrying on, you would have thought they were watching a Laurel and Hardy movie. Lisa, in stark contrast, didn't show a trace of interest or emotion, but acted as if she were sitting in a train station waiting for the 8:30 local to East Chugwater.

Isaac didn't cut up for long, though. Soon enough a very fierce expression replaced his hilarity. In that husky voice that was so unnerving, he asked Esau to hand him the gun, then sent him off to start up a car. Esau nodded, saying, "Yes, yes, of course," in a very subservient manner, and left the room. There certainly wasn't any doubt left as to who was in charge. A minute later you could hear the mechanical grinding of one of those automatic garage-door openers.

"Have you got some rope in the house?" Isaac asked Mrs. Hurlbett. She seemed bewildered by the question.

"Rope, Kitty," her husband coached her in an impatient tone of voice.

"There's some twine in the kitchen drawer."

"Would you get it for us?" Dr. Hurlbett said.

"Yes, dear," she said with a forced, spastic smile and a terrified look in her eyes. She left the room touching pieces of furniture and the walls as though she wasn't sure if she were real anymore. It began to occur to me that they weren't going to plug me there in the Hurlbetts' house after all but were planning to take me somewhere else. I thought about their neighbors, like the man walking his poodle the night before, doing mundane things all around us in their expensive homes: watching TV, grilling steaks. Some of them were probably the very "pillars of our Capital community" who had supposedly phoned Dan LaMott to complain about my newspaper articles.

Meanwhile, Esau returned from the garage and Mrs. Hurlbett came back from the kitchen with a big ball of that scratchy brown utility twine that people use to tie up packages for the mail. Isaac supervised while Esau tied my hands behind my back. When that was accomplished they marched me downstairs.

A white Mercedes-Benz sedan stood idling in the garage. Beyond the open door, the street was quiet in the gathering darkness. Esau got into the driver's seat. I was shoved into the back. Dr. Hurlbett got in on my right, Mrs. Hurlbett on my left. She was wearing some kind of perfume that did not cover up an acrid bodily smell under it, an odor I'd encountered before in police stations and courtrooms, the smell of someone scared senseless. Rebecca sat on Dr. Hurlbett's lap. Isaac guided Lisa into the front seat and got in beside her. Then we were off.

The car headed out of Minerva Park proper and got on the expressway loop that connected the northern suburbs with downtown. Most of the way Rebecca teased Dr. Hurlbett as she sat on his lap. She'd nuzzle up to him and put her tongue in his ear and giggle, and reach inside his sports coat and rub his chest, and say, "Mmmm." He seemed somewhat embarrassed by it, and asked her once under his breath to stop it, but even so you sensed that the two of them had been intimate before under less problematical circumstances. Mrs. Hurlbett turned her face to the window and pretended not to notice, but there was no way she could have missed it, the way Rebecca was giggling.

We got off the expressway at the Tilden Square exit and drove up Broadway, the street that had once been the center of the Capital's nightlife before the advent of Plaza Boulevard and all its plastic wonders. Now Broadway was a ghost town, especially on a Friday night, except for a couple of winos enjoying their freedom from the nearby bus station in the balmy weather. Farther up Old Dutch Hill, topped by its cluster of Gothic state government buildings, a police squad car with two officers inside idled in front of the deserted Court of Appeals. We drove right past them. I certainly didn't have time to yell anything, and besides, our windows were closed and the air-conditioning was on.

Eventually we turned up Union Street and pulled in front of the house, number 214, where I had interviewed "Isaac" (that is, Esau) two weeks before. Just seeing the front of the building and remembering that hot, rainy day overwhelmed me with regret that I'd ever picked the motherfuckers to write about in the first place. I almost wished Charlie Boland had switched me over to the city desk before then—not that I would have stood for it. But at least I might have quit two weeks earlier and not gotten killed.

Esau helped Mrs. Hurlbett out of the car. Rebecca looked after Lisa, who was able to walk by herself with no problem—except that she seemed to comply like a robot with anything she was told. No drugs that I was familiar with would make somebody behave that way. Isaac prodded me upstairs by poking the barrel of his pistol into my rear end, like a suppository. "Move it, asshole," he whispered and giggled. His viciousness could be very creative. Esau unlocked the front door and we all went in.

The house was quiet. None of the other group members seemed to be there anymore. Without any ceremony, as if they'd planned it all out in advance, Isaac and Esau took me down the hall through a series of dark rooms, a kitchen, and a pantry to a flight of stairs and then into the basement.

A bare bulb hung from a cobwebby rubber cord. Along one wall were a washer and dryer, but no laundry sink. At the far end was a tiny window covered with a decorative wrought-iron grill to keep burglars out. Next to it was a padlocked wooden door, probably a delivery entrance from when the house was built in the 1880s and not used for many years.

Isaac told me to stand still and not to try anything while he took somebody's shirt out of the dryer. He ripped it up until he had a piece of suitable length and then proceeded to gag me. It was very tight and was immediately uncomfortable. Esau had the big ball of twine from the Hurlbett's house. They pushed me over toward this vertical pipe in one of the corners, cut the twine on my wrists, and tied them back up around the pipe, then tied my ankles together and secured them to the pipe as well, winding the twine all around me threading it many times between my wrists and the pipe, and all up and down my body, including around my neck, using a lot of half hitches to secure me. They worked very methodically and used up the whole goddamn ball of twine.

Then, after admiring their work for a few moments, Isaac said, "I think that'll do nicely." Esau agreed and they turned to go. On his way out, instead of turning off the light, Isaac tapped it with the barrel of his gun. The bulb exploded with a pop and a grim little fanfare of sparks, and then I was alone in the dark.

CHAPTER 12

The way they had me trussed up, I couldn't move even to slide down the pipe into a sitting position on the floor. Now, I don't know if anyone's ever gagged you. Probably not, if you're like most people. But it's a hell of a lot more uncomfortable than you might gather from watching the old "Gunsmoke" reruns on TV. Take it from me.

In the first place, you can hardly breathe. In the second place, you can hardly swallow, because your tongue is all pushed in against your throat. And in the third place, the soft tissues on the inside of your lips and gums start to dry out almost immediately, and within a few hours the skin starts breaking open like overripe fruit. So, it's more than just uncomfortable—it's goddamn painful and frightening.

They didn't return within any reasonable amount of time, either. Not that I particularly wanted them to return, because I expected when they did it would be to finish me off. And not that reasonableness had anything to do with it, because obviously they were beyond that in my case. I just couldn't figure out what they were doing.

For a couple of hours I could hear the muffled sounds of things clunking against the floor upstairs, as though they were moving the furniture around. Then it stopped and there was only the occasional scuffing of small animals in the cellar. They sounded too minuscule to be rats. I figured they were probably mice. In any case, I wasn't alarmed because one of the few fears I *don't* happen to have is of rodents. Spiders I'm definitely put off by, but rats are no problem. I had a pair of white lab rats for my psych course in operant conditioning in college. I had to teach them to press a bar in a Skinner box to get food pellets as a reward. Their names were Elvis and Buddy, and I grew so fond of them that I eventually set them free at the Farm. It was probably a stupid thing to do in an agricultural community, but I didn't think of that until after I released them. Anyway, I couldn't have cared less whether there were rats down in the cellar.

What concerned me was the position they had me tied up in, hanging against the pipe. I had devised a way to hold my head down and let saliva dribble into the gag to moisten my lips and gums, but I had to keep doing it about every ten minutes. My neck began to cramp and I started to run out of saliva. Several more hours went by. Gray daylight seeped in through the single grimy window.

The next thing, which was rather disgusting, was that by dawn I had to take a leak. Very badly. It was pretty obvious that there weren't going to be any potty breaks. Eventually I couldn't hold it any longer and I had to let go in my pants. To be deprived of control over your body felt even more demeaning and demoralizing than being deprived of your freedom.

Meanwhile, my legs were getting badly cramped from standing up. My knees and hips ached. Shifting my weight back and forth from one leg to the other no longer helped alleviate the pain. But I couldn't slump against my bindings because the twine around my neck would strangle me. Of course I couldn't stay awake indefinitely, either, so it began to dawn on me that they could kill me just by leaving me alone down there. And it would probably be quite a slow and unpleasant death as well. That's when I really started to panic.

I strained my body against the twine and struggled to loosen my hands, but the panicky way I was doing it just made the scratchy twine bite into my wrists. The skin quickly got raw and I felt warm blood trickle down my fingers. Even so, I kept it up, in panicked, spasmodic intervals as the hours ticked by. But it was really no use, and eventually I started to cry. I even began wishing that one of the motherfuckers *would* come down and finish me off, I was so miserable and upset. But nobody did. So, I just remained there, like a little bug wrapped up in some big spider's web, waiting to have the life sucked out of me.

* * *

Sometime during the morning the muffled sound of things clunking around upstairs resumed. There were voices, too, but so indistinct that it was impossible to make out a single word. It went on for what seemed like hours. Of course in my situation time went by rather slowly, but I have a pretty good sense of direction, and the way the house was situated on the block, and which way Union Street ran (east–west), I knew that the grimy little window faced south. And so when the sunlight streamed directly in, I knew it was getting to be midafternoon. That's when I heard someone at the door.

A bolt was thrown. There were footsteps on the stairs. It was Isaac and he was alone. I noticed at once that he didn't have the gun in his hand, nor was it tucked into his waistband. But he was still wearing his sunglasses, even in the rather dim basement.

"How's my little lamb?" he inquired.

Apparently this was to be a social call.

I didn't even answer him by grunting through my gag. I just leaned up against the pipe and watched him walk slowly toward me. When he was about three steps away he stopped, reached behind himself, pulled the shiny pistol out from there, rammed back the barrel slide to put a cartridge in the chamber, and pointed it at the center of my forehead.

"When you wish upon a star," he sang in his gravelly voice, "makes no difference who you are."

At this point I started whimpering and making gerbil noises. I just couldn't help it, even though you could tell it delighted him.

"Say good-bye to everything you ever knew, to everyone you ever loved," he told me, and oddly enough I began to do just that. I began to breathe in shorter and shorter breaths, I was so frightened, and finally lost control of my bowels as well. Faces whirled in my brain: my mother and father, Philip, friends from school, Barbara Frye, Jeanie Goldstone, Jamie, even Merle Lyons. Not that I loved the guy. His stupid face just popped into my mind, and the harder I tried to get rid of it, the longer it stayed there, until I realized that it was the image I would carry into oblivion. Then Isaac pulled the trigger.

"Kssssh!" He made the sound of a gunshot with his voice, like children do. The hammer had clicked emptily. "Just kidding," he added and went into a short fit of hysterics. "Don't take it personally," he blurted out, trying to control his laughter.

At that point I actually fainted, I was under such a mental strain, but I came to about thirty seconds later gagging for air because as I slumped forward the twine started choking me. The next thing I knew, Isaac was yanking duct tape off a roll. He laid a strip over my mouth, across the whole gag and everything, and taped my head to the pipe so I couldn't move it. Then he put the gun back behind his waist and took a folding knife out of his pocket. He opened it up and leaned forward so that I could feel his breath in my face.

"Did you poop in your pants?" he asked. "*Pee-yoo*, do you stink!"

Holding the knife sort of like a pen, and humming "When You Wish Upon a Star," he started cutting something on my forehead. I felt the blade break the skin while the blood began to run into my eyes. It did no good to scream because the gag and the tape completely stifled it, but I did anyway because that's what you naturally do when some lunatic is carving his initials on your forehead. If you think it's no fun going to the dentist, where the guy gives you anesthesia, and has your best interests in mind, imagine what it's like to have someone like Isaac working on you.

In any case, he soon finished what he was doing, went and got the shirt that he'd torn up to make my gag, blotted away some of the blood to admire what he had carved on my head, gave a little grunt of approval, wiped off his blade, and went back upstairs. When he was gone I was actually grateful that he hadn't done something worse, like cut my dick off. Actually, it was unfortunate that I even thought of that, because as soon as I did I figured that would be next.

*   *   *

The light in the grimy little window became a nauseating orange-gray color, then just gray, and I was enveloped in darkness again. Isaac did not return. It was a blessing in disguise that he had taped my head to the pipe, because it allowed me to get a little bit of sleep without strangling myself—and by this time I had crossed the mental frontier into the realm of utter exhaustion. I figured out a way to take the weight off my feet and lower legs by pushing my knees against several loops of the twine and just sort of hanging suspended there. It was such a relief that I fell asleep almost at once.

When I woke up it was still dark. I don't know how long I had been asleep, but I don't think it was very long because what woke me up is that my knees slipped out of the loops of twine. After that I entered a very peculiar state of mind where I was no longer quite sure whether I was asleep or awake or on my way to being dead. I began to hear voices, especially Philip's. Then I'd hear my own voice and snap out of it realizing that I was dreaming, but unsure in the darkness if I had truly woken up. Then I'd drift off and hear the voices again.

Eventually daylight seeped into the basement. I was hallucinating fairly steadily now. I knew they were hallucinations because the images of people and the voices I heard were so fragmentary and disjointed, but even knowing what they were didn't stop them from happening. Meanwhile, my mouth was bone dry. My tongue had swollen and felt like a big dusty piece of meat in my mouth. I just hung there making mooing noises, trying to remind myself that I was at least still alive.

Sometime after dawn I heard a toilet flush, so I knew somebody was still in the house. But there was no more clunking around of large objects. I had really lost my grip on the passage of time by then, but eventually I heard the bolt thrown at the top of the stairs and slow footsteps coming down.

It was Esau. He stood across the room looking at me for a while, then came closer. The silvery automatic pistol hung limply in his hand at his side as though he was carrying a dead fish. His eyes looked almost crossed in concentration. It was then I knew that he was the Children's official company executioner. Isaac only played at mutilation and sadism, but it was Esau who came now to deliver the death stroke. I was screaming the whole time, except the noise that rose in my throat was not anything properly describable as a scream. It was just a hollow sound, like wind blowing through a drainpipe, or like in a dream, where you feel yourself trying to scream but nothing comes out.

With a jerky movement, he held up the gun. I shut my eyes waiting for the bullet to darken my mind forever. He fired off the whole clip, seven rounds. I was absolutely astonished that getting shot was so painless. I figured I must be in shock, that my consciousness would slip away in a matter of moments, like water going down a drain. But when I felt his warm breath on my face I realized that I was still alive, that I hadn't been shot at all, not once.

I opened my eyes. He was right in front of me. I could smell him. Something bright flashed. There was a ripping, tearing noise all the way up my torso to under my chin. Again I thought my body had been mortally assailed, that he had cut me open from crotch to tonsils with a knife, and once again I was amazed that it didn't hurt. I toppled over and hit the concrete floor. Then I felt him hovering over me, felt his breath in my ear, and heard the words, a hoarse whisper, saying, "Help me. Please help me."

His footsteps retreated across the room and up the creaking wooden stairs. The door shut. I passed out.

* * *

I didn't know how long I remained unconscious on the floor, but on the basis of what happened next, I'd say it wasn't much more than an hour or so. When I did come around I hardly wanted to move off the dirty cement floor, my body hurt so much. But also, you see, I wasn't yet aware that my hands were free, in the fully conscious sense that one grasps an idea and then proceeds to do something about it. When I managed to roll over onto my side, my left arm flopped out in front of me and it became obvious that my wrists had indeed been cut loose. I brought my left hand up to my face and tried to pull the gag off my mouth, but I couldn't manage it. To get it off, I realized, I would somehow have to sit up and use both hands to untie it. When I did sit up the pain in my hips and shoulders was just this side of incredible.

When I finally got the damn thing off the smell of the rag that had been stuffed in my mouth almost knocked me out again. I flung it as far away from me as I could. My tongue wouldn't move at first, and the soft tissues inside felt like they had been spray-painted with glossy enamel.

If you're like me, you've spent enough time in Laundromats to know pretty goddamn well that you can get water out of a washer. On my hands and knees I crawled slowly over to the one against the wall, reached up, and pulled myself upright. It was a Monkey Ward top-loader. Hunched over it, I turned the cycle selector to "regular wash" and pulled the center knob. Beautiful water started gushing out of the slots inside. It was warm water, but I didn't give a shit. I was so thirsty that I just about dove headfirst into the machine. After I had consumed a gallon or so, I realized how much noise it would make when the agitator started jumping up and down, so I shut it off. Then I slumped to the floor once more as my tissues began to restore themselves.

There were no more noises or voices coming from the upstairs anymore. If someone had heard me turn on the washer, they hadn't come down to see what I was doing still alive. I suspected that there was nobody left up there, but there was no way to confirm it without going up, and I wasn't about to do that. In fact, as soon as I proved to myself that I could actually stand up and walk, I set about trying to figure a way to get out the back door.

The window was out of the question because of the iron

grillwork. Besides, I doubted it was large enough to squeeze through. But the door was padlocked solid, and its hasp was designed so that you couldn't get at the screw heads. So the only other choice was to take the door off its three hinges. The trouble was, I didn't have a screwdriver. I looked around the basement, but there was nothing resembling a screwdriver anywhere, not so much as an old butter knife. Finally, I pulled the dryer out from the wall, because it was a hell of a lot lighter than the washer, trying to not make any noise, and rummaged around inside the back of the machine looking for a piece of metal I could use. I found it in the form of a flange that was part of the motor mount. I was able to unbolt it with a quarter from my pocket.

It took me at least half an hour to get the goddamn hinges off, and even then the door wouldn't swing free because it had been painted about fifty times and all the coats had dried in the crack between the door and the jamb. I was really getting demoralized, and dizzy, too, and at one point I had to stop for more water. But the wood around the doorjamb turned out to be old and punky, and after a little more gouging and prying, the goddamn thing worked free and fell inward on me.

I was disheartened all over again when I pulled it out of the way and looked outside because there was a metal grill at the top of the short stairway just like the one that protected the window. But the lock was all rusted out and the hinges crumbled as soon as I pulled in on the grill. One step up, and I was free.

The rear of the house was a courtyard garden. Someone had been growing flowers there in orderly raised beds. A brick wall about eight feet high surrounded the space on the other three sides. I limped quickly across the courtyard to the rear wall, jumped up, and caught the top with my fingers and managed to pull myself up and over it. I landed in the adjoining garden behind a house facing the next street over. It was full of roses.

To my amazement, and no doubt to their horror, I confronted an elderly couple who had been sitting there at a glass-topped table eating croissants and reading the newspaper. When I suddenly appeared, with my odiferous clothes and my forehead smeared with blood, they both stood up abruptly, knocking over the glass-topped table in the process. It crashed on the flagstones. The old man drew the woman close to himself as though to gallantly protect her from me. The sound of my own voice startled me, it came out so strange and froggy-sounding:

"Please!" I pleaded with them. "How do I get out of here?"

The old man pointed to the side of the house. It was an alleyway leading to the street. I squeezed past the Volvo parked there and burst into the street, then started limping as fast as possible down to police headquarters, which was in a brand-new building on Elk Street behind the state Motor Vehicle Bureau.

* * *

When I staggered up to the front desk at the Capital police headquarters, the receptionist, a young black female officer in uniform, looked at me as if I had just escaped an alcohol detox center by way of Okefenokee Swamp. I did have on a decent tan poplin summer suit, and my $100 English shoes. But the jacket was ripped in several places, and streaked with blood, and the pants were shit in, and the shoes were peed on, and my forehead was all sliced up, so altogether I didn't present a very appetizing picture—not to mention the smell.

In the froggy voice that I'd acquired from being gagged and deprived of water, I asked to see a detective. I also apologized for being so disgusting, but said I couldn't help it. I think she misunderstood me. In any event, she pushed a button on her phone console and in a few minutes a tall, barrel-chested plainclothesman about fifty years old stepped out of the elevator. The receptionist dipped her head to indicate that I was the one who asked to see him. He introduced himself as Detective Drysdale and told me to follow him upstairs.

In the elevator I explained that I looked so disgusting because a bunch of lunatics had locked me in a cellar for two days, that I was a reporter for the T-H (not strictly true anymore), and that he could check with Charlie Boland if he didn't believe me. Then I asked him if I could give $30 to someone to go out and get me some clean clothes. He said they had some coveralls for me, and would permit me to take a shower in the officers' changing room. In fact, he took me directly there, probably because I was too odiferous to sit down and talk to in my present condition.

When we got there and I looked in the mirror, I could see another reason my appearance was so startling. Isaac had carved the word *SHIT* on my forehead in letters two inches high. I got out of my suit and underwear and stuck them all in the plastic bag that Drysdale gave me. The showers were like the ones they have in a school locker room, and Drysdale stood at the entrance listening to my story while I washed all the dried blood and crud off.

I proceeded to tell him the whole goddamn story from top to bottom—about my investigation of the group on the original charity fraud rap, and the threatening calls, and meeting Debbie Clothier's parents, and about the Children cutting off my cat's head and mailing it to me, and the trip to California, and Steven Strunk's murder, and me coming back to check out the farm in Vermont, and finding Lisa Hurlbett there, and about Jamie and their parents, and being abducted and tied up in the goddamn basement and having guns pointed at me and words carved in my head—the whole insane saga from A to Z. The only part I deliberately omitted was that I quit my job on Friday because Dan LaMott took me off the story.

By that time I was drying off, and another officer had brought in a pair of blue police coveralls for me to wear. They had a professional first-aid kit there and Drysdale helped me put antiseptic on my cut-up forehead and also wrap a gauze bandage around it like a giant headband. Finally he told me to follow him into his office.

I don't know how coherent all this sounded to him and I couldn't tell what he'd thought of my story. Even though I was clean, I was still very strung out. I'd gone practically without any sleep for almost three days. I hadn't had anything to eat since that Chinese lunch on Friday. I mentioned it to Drysdale and he sent the officer down the hall to the snack machine.

In the meantime he leaned across his desk with his hands

folded and in a calm, earnest, reassuring voice he said, "These are serious allegations, Mr. Graff. Do you know what I'm going to do?"

I said, "No."

"I'm going to call up Judge Theobold and get a warrant, and then we're going up the hill to this place you say you were detained and see what these people have to say for themselves."

I told him that was great, but that I doubted any of them were still there. I suggested they try Dr. Hurlbett's house in Minerva Park or the farm in Vermont.

"I'll have that warrant in fifteen minutes," he said, picking up his phone.

The uniformed officer returned with a Snickers bar, a packet of those yellow cheese crackers filled with peanut butter, and a grape soda. I tore the wrapper off the candy bar and started to devour it. On the first mouthful it pulled out the tooth with the root canal in it that Isaac had loosened all the way back in California. I removed this big disgusting glob of caramel, peanuts, chocolate, and nougat from my mouth and tried to find the tooth enveloped in it. You could tell this grossed out Drysdale and the other cop, but there was just no way to be suave about it. I could feel the empty space back there with my tongue. It was so depressing.

A short while later we were heading back downstairs in the elevator, this time to the basement level. It was the parking garage, filled with red-and-white squad cars. We were joined at the curb by a second plainclothesman, introduced to me by Drysdale as his partner Lieutenant Nunn. He was dark-haired and sallow-skinned, as if daylight was not his natural element, and he chewed his cigarette filter. He wore a porkpie hat with one of those plastic rain covers over it, even though it was a perfectly gorgeous day.

A green unmarked car pulled up to the curb and stopped. The cop who had bought me the candy was behind the wheel. Drysdale and I got in the back. Nunn rode shotgun. It was about a two-minute drive to the house on Union Street.

They double-parked in front of it. We all got out and

climbed the stairs. The blinds were drawn in the front bay window. I also noticed that the little brass plaque above the doorbell that had said *The Lyman Foundation* was no longer there. You could see the four little screw holes in the wood where it had been removed.

When it became obvious that nobody was going to answer the doorbell, Drysdale told the driver to force entry. The officer went back to the car and retrieved a black valise from the trunk. It contained skeleton keys and dozens of tools. He must have known what the hell he was doing, too, because he had that front door open in about thirty seconds flat. I followed the detectives inside. The house had been stripped bare.

It didn't really surprise me, considering all the clunking noises I'd heard during my time there.

"You say this was some kind of commune?" Nunn remarked with unmistakable sarcasm. The floorboards creaked as he ambled about what had been the parlor where I first interviewed Esau. Drysdale wanted to look upstairs, too, so I followed them. There wasn't so much as a hairpin to be found anywhere. It was as if a crew had gone through the place with industrial vacuum cleaners.

"Sure doesn't look like any commune to me," the driver observed.

"Shut up, Belotti," Drysdale said.

Then we all traipsed back downstairs and through the pantry and the kitchen. The door leading to the basement was still bolted. We went down. It was just the way I'd left it an hour before, and to be honest with you, it made me feel light-headed and nauseated to be there again. I showed them the morass of twine I'd been bound up in, and the gag and the pipe I was tied to. You could even see the black smudges of blood around it, where my cuts had dripped.

Drysdale told the driver to collect the twine and the gag and put them in a plastic bag. A few minutes later we were back at police headquarters.

Two other plainclothes officers were waiting in Drysdale's office. I was told to wait in another room down the hall with Belotti. About ten minutes more ticked by. I was getting more

and more nervous. Finally the phone on the otherwise bare
table rang. Belotti was told to bring me back to Drysdale's
office. They had an empty seat for me. Of the others, only
Drysdale was sitting.

"Mr. Graff," he began, now leaning back in his chair in his
relaxed manner. "Do you have something personal against Dr.
and Mrs. Arthur Hurlbett?"

I was stunned, but I should have seen it coming.

"You could put it that way. They tried to kill me and I intend
to press goddamn charges."

"Mr. Graff, this is Lieutenant Gould and Sergeant Switzer."
He indicated the two new plainclothesmen. "They've just
come back from Minerva Park where they talked with the
Hurlbetts—"

"You went up there and *talked* to them!" I retorted indig-
nantly. "You should have arrested them."

"Calm down—"

"Did you happen to notice a green Datsun 310-B parked out
in front of their house, by any chance, with the right headlight
shot out?"

Gould or Switzer, whoever it was, shook his head to indicate
no.

"You see—they ditched my goddamn car now!"

"Mr. Graff," Drysdale raised his voice for the first time, "I'll
make it short and sweet—they deny that they took part in any
alleged abduction, they deny that they are officials of any religious organization, they say their daughter lives in British
Columbia and has for quite some time, and they allege that
you are conducting some kind of personal campaign of harass-
ment against them—"

"They're lying."

"—and furthermore, your boss, or *former* boss I should say,
Mr. Boland, says that you were fired on Friday because you
refused to desist from 'hounding'—his word—'*hounding*' individuals in the community over the question of religious prefer-
ence—"

"That's horseshit too. I quit, I didn't get fired."

"May I finish, Mr. Graff? Would you let me finish?"

"Okay. Finish."

"Right now, I'm not sure what to believe. Or who. You say they did such and such. They deny it. One thing I do know, Mr. Graff—Dr. Hurlbett is a well-regarded physician here in the Capital, and we're not going to rush him down here and book him on somebody's say-so without some evidence that he has broken the law. For that matter, we're not going to book you either, Mr. Graff. So, this is what I suggest—let us take you down to Capital Med this afternoon, check you out—"

"Check me out?" I said, knowing what that meant in police argot. "For drugs?"

Drysdale nodded with his eyelids closed.

"That's the stupidest thing I ever heard."

Drysdale recoiled slightly.

"It may seem that way to you, Mr. Graff," he responded evenly, "but we'd like to do it anyway, and we'd appreciate your cooperation. If you're clean, you have nothing to hide."

"Clean! I hardly even drink, for godsake. Who told you I was a drug addict? Here, look for yourselves—"

I started undoing the sleeves of the coveralls to show these bozos there were no tracks on my arms. But they didn't want to see it.

"Roll down your sleeves, Mr. Graff. They'll take blood and urine samples at the hospital. I'm just asking you to cooperate with us on this, and once it's out of the way, we'll have a clearer picture of what's really going on here. Okay?"

I was tempted to keep arguing, but my better judgment told me it would do absolutely no good, so I decided to go along with the stupid tests, which I had no fear of flunking whatsoever, of course. We all plodded downstairs again to the parking garage. This time there was an ambulance waiting.

* * *

Considering what I'd been through, and how I had first looked when I went down there, and the fact that no one seemed to be believing me, you might think the sight of an ambulance would provoke some serious paranoia—the men in the white coats coming to take you away and all that. But I knew from working as a reporter that it was just another tiny example of how blatantly corrupt Mayor Peavy's administration was. You see, the cops got a kickback every time they called a favored ambulance service, whether it was needed or not. Obviously they could have taken me down to the hospital in a squad car. But now I would end up getting billed $75 for an ambulance ride, and the cops would get a piece of it. So, the sight of the ambulance didn't freak me out. It just pissed me off.

Sergeant Switzer got in the back with me. We sat there on the stretcher the whole way down. The driver didn't turn on his siren or anything. It was just a stupid waste of money.

Capital Med is an enormous complex of affiliated hospitals, one of the largest in the Northeast. It's also the place where every accident victim in a fifty-mile radius ends up being taken, so the emergency room is like Grand Central Station.

Switzer informed the nurse at the main desk what we were there for. She told us to have a seat in the waiting area. This displeased Switzer, who must have expected preferential treatment, but the place was a madhouse and the nurse refused to argue about it. So, we sat down. The waiting area was a room about the size of a grammar school cafeteria with two dozen rows of turquoise blow-molded plastic seats.

During my time on the *T-H* there had been a major scandal surrounding the Capital Med emergency room, one of the few negative stories about public institutions that our reporters were allowed to pursue. On three separate occasions people had died right in their seats in the waiting area before anybody paid attention to them. The first was an elderly black man who had severed a major artery in his leg with a chain saw. He was wearing high rubber boots and bled to death right in his chair without anybody realizing it. The second was a bag lady who died in her chair of pneumonia. The third and most tragic was a woman in labor who didn't speak English and was hassled about not being a U.S. citizen and therefore not entitled to Medicaid benefits. While they were arguing about it—and ignoring her—she hemorrhaged and died, and so did the baby, making it four victims altogether. A doctor was "disciplined" in the last case, and that was the end of it for the time being.

I knew it would probably be a couple of hours before they called us. I hoped that Switzer might get bored out of his mind in the process, and I did my best to help matters along by deliberately not having a conversation with him. I read a whole pile of *Reader's Digests* that they had stacked on a table. Several times, Switzer himself tried to strike up a little chitchat, but I managed to thwart each attempt without being nasty or anything.

My strategy paid off. About a half an hour after we sat down, I could see that Switzer was growing antsy. He started muttering "Christ," and "Jesus," and commenting on the hospital's chaotic operation. I nodded my head and agreed with him to egg him on.

Another quarter of an hour inched by. Finally he said, "Look, Mr. Graff, do you think I can trust you to stay here and take these tests by yourself?" He went on to explain that his work shift was technically over at three o'clock, and that he was supposed to take his son to a Little League game in Woosterville. He couldn't have found a more sympathetic ear. "Just have the samples taken," he reiterated, "and we'll be in touch with you tomorrow, okay? Either Lieutenants Gould or Nunn or myself."

"Hey, Sergeant, nobody wants to get this thing straightened out more than I do," I assured him.

"I think they got it all wrong," he said. "You're no druggie."

"Thanks for the vote of confidence."

"But can I trust you to stick around?"

"You can put money on it."

"Okay, then. I'm gonna get going."

He stood up.

"I'll be waiting to hear from you guys."

"Just take the tests."

"I will," I reassured him. "Voluntarily. Don't you worry."

And so he left. The Capital police are not, shall we say, the most conscientious law-enforcement service in our republic. Especially when there's no loose cash involved.

About five minutes after he split I got up and walked out of the emergency room. There was a drugstore two blocks away. I called a cab from a pay phone there and went home.

CHAPTER 13

I had the cab driver drop me off two buildings behind my own, then skulked back and entered through the laundry room. The apartment was the same appalling mess as when I'd left it. But as soon as I entered I noticed that the furniture was not piled up quite the way I remembered it, and coming closer I saw that somebody with a glass cutter had cut a neat, rectangular hole in the sliding door to the patio. In fact it was still partly open. What's more—and to my delight—I realized that the stupid business with the broken glass and the tacks had worked perfectly. There was a good-sized dark reddish stain on the sofa, a diagonal splash on the backrest, and more splatters on the carpet around the piled-up furniture. Evidently the person had entered, tried to climb in over all the piled-up stuff, and slashed himself pretty good in the process of groping around. There were several dried blood smears on the coffee table, which had been flung out of the way in order for the person to get back out. Finally there were some excellent partial hand-prints, including the finger pads, on the wall adjoining the patio door.

I stole into the kitchen and pulled a cooking knife out of its wooden base, then crept on tiptoes into the bedroom. Nobody was hiding there, or in the closet, or the bathroom, thank God. I collapsed on the bed for a minute and lay on my back. For the first time in years I could have closed my eyes and fallen asleep instantly. Of course I don't recommend being bound and gagged for two days as a cure for insomnia. Anyway, I made myself get up.

My notebook from California with Jeanie Goldstone's phone number in it was on my dresser. The clock said ten minutes to four, meaning it was ten minutes to one Pacific time. I dialed. Her phone rang five times. I was about to hang up when she finally picked it up. Then there was a *thunk* over the line, as if she had dropped the receiver.

"Jeanie . . . ?"

"Hold on. I keep dropping the damn thing," she said with a giggle. "Who is this?"

"Grover Graff."

"Grover . . . ! My goodness! Why, it doesn't sound anything like you." There was some more giggling and strange background noises, as though somebody else was there. Jeanie said, "Ssssshhhh!"

"It's me all right," I told her.

"Where are you?"

"I'm back East, at home. I—"

"Are you all right?"

"I'm okay now. A few hours ago it was touch and go."

"What happened—"

"I don't have time to tell you about it, Jeanie. I called to tell you that you should notify the cops."

"I already did. On Thursday."

"You did?"

"Yes. After you left. I'm sorry, but I had to. Anyway, they busted the place. They're holding seventeen kids in San Rafael on suspicion of murder."

"For killing Strunk."

"For killing him and the girl."

"They found her? Debbie Clothier?"

"I'm afraid so. In San Pablo Bay, two weeks ago, long before you ever even came here. Only they didn't know who it was until I told them about you coming out to look for her."

"God, that's terrible."

"Are you—"

"I have to go now, Jeanie. I'm sorry. I'll call back. Can't tell you when, though. 'Bye."

It seemed pretty obvious that the sky was falling in on the Children of Abraham, and it didn't take long to realize that the Hurlbetts' choices were now pretty much reduced to one option: leaving the country. But the police had talked to them up in Minerva Park just a couple of hours ago. And you'd have thought that if the Hurlbetts were running around madly packing their stuff that the detectives might have noticed. That was when I decided to go up there myself. I changed out of the stupid coveralls into a pair of jeans, running shoes, a dark T-shirt, and Philip's old leather jacket.

* * *

The motorcycle checked out okay. Nobody had clipped the cables or snipped the brake lines. I was glad that I had moved it across the complex. It started on the first kick. Once you got on the expressway loop, Minerva Park was only a ten-minute drive from my apartment, but I had to make one urgent stop first.

As I already told you, Rollie Tuttle and his wife lived in a bungalow in a neighborhood of tidy but identically ugly little bungalows set practically shoulder to shoulder on a street rather remarkable for its total lack of trees. In the harsh afternoon sun of a warm June day they looked especially depressing. As I had anticipated, Rollie's four-wheel-drive Bronco was not in the driveway—on a day like this there was only one conceivable place Rollie would be: on a trout stream somewhere—but a green Chevy Citation was there. Walking up the little curved slate pathway to their front door, I racked my brain trying to remember Rollie's wife's name. I had met her only a couple of times, most recently at the Tuttles' B.Y.O.B. Christmas party in December, but I was hoping she'd remember me.

She answered the bell wearing this sad little Sunday-best

puffy yellow dress with her hair all sprayed and fluffed out and a frilly white apron on. The house was full of a delicious baking smell. No doubt she was getting Sunday supper together for the return of the Great Outdoorsman. At first she didn't seem to recognize me. In fact, she seemed downright alarmed at the sight of me. But then I realized it must have been the gauze bandage wrapped around my forehead that threw her.

"Yes . . . ?" she said in a cracked little voice.

"Uh, Mrs. Tuttle, I don't know if you remember me. I'm Grover Graff, the guy who sits next to your husband at the newspaper office."

"Oh, yes, yes, come in," she said, suddenly exuberant. Her face lit up as if she was tickled pink to see me. Actually, you suspected that she was glad to see anybody even slightly familiar, because it must have been lonely as hell sitting there in her crummy bungalow in a nice dress all by herself on a gorgeous Sunday afternoon, unless she was a complete moron—and even morons have feelings.

But then, just as suddenly, her smile turned into a frown again. She glanced down into the blue shag carpet as if she was afraid to look me in the eye and said, "Oh, Grover, I heard you got fired. Rollie told me." She held her hand up in front of her mouth, as if she had let slip something unmentionable. Apparently she was unsure if it was okay to even talk to me since I had become a person of ill repute.

"No, no, no," I tried to assure her, "it's all a silly misunderstanding. I quit, actually. But it was all silly and emotional. I'll probably be right back at my desk on Monday."

That was complete horseshit, of course. I was quite sure that my career at the *Times-Herald* was over. But the fib seemed to brighten her up a little.

"Oh . . ." she said. "Well, that's good."

"The whole thing was blown out of proportion, believe me. It was nothing, really."

"Would you like a cup of coffee?"

"Thank you, I would, Mrs. Tuttle." I felt awkward calling her Mrs. Tuttle, but it was the only way I could cover up for not remembering her first name. Anyway, I followed her into the kitchen. She had an electric pot all warmed up on the counter with its little red light on. Next to it was a plate of chocolate chip cookies. She saw me eyeing them. I was still half-starved. Usually I can't even drink coffee, but I put in two spoonfuls of sugar and half a cup of milk—for nourishment.

"Please help yourself to a cookie," she said.

I wolfed down three of them, one right after another. You could tell she thought it was a little weird.

"Boy, are these great," I told her, scarfing down a fourth. "I was hoping Rollie might be home because I have a favor to ask him, but maybe you can help."

"Rollie's fishing the green drake hatch on the Battenkill," she said.

"The what?"

"The green drake hatch. It's a kind of a fly that the trout eat."

"Oh, really? You'd think it would be a kind of duck, a green drake."

"Yes, I thought so too at first. But it's a fly."

"Terrific. See, what I'd like to do, Mrs. Tuttle, is borrow one of Rollie's guns."

That froze her right up again.

"A gun . . . ? Whatever for, Grover?"

"To be honest with you, I need it for protection."

"From whom?"

"No one," I said stupidly. "I mean, just some people who might want to hurt me."

"Why would anybody want to hurt you, Grover?"

"It's rather complicated, Mrs. Tuttle, but I really don't have time to go into it. Believe me, though, it's a serious situation."

She looked at me for a moment, blankly. Then her forehead wrinkled, as though an attempt to comprehend had ended in failure.

"Grover, are you on drugs?" she asked in a timid voice.

"Do I look like I'm on drugs, Mrs. Tuttle?"

"Well . . . I don't know."

"Do I sound like it? Or act like it?"

"No. I don't know." She heaved a sigh. "Rollie said he thought you might be *on* something."

"Believe me, Mrs. Tuttle. I'm not *on* anything. I hardly even drink."

It really baffled me that everybody thought I was stoned on something, exactly what, I wish I knew—angel dust? smack? LSD? Frankly, I don't think Rollie could've spotted a real junkie unless it jumped up and bit him on the lips.

"Please, Mrs. Tuttle, I really don't have much time. I wouldn't ask this favor unless it was very important. Now, where does Rollie keep his guns?"

"Downstairs," she said.

"Are they locked up?"

"Yes."

"Do you have the key?"

"No."

"Great—"

"It's inside," she informed me. "In the bedroom." For all her uncertainty and trepidation, she still had the desire to please, to be a good hostess.

"Would you go get it, Mrs. Tuttle?"

"Are you sure it's okay?"

"Yes, it's okay," I reassured her.

She started walking out of the kitchen, but after a few steps she turned around and, shaking her head, said, "No, I'm sorry, Grover, but it just doesn't seem right somehow—"

At that point I'm afraid I completely lost my patience. I grabbed the first utensil I could lay my hands on, which happened to be a spatula, and pointed it in her face.

"If you don't get that key right away, Mrs. Tuttle—"

"I'll get it! I'll get it!" she cried, her worst fears about me realized.

Anyway, I followed her into the bedroom. The key was in Rollie's valet tray on top of his dresser. I asked her to come down to the basement with me and unlock the guns.

He kept them in a sheet-metal chest, sort of a steel footlocker. Mrs. Tuttle was shaking so badly that it took her almost a minute to get the key in the hole. Inside were four rifles: a pump shotgun, a bolt-action Weatherby .225, a lever-action Marlin 30-30, and a 20-gauge over/under field gun. Below these, in a separate compartment, were three pistols: a Smith & Wesson .357 magnum revolver, a Ruger .22 magnum automatic, and a huge reproduction Colt 1851 cap and ball revolver. There was plenty of ammunition. I loaded the .357 and stashed a handful of loose cartridges in my pocket. I also took the .22. Its clip held nine rounds and there was a spare clip as well. I put both of the guns on safety and tucked them in my waistband, the .357 in front and the .22 automatic behind me. You couldn't see them under my flight jacket.

"We better go upstairs now," I told Mrs. Tuttle, trying to act as nice as possible under the circumstances. We went back to the kitchen. She sat down at the Formica table with the most awful look of resignation on her face, as if her world had come to an end, or was just about to.

"Mrs. Tut—I'm sorry, but would you mind telling me your first name? I'm afraid I've forgotten it."

"G-G-Ginger!" she stammered and then burst into tears.

"Look, I'm sorry I had to force you like this. But please understand, I'm not stealing these guns. I'll bring them back tomorrow, if I can. Okay? Can you hear me, Ginger?"

She nodded her head, still sobbing.

"Don't worry, I'll pay for any bullets I use, okay? You can tell Rollie that I was here and exactly what happened, and say I'll try to call him as soon as possible, okay?"

She nodded again, very rapidly, as though she were scared to death.

"Okay, then, Ginger. I'm going to leave now."

I took a few steps toward the door.

"And don't forget to tell Rollie I said thanks a lot."

It wasn't until I was halfway up the street on the cycle that I realized what must have been going through her mind: she probably thought I was going to shoot Charlie Boland.

* * *

I drove right past the Hurlbetts' house in Minerva Park. With a full-face helmet and a tinted windscreen, I was indistin-

guishable from any other motorcyclist in America. One thing
was immediately apparent: my car was gone. They had ditched
it somewhere, all right. It really pissed me off to picture them
in there, lying to the cops, while for all they knew I was hanging from a water pipe on Union Street with a bullet in my head.

I parked my bike around a curve, three houses away from
theirs, and skulked between two of the houses to the rear. You
couldn't call it a backyard, really, because the properties were
larger than that. It was park-like back there. Behind the house
to my left was an elaborate rose garden with many varieties
blooming in rows. Nobody was around. I stole through the
garden to a juniper hedge and carefully slipped through it.
The next property over had a tennis court. The surface was
old-fashioned red clay, all lined and fairly well maintained.
The fence around it was an old one made of four-by-fours and
chicken wire. I crept past it. As I did, a swimming pool came
into view. A mustachioed middle-aged man was lounging beside it alone, wearing sunglasses and smoking a cigar. He held
the New York *Times* Sunday magazine in his hands. You could
describe him as dapper-looking, except that he wasn't wearing
a stitch of clothing. Of course when he saw me he lowered the
magazine over his privates and took the cigar out of his mouth.

"It's okay," I told him. "I'm a friend of the Hurlbetts."

He nodded his head to indicate that he understood, but you
could tell that he was suspicious.

"They're the next house over," he said.

"They are? Great," I said. "It's been a while since I dropped
by to visit. You mind if I just tiptoe the rest of the way over? I
won't step on your daffodils."

He shrugged his shoulders and said, "Sure." Then he returned to his newspaper.

"Uh, sir," I said, trying to allay his suspicions, "do you
happen to know if the Red Sox won yesterday?"

"The Yanks won."

"Do you remember the score offhand?"

"No."

"Okay. Well, thanks anyway."

"Right."

Of course the ironic thing was that I was trying to act like a normal harmless person, but in fact I had two pistols tucked under my jacket. So it just goes to show you that you have good reason to be nervous when someone comes pussyfooting across your lawn. Anyway, I waved good-bye and ducked behind a clump of lilac bushes that separated his property from the Hurlbetts.

I crept up to a rear door, which I believed led to the kitchen. To gain entry was a simple matter of breaking one of the diamond-shaped windowpanes in the door, reaching in, and opening the lock. I waited inside the pantry for a few moments to see if anyone would react to the tinkle of broken glass. The house was silent.

I stole through the kitchen remembering almost word for word the quarrel between Jamie and his father so many years ago. It was dim inside the old house. I tiptoed down a somber hallway, through the dining room into the library. Seeing it again made my stomach turn, thinking what a chump I was.

It was pretty obvious that nobody was home. I quit pussyfooting around and hurried to look upstairs. Evidently the Hurlbetts slept in separate bedrooms, because two rooms contained unmade beds and both were in a state of disarray. In the first, a louvered closet door was thrown open and several articles of men's clothing lay on the floor, as though someone had grabbed a few garments in a hurry and not bothered to pick up things that fell off their hangers. In the other room quite a few dresses and women's slacks were laid out on the bed. A medium-size Louis Vuitton suitcase had been tossed aside empty, as if there hadn't been time or room for it. Numerous plastic prescription containers stood on a dresser top. They were for medications like Dilaudid, Percodan, and Seconal, all made out to different names and empty. A bottle of skin cream lay overturned beside them in a goopy, aromatic puddle.

Unless they were en route to a major airport at that minute, there was one last chance to catch up with them. I hurried downstairs and out the front door, then ran down the street to my motorcycle.

CHAPTER 14

From the edge of the woods I saw a young woman backing a white Mercedes sedan close to the front door of the farmhouse. She got out, went around to the rear and opened the trunk, then vanished inside the house.

I'd left the bike off the road a quarter mile back in a little dirt cul-de-sac where the remains of several campfires suggested it was a place that local teenagers came to drink beer and brag about their sexual exploits. Between myself and the house now was about two hundred yards of scrubby field and then the smaller guesthouse. When the girl finished moving the Mercedes and had gone back inside, I left the woods and dashed to the rear of the guesthouse. It seemed to be empty. At least you couldn't hear anyone in there from outside the window. When I got my breath back I made a shorter dash from the rear of the guesthouse to the far end of the main house's wing. This time I could hear voices inside through a closed window, the words unclear. It was harder to get my breath back because I was scared.

I peeked around the corner to the rear of the house. Two U-Haul trucks were parked over by the barn. No one was in the garden. I heard a car door *thunk* around in the front. All of a sudden somebody barged out of the mudroom door, about fifty feet away. He didn't see me, though, because he headed immediately toward the barn, in the opposite direction from where I was hiding. Though I could only see him from behind, Jacob's red hair gave away his identity. He was carrying two plastic garbage bags filled with something bulky but not too heavy. You could tell by the way he carried them, over his shoulder, like Santa Claus. When he entered the barn I left my hiding place behind the wall, bolted up to the mudroom, and slipped in through the screen door.

I hid in the corner, just to the right of the screen door, standing with my feet in a bushel basket full of dirty work gloves. Within the house all manner of a commotion could be heard—footsteps of people clomping up and down stairs, voices saying *get this* and *get that.* I drew the .357 out of my flight jacket and switched off the safety, then held it over my head in my right hand. My heart was pumping so hard I was afraid someone might actually hear it. A moment later footsteps scuffed lightly on the gravel outside the door. The screen door creaked. Jacob came in the mudroom. I let him take a few steps, then leveled the pistol at the center of his back.

"Hold it."

Unfortunately my throat was so dry that the words came out in a hoarse, froggy-sounding rasp, and I had to repeat myself. He stopped, though, and slowly turned around. For a few seconds, when he first recognized me, you could practically see the wheels spinning in his head while he decided whether to run, or go for me, or just stay where he was. To be honest, I had severe doubts about whether I could pull the trigger on somebody under any circumstances. And I think Jacob sensed it. But I could also tell from the look on his face that he had decided to give me the benefit of the doubt.

"Remember me?" I asked.

"Yes."

"Where's everybody going?"

"Who?" he said.

"You. The Hurlbetts, Isaac. Tell me."

"I don't know."

"What's going on inside, then?"

"Holy Spirit service."

"I bet."

He made a nervous, petulant face. Perspiration was beginning to bead on his forehead.

"Listen carefully to what I say," I told him. "Do exactly what I tell you. Understand?"

He nodded.

"Okay, turn around. Real slowly."

He obliged. He was wearing a polo shirt, Banlon or some goddamn thing. I told him to hold still, grabbed a fistful of his shirt around the back of his neck and twisted it real tight, so the front would cut off his air supply if he struggled. He chose this opportunity to try to elbow me in the stomach, but the blow missed completely. I rapped him smartly on the head with the butt of my gun. He uttered a little cry of pain. I told him to shut up and then stuck the gun barrel against his spine, where he couldn't elbow it, trying to impress upon him the need to cooperate. Finally he quit struggling. I relaxed the tension on his throat so he could get more air.

"Where's the nearest telephone?" I asked him.

"Inside."

"Where inside?" I jerked his shirt up against his throat.

"Living room," he gasped.

"Where are the Hurlbetts?"

"Inside."

"Where inside? I swear to God, if you don't start giving me straight answers, you're going to regret it."

"I don't know where. Upstairs. Downstairs. Please, I don't know."

There was a window in the door that led to the kitchen. You could see inside. No one was in there.

"Okay," I said. "We're going to go into the kitchen. Turn the doorknob slowly. Go inside and proceed to the swinging door on the far side. Stop there and don't try anything. I'll be right behind you all the way. Got it?"

"Yes."

"Go ahead."

He did exactly as I instructed. I maintained a firm grip on him the whole time and kept the gun barrel jammed against his spine. When we got to the swinging door I opened it a crack and peered out. Nobody was in the dining room, but I could see a blond girl with glasses standing in the living room.

"What's her name?" I whispered.

"R-Rachel."

"Okay, here's what I want you to do—call her over here. Tell her that you tripped out in the barn and cut your hand real badly on some broken glass. Tell her to go get Dr. Hurlbett. Got it?"

"Yes."

"Go ahead."

I let him stick his face out the door but stayed hidden behind him, holding on tight to him.

"Rachel. Please come here for a minute," he called to her.

You could hear her pad over on the creaky old floorboards.

"I . . . I tripped in the barn," he began haltingly. "I . . . I cut my hand pretty bad on some . . . some broken glass. Please ask Father Abraham to . . . to come here."

"Are you okay?" she said. "Let me see it."

I drilled the gun barrel into his back. He flinched.

"No, Rachel," he said. "It's pretty gory. Just get Father Abraham."

"All right," she agreed.

You could hear her pad away. We waited. Jacob was sweating through his shirt. Shortly there was a sort of hubbub as Dr. Hurlbett swept into the dining room followed by the girl.

". . . we really don't have time for this sort of thing," he was grumbling at her. "Well, where is he?"

When he was just a few steps short of the door, I kicked it open with my foot, at the same time shoving Jacob forward. He collided with Rachel, lost his balance and tripped over her, and struck his head on an edge of the dining table. Dr. Hurlbett and I stood face-to-face. The gun seemed to make a quick and deep impression on him.

"Turn around," I told him.

His mouth started grinding in that determined manner, as if

his dentures hurt. The machinations of his brain could easily
be read in the way his eyes darted around the room.

"It was always them, son," he said in a low voice, as though
he didn't want the girl to hear. "We were helpless to stop
them."

"Shut up and turn around, sir," I repeated. When he balked
I spun him around by the shoulder and grabbed a handful of
his shirt collar. He was wearing a tropical-weight dark gray suit
and a shirt and tie, so there was a lot to hold on to. He
struggled until I yanked the knot of his tie into his Adam's
apple. Meanwhile, Jacob was down on all fours shaking his
head, trying to clear the cobwebs out from the blow he had
received off the table, while Rachel squatted beside him, cow-
ering. I told them both to get up. The doorway between the
living room and the dining room was a wide arch, with eight
feet of wall on either side. With the gun muzzle held up beside
his ear, I dragged Dr. Hurlbett over behind the near wall.

"Rachel," I whispered. "Stand in the middle of the doorway.
Shout into the house that Father Abraham wants everybody to
come down to the living room. Tell them he has a few words to
say to everybody before he leaves."

Rachel looked plaintively at Dr. Hurlbett.

"Do as he says, Rachel," Dr. Hurlbett told her.

"Wait a minute," I said. "Jacob, stand right behind her."

He did.

"Go ahead, Rachel," I said.

"Everybody!" Rachel hollered. "Everybody, come down to
the Holy Spirit room. Everybody! Father Abraham wants to
talk to us before he leaves."

Footsteps resounded on the stairway practically at once. A
screen door slammed in front as people streamed in from
outside. There was excited chattering as the room noisily filled
up. I waited a minute. Then, still holding Dr. Hurlbett by the
collar, I stepped out from behind the wall. A collective gasp
was let out when they saw me beside him with the gun.

"Everybody against the wall by the fireplace," I said. There
was a great deal of confusion. I fired a round into the ceiling.
The reverberation of the report inside the house was quite

impressive. They all shut up and clustered against the far wall around the fireplace. I told Jacob and Rachel to join them.

The whole gang was there, except for Esau. Isaac stood just about at center, several of the girls, including Rebecca, clustered around him. He had on his sunglasses, as usual, and a dark suit along with his usual black turtleneck. Mrs. Hurlbett sank down on the sofa beside Lisa, the one looking terrified, the other totally dazed and impassive. There were twenty-five of them in all.

"Where's Esau?" I asked.

Nobody answered. There was near total silence except for a fly buzzing around the room and birds singing in the evening sunlight outside.

"Did you kill Esau too?" I asked Dr. Hurlbett and drilled the gun muzzle into the little hollow behind his ear.

"You're hurting me," was all he said.

"I know," I said. "Give me your passport."

He reached inside his jacket with his right hand and drew out the gray booklet with the gold seal of the United States printed on the cover.

"Hold it up right over your head," I told him. He did. "Okay, now, don't move a muscle." I cocked the hammer of the .357. The complex sound of various gun parts clicking into place seemed to have the desired cautioning effect. His gnarled reddened hand, with its fingers misshapen talonlike from arthritis, trembled. I let go of his shirt collar for a moment, took the passport away from him, stuck it in the back pocket of my jeans, and grabbed his shirt again. "All right, put your hand down," I told him. "Rachel?"

"Yes."

"Bring Mrs. Hurlbett's passport over here and hand it to Dr. Hurlbett. Get Isaac's too."

"Fuck you, my little lamb, I don't have a passport," Isaac snarled back at me.

"Of course you do," I said.

"If I did, I wouldn't hand it over to you, you filth."

The shrewd fucker knew that I wasn't in a position to come over and take it away from him, let alone search him for the passport. Then there was the question of his gun—the silver automatic. At first I'd assumed he had it on him. But he'd had ample opportunity to pull it on me by now or—more his style —hold it up to one of the girls' heads and threaten to blow her brains out if I didn't let him go, so I began to suspect that he wasn't carrying it. Then again, I was afraid to force the issue and ask him for it, thinking he'd sooner fire it at me than hand it over.

"Okay, forget the other passports," I said. "Rachel, go to the telephone." It was on a low table next to the sofa to the left of where Lisa was sitting. She went over to it. "What I want you to do is call the police in Manchester. Tell them exactly where we are. Tell them that the people who committed the Hurlbett murder are here. Understand?"

Mrs. Hurlbett let out a wild sob and began rocking back and forth in her seat with her hands clasped around herself, crying. Murmurs rose out of the group.

"Be quiet," I told them.

Meanwhile, Rachel just stared dumbly at the phone.

"Go ahead," I told her, "do it."

"I don't know the number," she said.

"Dial the operator and ask her to connect you."

Isaac laughed in his distinctive, gravelly way. Rachel finally picked up the phone and dialed "o." She followed my instructions, told the police what I'd said to tell them, and hung up with a sort of hang-dog expression on her face. Then we waited.

A quarter of an hour passed and no police arrived. It was getting late. That special sort of deep yellow sunlight you only see in the country on a summer evening poured through the front window. That's when I happened to realize that it was June 21, the longest day of the year. Still, even on the longest day, night eventually falls.

Another ten minutes went by and no one came. My arms were aching from holding on to Dr. Hurlbett's collar and from holding the gun up to his head.

"You didn't really call them, did you, Rachel?" I said.

"Sure I did."

"Then how come they're not here?"

"I don't know."

"I don't think you really spoke to them."

"I did."

"Okay, everybody—"

"I swear—"

"Shut up, Rachel. Get away from the telephone." She did. "Dr. Hurlbett, I'm going to let go of you. I want you to lie down on the floor, on your stomach, with your hands behind your head. Understand?"

"Yes."

"All right. Lie down."

He did.

Brandishing the gun and keeping my eyes on all of them, I went over to the low table and picked up the phone. There was no dial tone. It was dead. It was certainly a first-rate acting job on Rachel's part. I pulled on the cord. It offered no resistance. At the end were four frayed colored wires. I was so furious, I picked up the whole telephone and dashed it onto the floor near Dr. Hurlbett's head. Isaac laughed again.

"Shut up," I told him. I couldn't think straight. Of course he didn't shut up, but by then I'd had quite enough of his shenanigans and I decided to put an end to it.

"You." I pointed to the youngest boy, Ishbak. "Take off your shirt." He seemed bewildered. "Go on, take it off!" He did. It was a button-down oxford, good strong cloth. "Jacob, take off your shirt too." He did. "Rip it in half. Go ahead! Do what I tell you!" He ripped it in half. "Okay, I want you to tie Isaac's wrists behind his back with that shirt. And Jacob. I want you to gag him. One at a time. Isaac, come stand in the center of the room."

"Can't make me," he said childishly. "Dirty shitball."

"I'm not going to ask you again," I said, leveling the gun at him.

"*Nyah nyah nyah nyah nyah,*" he sang like a little kid and then put his thumbs in his ears, waggled his fingers, and blew a raspberry at me. Some of the others laughed. I squeezed the trigger and blew off the middle finger of his right hand. Blood splattered the white wall behind him. Isaac crumpled on the carpet, clutching his hand. Several of the girls shrieked.

"Godless shit," one yelled at me.

"My finger!" Isaac screamed. "Oh, God!"

"Here it is!" a girl said, picking up something that looked like a vienna sausage.

"Give it to me!" Isaac screamed. She did. He actually tried to fit it back in place, but blood was squirting out of the stump, and he must have realized it was useless, so he threw it at me, screaming, "You fucking filth!"

Dr. Hurlbett even raised his head to look, perhaps out of medical curiosity, I don't know, but I told him to put his face back against the floor and he did. Mrs. Hurlbett continued to wail. Isaac tore off his suit jacket and wrapped it around his right hand, rocking back and forth on his knees as the initial shock wore off and he began to really start feeling the pain. His sunglasses had flown off with the force of the bullet and for the first time you could see his eyes. They were large and hooded and tilted down at the corners.

Some of the others were still shouting things at me and crying and carrying on. I yelled at them to shut up and, miraculously, they did. When they were quiet again I told Jacob to go ahead and tie Isaac's wrists together behind his back and to gag him. Isaac threatened them and called them names, but he submitted all the same, and by now the others were too afraid not to do what I said. Then I told Ishbak to pull the mounting cord out of the telephone that I had smashed on the floor and to tie up Dr. Hurlbett's wrists the same way.

"Now, help them both up onto their feet."

Dr. Hurlbett obliged, but Isaac just went limp, like the protesters during the Vietnam War used to do. I knew he wasn't unconscious, because his large eyes were open and glaring right at me full of malice.

"All right, listen carefully to me," I said. "Mrs. Hurlbett—"

She gave a little yelp and sat up straight with a start.

"—stand up, and help your daughter up too."

She did, and held on to Lisa at the elbow. Lisa brushed a

loose strand of hair out of her face. It was the only voluntary movement I'd yet seen her perform.

"Dr. Hurlbett, stand beside Lisa."

He complied, a haughty, glowering look on his face, as though it might help him to maintain his respectability.

"Isaac, either stand up or you're going to be dragged out by your feet."

He made some sounds through his gag that sounded vaguely like the words *fuck you* followed by laughter.

"Okay, fine," I said. "Jacob, when I say so, start dragging him out of the house through the front door. Dr. Hurlbett, Mrs. Hurlbett. You follow directly behind with Lisa. The rest of you follow behind them. When you get outside I want you to stand in a tight group to the right of that Mercedes parked out there, about twice as far away as you are to me now. Does everybody understand?"

Several said they did. Jacob and Dr. Hurlbett said yes. Mrs. Hurlbett nodded fearfully. Isaac farted. A few of the others laughed, one gave Isaac the high sign, but by and large they were a pretty glum and submissive bunch now. I picked up the telephone and yanked out the coiled handset cord.

"Go ahead, start dragging him," I told Jacob.

With me leading the way, slowly walking backward and keeping the gun trained on them, we formed a sort of procession out of the house. It went very smoothly, except that Isaac was humming a song that sounded like "We Shall Overcome" as he was dragged by his ankles out of the living room and through the hall. Outside, Jacob picked him up like a sack of potatoes and carried him down the three front steps. I glanced inside the passenger compartment of the Mercedes. The keys were in the ignition. When everybody was out of the house and standing where they were supposed to, I went around to the rear of the car and unlocked the trunk. There was a bunch of luggage inside, six pieces in all. I chucked it all out on the grass.

"Okay, Jacob. Put him in here."

"Put him in the trunk?"

"That's right."

Isaac hollered through his gag. When Jacob tried to pick him up he started kicking and screaming. I told two of the other guys to come over and help by each grabbing a leg. They looked quite daunted, but finally got ahold of Isaac and stuck him in the trunk. I could still hear him inside with the lid closed, yelling and kicking, and the car rocked eerily from his struggling.

When Isaac was safely stowed away I asked Mrs. Hurlbett to help Lisa into the rear seat, driver's side, and for her to get in the rear seat, passenger side. Then I asked Dr. Hurlbett to get in the front passenger seat, and told Jacob to tie the old man's neck to the headrest with the other length of telephone cord. With his wrists also bound behind his back, I was satisfied that he wouldn't cause me any problems. I would have liked to bring in Jacob and Rebecca, too, but it wasn't practical to cram any more people in the car, and I felt that even if they fled the immediate area, the police would catch up with them sooner or later.

Finally I told Jacob and his helpers to go stand with the others. When they were all a safe distance away, I climbed in behind the wheel with a profound feeling of relief. The engine started up perfectly. I stuck the .357 inside my flight jacket and put the transmission in drive. It was one of those automatic stick shifts on the floor. It clunked reassuringly into gear. I had just stepped on the gas when Dr. Hurlbett reached over with his foot and tapped the transmission into reverse. Suddenly the car hurtled backward and slammed into the front steps with a terrific force. The trunk lid sprung open. Mrs. Hurlbett shrieked.

"Goddamn you!" I yelled at Dr. Hurlbett and struck him several times in the face with the flat of my hand. He could only move his head back and forth, the way his neck was tied to the headrest, so he couldn't really avoid the blows. Still, he kept trying to kick me. I had to take the gun out and whomp him in the face with the barrel before he would stop. Blood gushed from his nose.

I put the car back in forward gear and tried to drive away from there, but the engine just revved as if the car was in neutral. What happened, I realized, was that the car's rear bumper had become hung up on the front step of the house and the wheels weren't making contact with the ground.

Meanwhile, the others, who I had made assemble in a tight group over to the side, all began to scatter in every direction. I jumped out of the car and fired a couple of rounds into the air, yelling, "Freeze!" But only a few of the slower ones stopped in their tracks. The rest made it to the woods or around the other side of the house. I was trying to think of which of the several other cars I might be able to use instead, and wondering how to move the Hurlbetts and Isaac into it, and how to start the goddamn thing, when I heard the screen door creak behind me.

I wheeled around. Jacob stood there looking down the barrel of a shotgun at me. I dove in front of the Mercedes just as he fired, then heard him pump another shell into the chamber. Isaac picked just that moment to start screaming and kicking inside the sprung-open trunk. It must have distracted Jacob for a split second, because when I popped up he was looking down into it. My shot took off most of the top of his head above the eyebrows. A pink cloud seemed to hang over the white trunk lid as he went spinning backward like an oversized rag doll through the screen door.

That's when I gave up trying to bring any of them to the police myself. Instead, I threw open the rear door of the Mercedes, grabbed Lisa by the hand, and tried to simply make a run for it, with her, to my motorcycle. Unfortunately, she was not of a mind to cooperate. I had to practically drag her up the driveway to the road. She would follow along for a dozen steps, then seem to forget what she was doing. I would have to yank her forward. Twice she stumbled and fell, and sat befuddled in the dust while I yelled at her to get up. Meanwhile, I could hear all sorts of screams and shouts coming from back at the house, and I was afraid that pretty soon they'd be coming after me again.

Eventually, though, I managed to drag and cajole Lisa down the road to that little dirt cul-de-sac where I had left the Virago. My hand was shaking so badly I could hardly fit the key in the ignition. I jumped on the kick start and got it going. There was only one helmet, and I put it on Lisa. But then she seemed to have no conception of what I wanted her to do—to sit on the bike. I tried to show her how to climb on the seat, but she just stood there with a glazed expression, not even watching me. I even tried to pick her up and put her on the damn thing, but she was too heavy for me to lift.

Finally I had to face the fact that I just had to leave her there. So, I took the helmet off her and put it on my own head, and made her lie down in the weeds, telling her to please stay there and not move, *please*, and that I'd be back soon with help. I don't know if she understood a single word I said, but she did stay there on the ground. I climbed back on the bike, pulled the clutch lever in, and banged the gear shift into first with my foot. As soon as I spun out onto the road I saw a silver BMW barreling down at me from the direction of the farm. Of course it was a dead end down there, so it couldn't have come from anywhere else. And I thought I saw a head of snowy-white hair behind the wheel.

*   *   *

Did you ever notice that when you really need a cop around, they're never there? If you're tooling down the thruway at fifty-nine miles per hour, there's sure to be a state trooper behind every lilac bush on the median strip, with his radar unit trained on you. But just have a breakdown on that same thruway in a snowstorm in February when it's six degrees below zero, and forget it, you won't see a cop if you wait there for a week. The same thing applies when some crazy motherfucker is trying to kill you.

When I came off that dirt road onto the county highway, I was already doing sixty, and then on the blacktop I opened it up to ninety on the straightaways. He was right on my tail the whole time, passing other cars as I passed them, all the way into Manchester. I'd never driven the bike so fast in the year that I owned it and it was scaring the shit out of me, not to mention him behind me trying to run me off the goddamn road. I'd hoped that our reckless driving would attract the attention of a police officer, but naturally this was not to be.

By the time we reached the center of town, I was still going at least fifty. The sidewalks were full of gaping tourists. There was no way I could stop without him plowing into me. I did scream "Help!" as we streaked through the village, but with a full-face helmet on it was like yelling with a goldfish bowl over your head, and nobody seemed to hear a thing.

So, before you knew it we were barreling right out the south end of town, accelerating again and running a red light just past the Orvis Store at more than seventy miles per hour. Still, no cops appeared. Eventually, Main Street turned into Route 7. South of town it was an "improved" highway with a third passing lane in the middle and extra-wide shoulders. To tell you the truth, I was terrified of driving any faster than ninety, and sooner or later, I realized, racing flat out on a good highway, he was going to get me.

Then, on the right, we passed the entrance to the Mount Skytop scenic drive, a privately maintained tourist attraction that led up an extremely winding road to a parking lot on the summit with telescopic viewers and a snack bar. Barbara Frye had made me go up there with her on one of our first dates. I had anxiety attacks the whole time we stayed up there. Anyway, I thought if I could only somehow get on that road, he'd have a real problem steering with those gnarly, fucked-up arthritic hands of his. And if by some miracle he managed to follow me all the way up to the top, I could turn around on him in the summit parking lot and get him going back down, where he'd have an even better chance of killing himself.

In any case, I had to act fast, because Route 7 was looking real straight up ahead, and he was closing in on me. I cut across the passing lane and the northbound lane between two oncoming cars. That experience in itself was enough to land me on a psychiatrist's couch for a year. But somehow I survived without killing myself and half a dozen innocent people, and I made it over to the paved shoulder, where I punched the gears back down trying to decelerate. It took me a quarter of a mile to stop.

Meanwhile, a couple of hundred yards ahead, the BMW sat pulled over on the opposite shoulder, no doubt watching to see what I would do next. I edged into traffic in the north-bound lane. In my left rearview mirror I saw the BMW pull a U-turn, cutting in front of a fast-moving pickup truck and causing the driver of that vehicle to swerve off the road into a hayfield. I punched the Virago into top gear. The BMW moved ahead in the passing lane.

A single chain strung between a couple of Indian totem poles blocked the entrance to the scenic drive. A green and white sign hanging from it said "Closed for the Day." I easily drove up over the curb and around the vacant ticket kiosk onto the drive and started up the mountain. I had made the first hairpin when I heard the BMW crash through the chain below.

It quickly became obvious that I was right about him having trouble on the curves. I could hear his tires squeal as he over-steered and then corrected. Negotiating the turns was not really a problem for me and I even slowed down somewhat on purpose to stay within his sight and taunt him. As we drove higher and higher the view of the surrounding countryside opened up, and to the west a sinking red sun shimmered just above the horizon.

Eventually we reached the summit. The parking lot was empty. I drove around the perimeter of it to the far side where the snack bar was located and stopped there. Moments later the BMW appeared and came to a stop at the entrance to the lot, as though he were looking for me. Then he gunned his engine and came at me. I waited a couple of seconds, cranked open my throttle, and swerved out of his path. He jumped the curb and bashed into a steel trash can on the path to the snack bar.

Now I waited on the opposite side of the lot. He backed away from the trash can, then sped at me again. I managed to swerve away from him again. This time he didn't jump a curb but came to a screeching halt, shifted gears, and started charging at me in reverse. As I evaded him, and swerved around to his left, he shifted back into forward gear and almost nailed me broadside but missed by a few feet. The parking lot was like a bull ring and I suddenly felt like a matador goading a big dumb danger-ous beast.

Unfortunately I was the one who fucked up first. He'd given up charging at me and now was slowly circling, stalking me around the outer edge of the lot. We got going faster, and a little faster, and soon he was chasing me around in a circle at a pretty good clip. That's when I tried to cut across the center of the lot and lure him back down the road. But I hit a patch of loose gravel and my rear wheel spun out from under me. The bike went into a sickening, spinning slide, and came to rest with my left leg pinned under the tank. The pain in my knee was beyond belief. Meanwhile, Rollie's .357 skittered loose across the asphalt. I waited for the motherfucker to run me over, but the BMW came to a halt about ten yards away. Dr. Hurlbett leaned his head out the window, flecks of dried blood around his nostrils and upper lip where I'd hit him, and his jaws were grinding in that determined way of his. The car's windshield reflected the red half-circle of sun going down behind me.

"Give me the passport, son," he said.

I flipped up my face shield.

"What's the matter?" I said. "Afraid to get blood all over it?"

"If you give it to me, there won't be any more problems, I assure you."

"Yeah, because I'll be dead, right?"

"Just let me have it, son."

"Why'd you kill Jamie?"

"The passport, son."

"Fuck you."

He drew his head back inside. I reached behind me and grabbed Rollie's automatic from my waistband and managed to pull my left leg out from under the tank. His transmission *thunked* into gear. The car lurched forward with a squeal. I rolled away from the Virago and pumped five shots through Dr. Hurlbett's windshield. He threw up his hands in a futile attempt to shield his face. The car crunched over the bike, swerved to the right, picked up speed, jumped the curb, smashed through a little white guard rail, and vanished over the edge of the mountain. There were an eerie few seconds of silence, then the noise of a crash followed by a more distant explosion, and a thin column of sooty black smoke that rose above the purple horizon where, moments before, the sun had gone down.

EPILOGUE

The aftermath of that wild summer evening in Vermont, including the trials of individuals who belonged to the Children of Abraham, is a subject that could fill a dozen volumes, if you included all the court transcripts.

My motorcycle, needless to say, was not drivable, nor would I have been in any condition to drive it, with a fractured left ankle and torn lateral and transverse ligaments of the left knee. I managed to limp about an eighth of the way down the scenic drive when a whole fleet of Vermont State Police cars intercepted me on their way up, alerted to the scene not only by a mysterious explosion that was visible clear down to Bennington, but by reports of highway irregularities involving a motorcyclist and somebody in a silver BMW.

After my release from the hospital in Bennington, I was taken to the state police headquarters and held in custody for thirty-six hours. It took that long for the investigators to even begin to understand what had really happened. In the meantime an impressive array of charges was lodged against me: suspicion of murder, illegal possession of a handgun, reckless endangerment, reckless driving, and trespassing. My bail was set at $200,000.

When the police first visited the Lyman Foundation farm, they found the body of Jacob where I last saw it, sprawled in the front entrance of the house in close proximity to a shotgun bearing his fingerprints. All the other alleged residents of the place were gone, with the exception of Katherine Hurlbett, sixty-one, who was found semiconscious in the rear seat of a Mercedes-Benz sedan suffering from shock, neck injuries, and what was later established to be barbiturate withdrawal.

Lisa Hurlbett, twenty-nine, was found early the next morning "wandering aimlessly" down State Highway 30 in a condition first misidentified as "shock" and again later misdiagnosed as acute catatonic schizophrenia.

The body of Dr. Arthur Hurlbett, seventy, was not recovered for almost twenty-four hours due to the ruggedness of the terrain on the western slope of Mount Skytop. It was burned beyond recognition and positive identification was made on the basis of dental records.

Lyman C. Weatherwax, thirty-one, also known as "Isaac," aka "Shitfingers," was apprehended two days later in the Dixie King Motel, Valdosta, Georgia, after seeking medical attention in the Lowndes County Infirmary for an infected hand resulting from a severed middle finger and creating a disturbance when proof of identity and county residence were requested for billing purposes.

Weatherwax was the son of actor Lloyd Weatherwax (d. 1978), star of the TV situation comedy "Toggles" (1964–69), the madcap adventures of an endearing British butler who inherits his employer's Palm Beach mansion and then has to contend with her rambunctious ghost. The elder Weatherwax worked only sporadically after the cancellation of his series. In 1976 he was a suspect in the shooting death of his ex-wife, Lyman's mother, the actress Lorna Buell. Released for lack of evidence, he committed suicide two years later. Her killer was never found.

Lyman C. Weatherwax grew up in Darien, Connecticut, where his mother lived. He spent summers in California with his father until Lloyd Weatherwax's visitation rights were cut off on account of failure to supervise the child, who, at age thirteen, was arrested twice for hustling in West Hollywood. Lyman Weatherwax attended the Mount Riga Academy in Salisbury, Connecticut, a school for "emotionally disadvantaged" youngsters. His records there recall a career distinguished only by several instances of cruelty to animals. He attended Goddard College in Vermont for two years, and the Art Institute of San Francisco for another.

From 1977 to 1982 he lived in the Bay Area, much of that time as a member of the Christian Overlord Brotherhood, for whose publication, *End-Times*, he contributed many drawings. In 1982, after an aborted attempt to take over the group's leadership, Weatherwax left California and returned to Vermont.

Randy Lewis Schneider, twenty-five, also known as "Esau," was found buried in the earthen floor of a barn on the Lyman Foundation Farm, along with a 9-mm nickel-plated Franzetti automatic pistol. The county coroner later established the cause of death as severing of the trachea and carotid arteries, i.e., a slit throat. Schneider, originally of Menlo Park, California, became acquainted with Weatherwax in the Christian Overlord Brotherhood organization and was cast out of the group with him after the botched takeover attempt. He accompanied Weatherwax to Vermont.

Leslie R. Blount, twenty-four, also known as "Jacob," originally of Winooski, Vermont, had been a dishwasher in a Manchester restaurant when he became acquainted with Weatherwax and Schneider. Between 1980 and 1983 he was a patient at the Vermont State Hospital in Burlington, where he was classified as "a severe thought problem." His release was later called "an administrative error."

Marcia Provo, twenty, also known as "Rebecca," was the daughter of a wealthy Vermont ski-center developer. Her teenage years were a record of formidable drug abuse, including three suicide attempts. She was a freshman at Bennington College when recruited by Lyman Weatherwax. She rapidly became one of his most ardent disciples and effective weapons.

William Sheffler, twenty-three, also known as "Ishmael," was the son of California evangelist Vernon Sheffler. At age fifteen William Sheffler was convicted with three others in connection with the ritual slaying of a Corte Madera youth. Sentenced as a youthful offender, he was confined for twenty-four months in the Youth Facility at Stockton. Before being recruited into the Christian Overlord Brotherhood by Weatherwax, he worked variously as an "artist's model," "professional escort," and "paid companion."

* * *

The strange fate that brought the Hurlbetts into the orbit of Lyman C. Weatherwax, that led to the death of their son and the maiming of their daughter, can be reconstructed from information that came out of the trials, at which Mrs. Hurlbett was one of the chief witnesses for the prosecution.

The connection began three years earlier when Dr. Hurlbett rented the Dorset farm, which he had acquired since his retirement, on a nine-month lease to Weatherwax and Schneider. Using it as a base of operations, they began to collect a group of disciples, chiefly young women, preaching a gospel that combined standard-issue scenarios of impending apocalypse with comic-book themes (the metal-headed people from the center of the earth), topped off with plenty of sex. Dr. Hurlbett was Marcia Provo's special project, and she soon brought him under Weatherwax's influence. Among the first things she persuaded him to do was to extend the group's lease on the property through the summer. She also gave his prescription pad quite a workout.

During this time Dr. Hurlbett also began serving as the group's banker. The town house on Union Street was purchased for both the convenience of his liaisons and for Weatherwax's recruiting purposes. Among the evidence gathered at the Dorset farm were videocassettes of Dr. Hurlbett engaging in sex acts with Provo and others, including two of the young men who resided there. They were made in case the need for blackmail arose, Provo later testified, but it never did. In the second year of his involvement with them, Dr. Hurlbett assumed the role of Father Abraham. Evidently he grew to relish his position within the group, one of seeming authority without responsibility.

"He got off on it," Provo said in court. She proved a chillingly garrulous witness once she had been granted immunity from prosecution in exchange for her valuable testimony. "And he served a very useful purpose."

It was only toward the end, after the fiasco of his son Jamie's death, that Dr. Hurlbett actually challenged Weatherwax's supremacy within the group, finally becoming the true authority figure, and then only because everybody was starting to panic, even Weatherwax himself.

"For a long time Isaac used to laugh at the old geezer behind his back, and make jokes about him when he wasn't around," Provo testified. "But when people started croaking [i.e., getting killed], Isaac just got too weird and a lot of us turned to him [Dr. Hurlbett]. He was at least thinking of a way to get some of us out."

I happened to be in a booth in the coffee shop across the street from the courthouse where one of Weatherwax's several trials took place when I overheard this bit of conversation in the next booth between the district attorney and his chief deputy prosecutor, who was the one actually trying the case. The deputy was going to summation before the jury that morning, and his boss was coaching him.

"An old man senses death breathing down his neck. Young women are made available to him. Sex is the one thing that keeps that old man's flame burning, and he will risk practically everything to hold on to that little spark of life!" the D.A. spoke in a dramatic whisper.

"Don't you think that sounds a little corny, Russ?" the deputy prosecutor reacted warily.

"Shit, Jim," the D.A. shot back, "it's the old bastards who are most susceptible, and the jury'll know that. Who are the guys who risk arrest and all these disgusting new diseases trying to pick up the world's ugliest whores down on Ninth Avenue in New York? It's not the twenty-year-old studs. It's the sixty-three-year-old bank presidents with the dried-up wives who feel themselves dying an inch a day but come alive for five minutes when they get a blow job in their Cadillac. This Hurlbett, once he got a whiff of these teenage chicks, he just went apeshit. He wasn't going to let go of it for anything."

"Is that what you want me to tell the jury?"

"Sure. Only dress it up, make it sound nice. . . ."

Katherine Hurlbett had already testified that she knew her husband was deeply involved with Weatherwax and company, and that he was frequently absent from their home for days at a time, but that her response was a retreat into the haze of prescription narcotics and barbiturates, liberally furnished by her husband. It wasn't until Jamie and Lisa appeared on the scene that she became truly alarmed, and by that time she lived in fear for her own life.

Known only to their mother and father—who understood what it really meant, and disapproved!—Jamie and Lisa Hurlbett had been living together for two years. I'm sure this is the reason Jamie became so secretive toward me in those last years, because I would have understood what it meant too. Lisa's life before that fateful spring can only be sketched, and her emotions guessed about. But evidently there had been men out West, and those men hadn't worked out for one reason or another, and so in the end she returned to the only relationship that had ever worked for her, and was welcomed back with open arms.

Now, the winter before he died, Jamie Hurlbett made a decision. He'd apparently concluded that their life in the cabin outside Lake Placid was too hard and too isolated from the world. Perhaps the perversity of it was finally getting to him and he was looking for a way out. Perhaps Lisa influenced him to make the move away from there. We'll never know. In any case, early that March they packed up his paints and easel and all her stuff and drove down to Dorset, Vermont, with the intention of moving into the guesthouse on their father's property. Jamie had lived there for a while in 1979, right after his father purchased the place—not in a ski chalet as Dr. Hurlbett had told me—until the old man decided to charge him rent just to be a hard-ass and Jamie left in a huff, his mother testified. Only *this* time when they arrived at the Dorset farm in Jamie's battered pickup, who should they find living on the property but Weatherwax and company.

The result was deadly antagonism. Jamie and Lisa apparently had no idea of their father's deep involvement with the group. When he asked his father to evict the Children, Dr. Hurlbett stalled. Of course Weatherwax first tried some of his usual tactics, but Jamie's long years of isolation, his deep misanthropy, had left him unsusceptible to having his mind fucked, and Lisa was too much in love with her brother to fall under another's spell, and so when this nut who called himself "Isaac" tried to seduce them, and then failing at it tried to intimidate them, Jamie told him to fuck off and get out. Why did Jamie and Lisa stay? They had no money and nowhere else to go. And they surely felt they had a right to be there. For a few weeks it is a standoff.

Then one night in April, following an argument between Jamie and Weatherwax, the Children break into the guesthouse and cart all of Jamie and Lisa's belongings out onto the lawn. A confrontation ensues, a struggle between Jamie and several of the men, including Weatherwax, in which Jamie is subdued by a blow to his head with a lug wrench—wielded by Blount ("Jacob"). The blow is not intended to kill Jamie, just quiet him down, but his skull cracks open. The Children are too paranoid to take him to a hospital and before morning Jamie dies. Lisa, meanwhile, has witnessed the whole thing.

She is now virtually held prisoner. Weatherwax, in the full flower of his perversity, tells her that her father is part of the gang. Naturally she refuses to believe it. He hauls out the videotapes. Lisa becomes hysterical. Father Abraham is summoned from Minerva Park. What to do? Oh, what to do?

Jamie is dead. There's no bringing him back. On the other hand, there's no calling the police either. Schneider ("Esau") is given the job of disposing of the body. This he accomplishes not very well, and within a week pieces of Jamie start turning up at town dumps across Vermont, where he stashed them. As his punishment for screwing up, Schneider's face is held over the burner of a stove. They give him the moniker "Shitfingers" and humiliate him. Then, when the attorney general's investigators, and nosy newspaper reporters, come around asking about the group's finances, he willingly switches identities with Weatherwax to protect his avatar.

Finally there is the problem with Lisa. What do you do about her? Let her go? Out of the question. Kill her? Father Abraham agonizes. As usual the resourceful Weatherwax comes up with an idea, an excellent alternative to death, and just perfect for a surgeon: a somewhat discredited procedure used frequently up until the 1950s, a procedure that renders the most obstreperous patient docile, a procedure so surprisingly simple, for its profound effects on the personality, that it can be performed on a dining-room table with a minimum of equipment and simple anesthesia. One approaches the brain's frontal lobe via the orbit, or eye socket, of the skull. A little flick of the blade is all it takes. Only, the surgeon's hands are not what they used to be, and he lacks the finesse of his halcyon days in practice. And that's what the old motherfucker did to Lisa.

* * *

I was released on bail, and one of my father's law partners represented me in the initial proceedings. The charges against me were eventually dropped. Back in the Capital, Rollie Tuttle dropped the complaint for stealing his guns.

I didn't return to the staff of the *Times-Herald*. The district attorneys of several jurisdictions made it clear that I would have to serve as a "professional trial witness" before they got done prosecuting everybody, so I've been commuting from one courtroom to another for over a year now. Lyman C. Weatherwax is currently serving a life sentence in the Vermont State Penitentiary at Warren, and when he comes up for parole in the year 2005, he can look forward to serving another life sentence in the state of California, where his friend William Sheffler is also doing time for both the Debbie Clothier and Steven Strunk killings.

Debbie Clothier proved to be as headstrong and troublesome for the Children of Abraham as she had been with her parents. She had first joined the Children in the Capital and then been flown out to California as "a gift" to Sheffler (Provo testified). Unluckily, she and Steve Strunk fell in love out there. Strunk tried to get her to leave the group with him. She agreed. Sheffler said no. She said she was leaving whether he liked it or not. He dosed her with PCP one night, then with some of the others took her out to the cliffs overlooking Stinson Beach. They built a big fire and held an all-night mindfucking session. Sometime before dawn Debbie Clothier leaped over the edge onto the wave-battered rocks far below. It was only a matter of days before the cold Pacific currents and the strong tides sucked her body through the Golden Gate and eventually into San Pablo Bay.

Some of the other Children of Abraham were ultimately convicted on a variety of lesser charges, ranging from simple conspiracy to credit-card fraud, but they won't be in jail long. Quite a few of the rest, like Marcia Provo, got off scot-free.

Which is why I can't tell you where this is being written. Of course Weatherwax did a pretty good job of branding me when he carved the word *SHIT* on my forehead in two-inch-high letters. I've had two series of skin grafts already and I still have to have another operation to get rid of the remaining scar tissue from the grafts.

But at least I don't have to worry about a job. The people who published this book want me to do another one on cults, only a made-up one this time. ("How about a group that practices cannibalism," my editor suggested.) They're crazy about the subject. Personally, I'd rather write something historical, something completely disconnected from this ridiculous century, maybe something with pirates or Indians in it. In fact, maybe I'll do it anyway, just to piss them off. I never was much of a company man.